The Result

Robert Cort

Published by Clink Street Publishing 2024

Copyright © 2024

First edition.

ISBN
– paperback 978-1-915785-37-4
– ebook 978-1-915785-38-1

This book is dedicated to the memory
of my parents, Harry and May Cort.

ALSO WRITTEN BY ROBERT CORT

THE IAN CAXTON THRILLER SERIES

www.robertcort.net

Chapter 1

"I have a problem, Ian, and I'm fairly sure you'll be able to help," said Charles. He had a very serious expression on his face. "If my grandfather's art collection is valued correctly at about 80 million pounds and this becomes public knowledge, then Mr. Taxman is going to seriously slam me for inheritance tax. I want you to prove conclusively, Ian, that the value of all these paintings is only... what? Shall we say, about ten million!"

Ian raised his eyebrows and a tiny smile appeared on his face.

Charles continued, "I can then pay Mr. Taxman a much lower figure, obtain probate and get on with the task of selling this property, my grandfather's house, 'Dexter's End'. In return, Ian, I have a proposition, which I'm hoping you'll be seriously tempted by. Achieve all this for me and I will then give you, totally free, the 'Madeleine B' painting. Yes, the one hanging on the wall in the hallway. By your own considered valuation, a snip at maybe between 25–30 million pounds. So, Ian Caxton, what do you say? Do we have a deal?"

Well, well, well, thought Ian. Now there's a challenge. He needed time to think this one through properly. "Interesting proposition, Charles. You know all this would be against the law. It's completely illegal."

"I know, but with all your knowledge and experience of the art market, I'm sure you've come across similar situations."

Ian smiled. The truth was, he hadn't. "I'll need some time, Charles. There's a lot to consider."

"Here, take this," said Charles, holding out a green folder containing photocopies of the correct provenances of all his grandfather's paintings. "Our only immediate problem is time. I need to obtain probate as quickly as possible. People like my solicitor, accountant and, I'm sure, Mr. Taxman, will be anxious to progress this matter very quickly."

Ian accepted the file and placed it under his arm. "Give me 48 hours."

"Fine," replied Charles. "Ring me. We can then discuss your decision."

The two men walked back into the hallway preparing to leave the house. Ian stopped to look again at the 'Madeleine B' painting. It still needed a good clean, but the sweaty palm of his left hand reminded him, this was a genuine Paul Gauguin. No doubt about that.

"Checking on your possible new acquisition?" asked Charles, with a teasing smile.

Ian smiled back and stepped out through the front doorway. "You really should put this picture, and all the other valuable paintings, in a bank vault."

Charles reset the burglar alarm, closed the front door and inserted a key into the lock. "Once I get probate sorted, they'll all be gone."

"I'll give you a lift to Virginia Water station," said Ian, as he walked towards his car parked in the driveway.

"Thanks," replied Charles. "If you drive out into the lane, I'll set the gate's lock and alarm system."

Ian put the green folder in the car's boot and opened the driver's door. Five minutes later the two men were driving through the Wentworth Estate. At the road junction with the A30 Ian steered the vehicle right and headed north towards Virginia Water.

When Ian stopped the car outside the railway station Charles opened the passenger door, but, before stepping out, he turned towards Ian and said, "Thanks for the lift. Look after those documents. I'll speak to you again in two days' time."

Ian nodded. "Bye for now."

Charles got out, waved and shut the door. Ian waved back and drove away. On his journey back home to Esher, Ian had only one thought on his mind. What would Andrei have done with a proposal like this?

When Ian arrived home, the house was quiet and empty. He checked his watch and realised Emma would still be on her way back from collecting Robert from school. He walked into the home office, sat down behind his desk and placed the green folder in front of him. He opened the flap and removed several clear plastic files. Counting them, Ian established there were 19 individual files, each with its own white label attached to the cover. Each label stated both the title of the painting and the artist's name. He flicked through each plastic folder until he came to the label saying, *'Fête Gloanec', Paul Gauguin ('Madeleine B')*. He then removed all the papers inside and started to read and make notes.

Once he'd finished, he returned the pages back into the plastic folder. Pondering on the situation, he leaned back in his chair and stared out of the window. Yes, he concluded, the provenance did appear to stack up. The painting is about the same size, 36.5 x 52.5 cm and everything about it says it is the real painting, not a fake or copy. Also, my instincts say it's the real painting too. Mmm, so why do we have two paintings both aspiring to be the original? Is the existing authorised version of 'Fête Gloanec', currently displayed in the Musée des Beaux-Arts d'Orléans, just a copy? It doesn't make much sense. Surely the French would have fully investigated their painting... or had they?

Ian decided he needed to see this French version for himself... and establish what the provenance, attached to that painting, actually said.

Viktor was sitting at his desk in the 'Taylor Fine Arts Gallery'. He was signing the papers which agreed to the sale of the gallery's premises lease. After checking the wording one final time, he scribbled his signature and handed the papers to Mary to deliver to Mr. Crawshaw.

Mary had discovered the new gallery premises only six days ago. It was located just along the road in Old Bond Street. Having spotted the 'To Let' sign in the window she'd immediately organised a viewing for her and Viktor for later that same day. They were both impressed and decided it would be perfect for their needs. It was ideally situated and had more floor space than their current gallery.

Whilst Mary delivered the legal papers to Mr. Crawshaw, Viktor had returned to his investigations into item 14 on Alexander's original listing of the paintings he and Ian had viewed at 'Dexter's End'. He was still convinced that Ian knew something... something that he hadn't noticed. It related to the 'Madeleine B' painting on the wall in the hallway. So far his research had identified the signature, 'Madeleine B', was an alias sometimes used by Paul Gauguin. Also, there appeared to be two pictures, titled 'Fête Gloanec'. One at 'Dexter's End' and a second on display in the French gallery, Musée des Beaux-Arts d'Orléans. So, what had Ian spotted? Why had the provenance for this 'Dexter's End' painting been so vague? Why was there an exact copy of the painting being displayed in the French museum? Were there two original 'Fête Gloanec' paintings? Or was one a copy? A fake?

Viktor leaned back in his chair and tried to think of another approach. Nothing, at the moment, seemed to make much sense.

Viktor's mind was suddenly distracted when his mobile phone started to ring. Answering the call, he was surprised to hear Ian's voice.

"Hello, Ian. I've just been thinking about you."

"Obviously expecting my call," replied Ian. "Anyway, I thought I ought to bring you up to date with regards to the painting collection at 'Dexter's End'."

Ian told Viktor about Charles's decision not to accept Alexander's offer for the painting collection. He then gave Viktor a selective version of his subsequent meeting with Charles. He explained that Charles had previously met Ian at Sotheby's, several years ago, and wanted him to personally handle the sale of the collection.

"I see," was Viktor's immediate reaction. "So, what happens now?"

"I need to look into Charles's paintings again. He's given me a more accurate record of each of the paintings' provenances. Some of the pictures are worth a lot more than we originally reported."

"I think we both thought that would be the case, but the paperwork we were given was really quite vague."

"I know," replied Ian. "But Charles had his reasons."

Chapter 2

On the final morning of May Ling's vacation in Antigua, Oscar slipped quietly out of bed. It was just after 5.50am. He left May continuing to sleep peacefully. He'd struggled to sleep himself, knowing he'd soon be back alone in his bed.

He quietly slipped on his dressing gown and walked into the kitchen to prepare breakfast. He wanted to make sure everything was fully prepared before they went for their early morning swim in the Caribbean Sea.

May had become very fond of Oscar's tropical fruits, nuts and cereals for breakfast. All very different to her usual quick Chinese dishes and coffee back home.

After preparing a huge bowl of mixed fresh fruits he placed it in the fridge and made himself a mug of coffee. Taking the drink through to his study he savoured and sipped the hot coffee whilst he waited for his computer to spring into life. After it had booted successfully, he checked his three favourite news websites but nothing really captured his attention. These websites were his main contact with what was happening in the outside world. He then switched his attention to his emails and found that Wesley, the owner of the 'Shell Gallery', wanted to have a meeting to discuss a particular problem. Wesley had briefly explained the situation but Oscar decided his reply could wait until May had left. He could then give the query his full attention.

Oscar sipped the last drops of his coffee and looked at his wristwatch. 6.45am. He looked out of the window and saw the first signs of sunrise. This was his usual time to swim in the Caribbean, before the sun became too hot.

He left the study and strolled back towards his bedroom. Quietly pushing open the door he noticed May was curled up and still fast asleep. He slowly walked to the side of his bed, sat down and listened to her rhythmic breathing. He leaned forward, pulled back the single cotton sheet and kissed her on the cheek. He then smiled and gently stroked her hair. Gradually, May began to stir. Opening her eyes and spotting Oscar, she sat up, smiled and kissed Oscar fully on his lips.

"Last morning, May," whispered Oscar, standing up from the bed. "There's a big sea out there waiting for us." Oscar wandered over to his wardrobe and selected a pair of blue swimming shorts.

May sat up, stretched and yawned. "What time is it?"

"Time for our swim," replied Oscar. He checked his watch. "Nearly seven o'clock. We've got three hours before I need to take you to the airport."

May got out of bed and Oscar watched her slim, naked body walk into the ensuite bathroom.

It was about an hour later when they both sat down at the kitchen table and began to eat their breakfast.

May had once again enjoyed her relaxing swim in the lovely warm sea. "I'm going to miss the Caribbean, Oscar. Our early morning swim is so refreshing and it gives me such a great appetite for breakfast."

"Is that all you'll miss?" teased Oscar. He tried to hold back a smile.

May smiled and placed her hand on the side of Oscar's face. "I'll miss you, too."

"I'll miss you too… a lot," said Oscar, looking deep into May's dark blue eyes. "It's been fabulous, you staying here."

"I've had a wonderful time. You are so lucky to be living on such a lovely island. It's all made me think."

"Think about what?" queried Oscar.

"The future. Our future. Beijing… and Hong Kong. I don't really want to go back. All I have there is work… and with the Chinese government, well, that's becoming more difficult and uncertain, by the day."

"You don't have to go back, May. It would be wonderful if you stayed here with me."

"I know. But even if I decided to move out here… permanently, or elsewhere, I'd still have a lot of sorting out to do first. I can't just drop everything… all the things I've worked so hard to achieve. A lot of people rely on me for their livelihood. I won't just walk out and let them down."

"No, of course. But, do you think we have a future… us together, I mean?"

"Yes, of course. It was wonderful meeting up with you again in Hong Kong. When you invited me to come and stay with you in Antigua, it was the highlight of my year. I counted the days until I left Hong Kong. We've got to keep in touch this time and see how we can move forward… together."

Oscar smiled. He could feel his emotions rising and wiped his right eye. "Of course we will. I don't mind returning to Hong Kong for a short holiday, but I'm not going back there to live again."

"I know," replied May. She stared down at the last three pieces of fruit in her bowl. "We need to talk about the future, Oscar. I know we're both going to be sad living apart."

The drive to the airport was a quiet journey. They were

both deep in thought. Everything that needed to be said had been discussed over the last few hours. May's eyes were focused on the passing countryside and the traffic, but her mind was thinking about the last few weeks with Oscar. It had been far more than just a wonderful holiday, it had been a time for her to relax and reflect on her life and ambitions. Her relationship with Oscar had blossomed and she was certain he was going to be an essential part of her future. She felt sad to be leaving, but tried to convince herself it would only be for a short period. But would it? When she arrived back in Hong Kong would she simply slot back into her old lifestyle and realise that the great time with Oscar was just that, a great time, a holiday romance, or was it something more special? Time would tell… one way or another.

Emma sat quietly in the home office. Ian was away at a business meeting and Robert was at school. She had reserved today to try and find the last missing link between the artist Georges Seurat and Pickles and Co. She opened up her computer and typed the list of all the information she'd recently established:

- *'Mademoiselle Chad' had been painted in 1889*
- *It had been purchased at an auction on the 14th November, 1902, by Barrett's the Jewellers for three shillings.*
- *Pickles and Co. owned the painting prior to the auction. They'd ceased trading earlier in 1902.*
- *Pickles and Co. had previously been based at 12 Cornmarket Street, Oxford.*
- *Prior to 1902, 12 Cornmarket Street was occupied by Pickles and Co. both as an art shop and as an agency from the offices upstairs.*
- *The agency specialised in purchasing and importing*

paintings by some of the post-impressionist artists living in France.

- *Georges Seurat died in 1891.*

Pondering on these facts, she gradually realised there were more questions still to be answered. Typing again she listed the following:

- *Was the painting purchased directly from the artist, or through a French agency link?*
- *Were there any other links or connections?*
- *What had happened to the painting during those first 13 years of its life?*
- *Was there a direct link between Pickles and Co. and Georges Seurat?*

Emma rechecked all her notes from earlier findings plus the information she'd obtained during her conversations with Jean at Barrett's the Jewellers. She was happy that the provenance dating all the way back to the 14th November 1902 would stand up to official scrutiny, but she also knew that without the missing information for its first 13 years, between 1889–1902, the painting would certainly be devalued. Ian had told her that without proven provenance for this critical period, the picture's value could well be reduced by many, many, thousands of pounds.

She sat back in her chair and pondered again on the challenge. How could she find out more about Pickles and Co.'s business dealings during those crucial 13 years?

Suddenly, Emma had an inspired thought. What had happened to all Pickles and Co.'s paintings and assets when they'd ceased trading? Presumably they were sold off by the official receiver. Did official receivers exist back in 1902? She made a note to find out. Who would they have been sold to? Would it be via an auction? Maybe. Could the buyer or buyers have obtained all Pickles and Co.'s records as well? After all, those records would contain valuable information, including the provenances for all Pickles and Co.'s paintings. Maybe, just maybe, those records would include the painting, 'Mademoiselle Chad'!

Emma stood up from her desk and walked over to Ian's collection of art books, on a large bookcase immediately behind his desk. She was not sure what she was looking for, or going to find, but hoped something useful might just turn up. After a few minutes she removed a book listing all the art galleries in the United Kingdom. The publication date was 1996. Obviously out of date, she thought, but maybe it would still give her a clue to all the old established UK galleries.

She then spotted and removed another large book. It was a comprehensive history of the Ashmolean Museum in Oxford. Pickles and Co. had been based in Oxford. Was there a connection? She carried both publications back to her desk and opened the galleries book, looking in the index for galleries located in and around the Oxford area. She then excluded all the galleries that didn't exist prior to 1910. The result was three galleries; she wrote down their names and telephone numbers.

Next, she opened the thick book titled 'The Ashmolean Museum' and found the section on the Pre-Raphaelite art collection. She established that the museum had built up a large collection of these paintings, but, more intriguingly, she also read that a group of young painters, sculptors and writers had, in 1848, formed an alliance known as the 'The Pre-Raphaelite Brotherhood'. Although she was disappointed to read that Georges Seurat was not part of this group, she wondered if there was still any possible link with Pickles and Co.

At least now, she thought, I'll have some more up-to-date information to present to Ian.

Later that evening, Ian and Emma were sitting on the settee in the lounge. Emma was summarising her new findings. Ian remained silent and was impressed with Emma's research.

Once she'd finished, Ian said, "That's all very interesting, what do you plan to do next?"

"Unless you have any other suggestions, I thought I'd make some telephone calls, ring the three galleries I've listed and maybe the Ashmolean Museum too. I'm hoping somewhere in this group I'll find my answer."

Ian had one additional idea, but decided to let Emma try her own options first. "Okay. Good luck. I think you're almost there."

Emma smiled. She was determined to crack this tortuous final leg of her investigations.

Chapter 3

Ian telephoned Viktor. "Vic, it's Ian. Fancy an adventure?"

"Hi, Ian. Of course. What are you suggesting?" Viktor was excited and curious.

"A short trip to France, to the Musée des Beaux-Arts d'Orléans."

"I knew it!" exclaimed Viktor. "You want to see their version of the 'Fête Gloanec'."

"Well done, Vic. I'm impressed. You've obviously been doing your homework," replied Ian, smiling to himself.

"It's that painting at 'Dexter's End', by 'Madeleine B'. That's Paul Gauguin's work. But which is the real painting? You think Charles's version is the real one, don't you?"

"That's what I want to find out. I want to understand why the French consider their painting the original because… I'm not convinced it is! I've got two seats booked on a private flight from Gatwick tomorrow morning. Do you want to join me?"

"Try and stop me. What time's the flight?"

Fifteen hours later, Ian and Viktor were on board a small Cessna private charter plane over the English Channel. They were the only two passengers.

Viktor looked at Ian and said, "I'm still not sure why you need to personally see the French museum's painting?"

Ian smiled. "I told Charles I thought his painting was the original, but I won't be totally sure until I've seen the museum's version, 'in the flesh', so to speak. I discussed the matter with Charles yesterday and told him my plan. There's serious inheritance tax implications for him, so we need to be sure which painting is the original."

"Yes, I see. But why did you want me to join you?"

Ian smiled and turned to look directly at Viktor. "For your expert opinion of course."

The French taxi arrived outside the front entrance to the Musée des Beaux-Arts d'Orléans. It was 1.45pm. Twenty minutes later they stood side by side, facing the painting titled 'Fête Gloanec' by Paul Gauguin. Written in French, the note at the side of the picture explained why it had been signed as 'Madeleine B'.

"It's much cleaner than the painting we saw at 'Dexter's End'," whispered Viktor, still inspecting every detail. "Otherwise, I don't see any difference."

As Ian inspected the painting a small grin appeared on his face. He had no itchy scalp, no sweaty palms this time. In hushed tones he whispered back to Viktor. "Vic, what you see in front of you is a good copy. It's not the original."

"Come on, Ian, you think it's a fake?" queried Viktor. "You can't decide just like that."

"This is not the real 'Fête Gloanec'. I just know. Unless… there are two!"

"Wow! If you're correct, well… this means there'll be massive implications."

Ian leaned forwards and tried to inspect the brush-strokes closer. "When you look at this painting, do you feel anything?"

"Feel? You mean, can I tell it's not the original? Well, no. Occasionally, I can see something in a painting that I think isn't quite right, but… well, in this case it looks fine. I'd need to put both copies next to each other and obviously get the experts to complete the usual scientific investigations. Then there are the provenances."

Ian nodded. "I don't get the same feeling with this picture that I did with the version at 'Dexter's End'… and my instincts are rarely wrong."

Viktor smiled and shook his head. He was definitely feeling bewildered and knew Ian had a sort of sixth sense when it came to paintings. Personally, he was feeling completely out of his depth. "Okay. What do we do now?"

Ian looked at his wristwatch. "What we do now is find a taxi. Our flight back to London leaves in two hours."

When Ian arrived home later that evening, he explained to Emma the details of his earlier conversations with Charles, and his findings from the visit to the Musée des Beaux-Arts d'Orléans.

"You're not going to go along with Charles's fraudulent proposals to avoid inheritance tax, are you?" asked Emma. She was alarmed that Ian was even mentioning this possible course of action.

"No. Of course not. Charles's suggestion is far too risky. Besides, it's not going to work either. You and I have previously agreed we don't need to be involved in illegal activity… or be unnecessarily greedy. No. I'm thinking of a much simpler and far better solution to Charles's problem."

Ian then outlined to Emma what he was planning.

After about 20 minutes Emma said, "Okay. It's quite a good idea. Borderline legal, but worth a try. When are you going to speak to Charles?"

"It's too late to ring him now," replied Ian. "But tomorrow I'll send him an email."

First thing the next morning Ian emailed Charles. He suggested they should meet as he'd got some information... and a new idea.

Five minutes later Charles replied and said he was at work, but would telephone him later that evening.

It was just after 9pm when Ian's mobile phone rang. The call was from Charles Owen.

"Hi, Ian. Your email sounded intriguing."

"Hello, Charles. Can we meet up? I've thought of another idea which... I think you'll be pleased with."

"Can't you tell me over the phone?" queried Charles. He was extremely busy at work.

"No, I don't think that would be very wise," replied Ian, in a serious tone.

Two days later, the two men met in Trafalgar Square. It was during Charles's lunch break. After a brief exchange of pleasantries, they sat on a bench far away from other people.

Ian started to speak, "I've thought of another route to help with your inheritance tax situation. As you know, I visited the Musée des Beaux-Arts d'Orléans the other day and stood within three feet of their version of the 'Fête Gloanec'. It's a fake, a copy, call it what you will, but your painting is the original."

"Well, that's good news, but I don't see how that helps me with my tax problem," replied Charles, a little confused.

"Their version is deemed to be the original, right? It has been accepted in the art market as the original, therefore yours must be a fake, a copy."

"But it isn't, you just said so."

Ian smiled. "Bear with me. I'd be prepared to arrange for someone to give you a low valuation on the picture that currently resides in your grandfather's hallway. The report would say it's a copy of the painting that currently hangs in the French museum. That valuation could then be presented for inheritance tax purposes. Once that's all gone through, and all the dust has finally settled, well, that's when we can get your painting professionally examined. Hopefully, the experts will conclude your version is the original and the museum's version is the copy."

Charles looked at Ian and then gradually smiled. "That sounds nice and sneaky, but, will it work?"

"I don't see why not… and in the meantime it's going to save you on inheritance tax: legally, well, sort of. We can look at some of your grandfather's other paintings at the same time."

"You think this scam will work with some of the other paintings?"

Ian stared at Charles with a scowl. "Charles, this isn't a scam. It's all above board and certainly more legal than the route you were thinking about. I still need to look in more detail at your grandfather's other paintings… and their provenances. We need to see how we can justify new and legal valuations for the taxman."

"Okay. Well done, Ian. Let's give it a go."

"One last thing, Charles." Ian was trying to convey his seriousness. "Your generous offer of your grandfather's 'Fête Gloanec'. I'm sorry, but I can't accept it as my reward. Once we've finalised the collection and the inheritance tax authorities have agreed to the paperwork, then you can decide what my contribution has been worth."

"Okay, Ian. Trusting aren't you?"

"In your business world I gather there's a saying, 'my word is my bond'."

Charles laughed and then leaned towards Ian. "You read too much fiction."

Chapter 4

Emma had made telephone calls to two of the well-established art galleries in the Oxford area. Unfortunately, neither seemed to have any knowledge of, or connection, with, Pickles and Co. They were also reluctant to search through all their old records to see if they'd previously had any dealings with them back in the late 1800s. Although now feeling slightly deflated, Emma decided to ring the third gallery before taking a break for lunch. She pressed the telephone numbers and waited for the call to be answered. She could hear the gallery phone ringing but nobody was answering. She was just about to hang up when suddenly she heard a male voice announce, "Barker's Gallery."

"Hello," announced Emma. "My name is Emma Caxton and I'm trying to find out if your company had any dealings with a particular Oxford art gallery and an agency in the late 19th century."

"The 19th century you say. You'll need to speak to our Mr. Clive Jackson; he's our archivist. He works part time and today is one of his days off."

"Which days does Mr. Jackson work?"

"Tuesdays and Thursdays, ten till three."

"Thank you," responded Emma. "I'll telephone again

tomorrow. Would it be possible to let him know I called please? My name is Emma Caxton."

"Okay, missus, I've made a note."

"Goodbye and thank you," replied Emma. Oh well, she thought, I'll just have to wait another day.

Emma sat back in her chair and wondered whether to contact the Ashmolean Museum now or leave it until later. However, something in her mind prompted her to google Clive Jackson at the Barker's Gallery, Oxford. She just wondered if there would be any additional information online.

Emma entered the details into her computer and, to her surprise, there was a positive response. She slowly read the results and immediately realised that Mr. Jackson was quite an expert on 18th and 19th century art. He'd got a number of titled letters after his name. She also established that he'd previously been employed at Christie's and the Ashmolean Museum, before retiring in 2015. Well, well, well, she thought, this is a turn up. I wonder if Ian has come across him?

Five minutes later Ian returned to their house and Emma called out to him. Ian walked through the hallway and joined her in the office.

"Ian, have you heard of a man named Clive Jackson? He's working part time at Barker's Gallery in Oxford. He used to work at Christie's and the Ashmolean Museum."

Ian smiled. "So, you've found Clive have you?"

"Oh, so you do know him."

"Know of him, but not personally met him. He's well thought of in the art world. How did you come across him?"

"After he retired from the Ashmolean Museum, he joined Barker's Gallery in Oxford. As I said, he now works part time as their archivist. I've made an appointment to ring him tomorrow," replied Emma, feeling quite pleased with herself.

"Excellent. Coincidentally, I was going to suggest you try and track him down if all your other avenues failed, but obviously you didn't need my help after all."

Emma smiled. "No, I didn't, did I?"

The next morning, just after ten o'clock, Emma telephoned Barker's Gallery and asked to be put through to Mr. Jackson.

"Hello, Jackson speaking."

"Good morning, Mr. Jackson. My name is Mrs. Emma Caxton."

"Did you telephone me yesterday?"

"Yes, that was me. I'm hoping you may be able to help me." Emma crossed her fingers in hope. "I'm trying to trace any companies that may have had any knowledge or previous dealings with a firm called Pickles and Co. They had an art gallery and agency based in Cornmarket Street, back in the 19th century."

"That's not a name I recall. Tell me what, in particular, you're looking for and I'll see if I can help?"

Emma gave Clive Jackson a summary of her research into the 'Mademoiselle Chad' painting to date.

"I see," responded Mr. Jackson. "So, you think you might have unearthed an original Seurat painting?"

"I hope so, especially after all the hard work I've put in."

"Mmm. It's a possibility, although there are a lot of fakes about. Have you taken your painting to an expert?"

"My husband used to work for Sotheby's. Ian Caxton."

"Oh, yes. I recognise the name now. I think I might have met him at some time. You say he doesn't work for Sotheby's anymore?"

Emma explained briefly what she and Ian were now doing.

"Well good luck to you both. Tricky occupation choice. I'll see what I can find from our records, Emma. Let me have your telephone number. It might be about a week, but I'll ring you."

Emma said thank you and gave him the numbers for both the landline and her mobile.

When Emma ended the call, she was feeling much more positive.

It was exactly seven days later that Emma's mobile phone rang.

"Emma? This is Clive Jackson."

"Oh hello, Mr. Jackson," replied Emma. She was in the kitchen and carried her phone through the hallway into the office.

"Well, I have a little bit of good news for you. Amongst our archives I found out that Pickles and Co. ceased trading and went into voluntary liquidation in early 1902. All their assets were subsequently sold at auction. We have a catalogue list of all the assets that were auctioned and a list of all the paintings Barker's Gallery purchased. Your painting was listed as Lot 72, but it wasn't one of the paintings we bought. Pickles and Co. would appear to have been well organised because all the paintings we bought from the auction came with satisfactory provenances. Before they ceased trading, it would also appear that we did actually do a little bit of business with them. Mainly buying a few of their imported French paintings."

"I see," said Emma, a little deflated. "But no extra information about my picture."

"No, sorry," responded Mr. Jackson. He could hear the disappointment in Emma's voice. "As I say, the paintings we bought all came with good provenances so, in theory, your people in Witney should have received the same. You should go back to them. They may still have the original paperwork."

"Thank you for your time and effort, Mr. Jackson."

"Let me know how it goes, Emma. I'm intrigued to know how it all works out."

"I will. Goodbye and thank you again."

Emma placed her mobile phone down on the desk and stared out of the window. It was now January and Ian was brushing the last of the snow from the driveway. She briefly shivered at the cold bleak view. All in all, she thought, it was definitely not a good day.

Chapter 5

"Ian? Is that you?" When he picked up the telephone, Ian discovered it was his father on the line.

"Hello, Dad, is everything okay?" replied Ian. Ian's father rarely telephoned and, when he did, Ian tended to assume there was an issue or a problem.

"Yes, fine. Your mother and I have just moved out of 'The Willows'. The sale goes through tomorrow and we're moving into 'Bluebell Cottage' on Friday. I thought you ought to know."

"Thanks, Dad. Are you and Mum still okay about it?"

"Your mother had a few emotional moments whilst sorting out some of our possessions. You know, what to keep, what to send to charity shops and what to throw out, but she seems fine now. We're both excited about our new future."

"I'm really pleased for you both, Dad. So's Emma. We both like 'Bluebell Cottage'. It's a good choice, a nice size for you both and a lovely location. Where are you staying tonight?"

"We've just got overnight bags and are staying in, what will become, our new local pub. We've booked in for two nights. They do bed and breakfast. Nice people."

"Well, that's one way to quickly meet some of your new neighbours."

"Come and see us when we're all settled in. Your mother wants to see Robert."

"We will, Dad. Give my love to Mum." Ian switched off the call.

"Who was that on the phone?" Emma reappeared from the garden.

"It was my father. They've moved out of 'The Willows'."

"I think they'll enjoy 'Bluebell Cottage'. Much less work and worry. I think it was your support and positivity that finally convinced them."

"Maybe, but you were very positive when we viewed the cottage with them too. They want us all to visit as soon as they've settled in."

"That's nice. We'll do that. By the way, Mr. Jackson at Barker's Gallery telephoned earlier and suggested I should try Barrett's again about the provenance. However, I was wondering, wouldn't the provenance have been passed on when they sold the painting? When I spoke to Jean last time, she said she'd given me all the information they had. Besides, contacting her again is a little tricky as I originally told her I was tracing family history, not investigating the provenance of a particular painting."

Ian nodded his head. "Jackson's probably right."

"Anyway," continued Emma, "I've now telephoned the Records Department at the Ashmolean Museum. I spoke to Mr. Giles, a nice young man, and he promised to investigate any historical connection the museum might have had with Pickles and Co. I'm hoping he'll ring me back later today."

"Fingers crossed then," replied Ian. "It's a pity, I really thought Clive Jackson would have come up trumps for you. Still, there's often snags when anybody investigates provenances. Let's hope you have better luck with the Ashmolean."

It was just after 3.30pm when Emma received the

telephone call on her mobile. She was driving along a country lane on her way to collect Robert from school. She slowly pulled into the side of the road next to a footpath sign and stopped. "Hello. Emma Caxton," she answered.

"Emma. John Giles at the Ashmolean Museum. I've checked our records and have some good news for you."

Emma closed her eyes and crossed her fingers. She just hoped…

"I've found the original auction catalogue you mentioned," continued John. "It appears we bought five paintings at the same auction. We've also got a list of all the paintings sold and separate copy files relating to their provenances."

"Really!" exclaimed Emma. Her heart was beating quickly now. "Tell me, John, can you look at the provenance listing please and tell me if it includes a painting titled 'Mademoiselle Chad' by the artist Georges Seurat."

"Just a minute, I'll have a look."

Emma squeezed the steering wheel in anticipation and excitement. She could hear a rustling of papers at the other end of the line. Come on, come on, please, please, she pleaded quietly to herself.

"Yes. Here we are. Now then. Er, yes… it would appear that Pickles and Co. purchased the painting via an agency in Paris, the Société des Artistes Indépendants, on the 23rd August 1890."

"Oh wow!" exclaimed Emma. "That's brilliant."

"I don't know if you are aware but, the Société des Artistes Indépendants was actually a group of painters in Paris. Georges Seurat was one of its founder members in 1884… or thereabouts. So really, your painting could be said to have been bought directly from the artist."

"That's fabulous news, John. Oh wow! You've been so helpful. Is there any chance I could have a photocopy of that information, please."

"Don't see why not. It's not classified information."

"I can come into Oxford and collect it," said Emma. She felt so excited and would have travelled all the way to France to get this result.

"Okay. When are you coming to Oxford?"

Emma removed her diary from her handbag and quickly flicked through the pages. "What about tomorrow afternoon… about four o'clock?"

"Yes, that's fine. I shall be here and I'll have the photocopy waiting for you."

"John, I don't know how to thank you. You've been so helpful. I look forward to meeting you tomorrow. Goodbye."

"Goodbye, Emma. I'm pleased I was able to help."

When Emma switched off her phone, she shouted out loud "Yes!" But what she hadn't noticed was that two women ramblers were crossing the road from the footpath directly behind her car. Once she did notice them, however, she suddenly felt embarrassed. The ramblers had heard her shout and both looked into her car before they carried on walking. Now they were both laughing and kept glancing back in Emma's direction.

"'Right," Emma said to herself, still feeling a little embarrassed, "I'm going to be late collecting Robert. I'd better get a move on."

After Emma arrived home with Robert, she quickly went into the office to speak to Ian. Excited and anxious to tell him, she summarised her telephone conversation with John Giles at the Ashmolean Museum.

"Well done you. That's brilliant," said Ian, and gave his wife a kiss and a hug.

"I want to take a gift for John, to say thank you. Any ideas?"

"Strictly speaking he's only been doing his job, but I can understand why you'd want to show your appreciation.

Without knowing him, it's difficult to know what to suggest; what about a nice bottle of whisky or some wine? Hopefully he won't be a teetotaller."

"I think wine would be a better choice. A selection of red and white."

"That should be acceptable. I'm really pleased for you, Emma. You've done this research all on your own."

"It's been hard work, but I did have some help from you. Mind, it's both rewarding and very satisfying to get to the end. Do you think this provenance will be accepted?"

"The only way to find out for sure is to get the painting authenticated by an expert. Someone whose opinion is really valued."

"Do you know anyone?" Emma's excitement was slowly being displaced by concern and a little doubt.

"No. But I do know someone who may have a suggestion. I'll contact her tomorrow morning."

Emma looked at Ian with a questioning look on her face. She wondered who exactly 'her' was.

Chapter 6

It was 12.30pm when Ian met Charles in the 'Hind's Head' public house, close to Leadenhall Market. It was Charles's suggestion and he'd ordered two pints of beer.

"I often use this pub for business meetings," said Charles, passing Ian his drink. "The seating's well spread out and it's not easy to be overheard. It's a popular after-work watering hole for city workers."

"This pub is fine," replied Ian. "Besides, it's far too wet and cold to meet outside in Trafalgar Square again."

They collected their drinks and sat at an empty table well away from the other customers. Ian opened his briefcase and removed a file of papers. He passed them over for Charles's inspection. "Here are the revised valuations I promised. They're based on the original provenances you produced on my first visit to 'Dexter's End'. The valuer I used has agreed to our fee and I think he's done a good job."

After putting his glass of beer down onto the table, Charles glanced at the papers. "You're sure the taxman will accept these?"

"I don't see why not," replied Ian, picking up his own glass of beer. "There are only three paintings that have had their valuations reduced. It should be all fine."

"I still don't understand why you wanted a third party

to provide these valuations. You and Vic completed them yourselves earlier. Why couldn't we just use those?" asked Charles.

Ian leaned forward and lowered his voice. "In a few months' time, you and I will be trying to prove that your version of the 'Fête Gloanec' is the original picture. It would look very odd, and potentially criminal, if my name was against the valuation for inheritance tax purposes as well."

"Good point," said Charles, with an understanding nod of his head. "I'll get these over to my accountant first thing in the morning. Everything else is now ready for submitting to the taxman."

"Good luck." Ian raised his glass and drank some of his beer.

Charles smiled. "If all works out as you think it will, I intend to resign from work and move abroad. I'm almost burnt out as it is."

"Money trading that bad?"

Charles stood up. "Let me get you another drink first and then I'll explain."

"No, no. I'm fine. Thanks anyway," replied Ian, holding on to his glass which was still half full.

Charles sat back down. "Yes, I work for a large investment bank, AKGI, just two minutes' walk from here. Joined straight from university. Initially I worked as an analyst. I enjoyed the work and the challenge. It's not so manic as a trader. Analysts like to think they're more intellectual than emotional." He gave a small smile and then carried on, "However, the hours are very long and working until 2am isn't unusual. You can forget your social life and your weekends. The salary and bonuses are a powerful pull. We really felt important, which is great when you're in your early 20s. Even so, I gradually realised it was becoming far too all-consuming, but I didn't really mind as they were paying me well. My main role was helping companies raise capital. This was done by either issuing stock, borrowing money, or assisting with mergers and acquisitions. We looked for investment opportunities for our wealthy clients as well. Some are really nice people, but mostly… well they're, let's just say, obnoxious."

Ian listened intently. This was all a new world to him. He sipped the last of his beer and wished he'd taken up Charles's offer of another pint, but then he remembered he still had to pick Robert up from school later that afternoon.

"As I say," continued Charles, "we work ridiculous hours. Mind, I'm one of the lucky ones. I've never been a person that needs more than about five hours' sleep at night. Some of my colleagues could often be found sleeping at their desks."

"I've never understood why bankers have to work such long hours. It must eventually become an inefficient way of doing things."

"Yes, it is, but you have to remember, if you didn't do it, others certainly would… and do. Without putting in the hours, you'd quickly be shown the door. After all, money trading is carried out 24 hours a day. New York, Tokyo, you name it, they all work long hours. Yes, financially, it's a very rewarding career, but only if you produce the figures. Sitting where I did, you could always see your career path. Your boss and his boss were both on the same floor. You look at them and think, I could do their job, so you work harder and longer hours. The pressure is always on to deliver. You have to be totally focused. Millions and billions of pounds are just numbers, but everything must be triple-checked. One false deal and you could be responsible for the bank, or a client, losing millions of pounds. Remember Nick Leeson at Barings Bank? It's so easy for some of the traders to get sucked in deeper and deeper. A couple of bad calls and you're really chasing and panicking.

Very quickly, tens of millions of losses can be billions lost with yet another wrong call."

Ian slowly shook his head and took a deep breath. He thought the art world could be pressurised at times, but this was all so very different.

Charles drank the last mouthful of his beer. "Thinking back, I used to live on coffee and any other drink that could keep me awake. I'd eat a quick sandwich, or some sort of microwave food, at about 3am. However, one good thing, I never had the need to go down the drugs route. I know some colleagues who have, just to try to stay awake. Cocaine, large quantities of alcohol and all sorts of self-medication. After my first two years I'd easily achieve over a 100,000 salary. That was doubled with my bonus and other extras. Other than top footballers, Ian, who else earns that level of money at 22? Anyway, I could put down a good deposit on a nice flat, just ten minutes' walk from the office. I planned to work this way for possibly ten years and then buy a property somewhere in the country – maybe set up my own vineyard. Trouble is, the whole thing becomes your life. It's addictive. You only speak, face to face, with people at work. You gradually dream of leaving, eating proper meals… and at a sensible hour. My mum hated what I was doing and regularly told me so. But when it comes to February… well, that's bonus time. Focus quickly shifts back to the job in hand. Back to the treadmill. Most people in the business are either sacked or wheeled out of the office in a body bag. I don't know of anyone who's worked in our bank for 25 years. Burnout is a real mental health issue in our business."

"And you think you're at burnout right now?"

Charles laughed, "Maybe, but not quite, not yet. I spoke to an ex-colleague a few weeks ago. He said you'll know when you're burnt out, because you'll gradually realise you hate the person you are and your family hates the person you've become. You hate going to work and the money is no longer the motivation it once was. The innate hunger for success has gone. At the moment, Ian, I still like myself… well, a little bit."

Ian smiled, more from acknowledging that he had been listening to every word Charles had said. Certainly, he didn't feel any of this was a laughing matter.

"Today, Ian, to answer your original question, I'm my boss's boss that I referred to earlier. I was promoted 18 months ago. I now look at the young kids joining our company and wish them the best of luck. They'll definitely need it. With the passing of my grandfather, this has given me a new chance… a new opportunity. I'm hoping your little scheme will give me the security, and the balls, to finally get out… before the ambulance men inevitably carry me out in my own zipped-up body bag."

Ian patted Charles on the shoulder, stood up and told him he had a train to catch. His departing words were, "No promises, Charles, but you might just want to start investigating available vineyards."

On the train journey back to Esher, Ian considered the discussion he'd just had. He could see why Charles wanted to get out of investment banking, despite only being in his early thirties. Ian just hoped his plans would work out and they'd both get the right result.

Time would tell.

At the same time as Ian was attending his meeting with Charles, Emma was driving towards Oxford. She was on the M40 and had just passed a sign saying, 'Oxford 15 miles'. She'd already decided it would be best to use the local 'Park & Ride' system. Ian had warned her that parking in the city centre was both difficult and expensive.

Just before leaving home Emma had set the satnav for the 'Park & Ride' on the eastern side of Oxford, just off the A40. Now, after exiting the M40 and joining the A40, her emotions were a mixture of excitement and apprehension. She was pleased she'd finally been able to assemble all the pieces making up the painting's provenance, but also wondered if all her hard work could still be in vain if the experts refused to verify her picture as the genuine work of Georges Seurat. Nothing was certain.

When Emma arrived at the 'Park & Ride' she was not totally sure how the system worked. However, after parking and getting out of her car, she could see a double-decker bus parked just behind a single-storey building. She walked over towards the building and purchased a ticket from one of the pay points. She then joined a small queue of people boarding the bus. She clarified with the driver that the bus would drop her off quite close to the centre of Oxford and that the return bus would collect her from a bus stop across the road.

As soon as she sat down, the bus started its journey. Emma had never been to Oxford before so she'd given herself some extra time to see the facades of the old colleges and visit a few of the shops. She'd remembered from the old television series *Morse*, that Oxford appeared to be a very interesting place to visit for a day. Now she hoped it was going to be both a very interesting and exceptional day.

Chapter 7

As the bus entered the outskirts of Oxford city centre, Emma started to see some of the famous spires in the distance. She thought they looked majestic, especially in the sunshine and against the clear blue February sky. She tried to remember if it was from an old poem, or was it Ben Johnson, who had referred to Oxford as 'the city of dreaming spires'? She could see why. For hundreds of years young people have been educated here. What dreams and ambitions they must have about their futures and careers. In years to come, she wondered if Robert would be clever enough to be accepted here?

When the bus finally arrived in the city centre, Emma alighted with most of the other passengers. She stood and looked for street signs to try and get her bearings. She then consulted her small tourist guide and the street map attached in the rear. Looking all around her, she headed in the direction of Cornmarket Street. She was eager to see number 12, the former gallery and office premises of Pickles and Co. It took Emma just a few minutes to arrive. She looked up and down the rows of properties, but was disappointed to see most were occupied by national chain shops, banks and some offices. She'd expected more independent shops and the construction of the buildings to be in a similar style to those of the nearby colleges. Walking down the street she eventually found number 12. She stood outside the three-storey building. It was located at the corner of Market Street. Once again, she was disappointed. Although she spotted a plaque with 1938 inscribed on it above the first floor window, the whole building had been totally remodelled since Pickles and Co. resided on this site. She hoped these disappointments were not going to be typical of her day.

Although Oxford has been classified as a city for many centuries, it is still, even today, only the size of a reasonable town. Her guide highlighted the fact that most of the interesting sites could be comfortably seen just by walking.

During the next hour Emma wandered up and down a lot of the old streets, lanes and alleyways. She identified the frontages of many of the colleges and explored the famous covered market. She also discovered a small wine shop and purchased two bottles of Chablis for John Giles.

Next to the wine shop, she noticed an empty bench and chose to sit down for a few moments to rest her legs. Looking all around her, she decided she must come back, with Ian and Robert, for a short break. There was so much to see and to do. Yes, she thought, a very interesting and historical city and certainly only one hour's exploration doesn't do the place its full justice.

Emma checked her watch and consulted her map again. She stood up and headed north, eventually joining Magdalen Street. She noted the famous St. Mary Magdalen church on her right-hand side and then further ahead the renowned 'Randolph Hotel'. After passing the hotel's front entrance, she turned left into Beaumont Street and immediately spotted the impressive Romanesque-style building of the Ashmolean Museum. She thought it looked even more impressive in real life than in the photographs she'd seen. Crossing the road and entering the outer courtyard, she walked by the majestic entrance portico. Through the huge entrance doorway, she arrived in the large and very impressive reception area.

For a building that supposedly dated back to the 17th century, Emma was surprised how modern and light the museum appeared. She checked her watch again: 3.57pm. She walked towards the reception desk, where a young lady smiled at her as she approached. "Good afternoon," said the receptionist. "My name is Jill. How can I help you?"

Emma smiled back and announced, "Hello, Jill, I have a meeting with Mr. John Giles at 4pm. My name is Emma Caxton."

"I'll give Mr. Giles a ring for you. Just a moment."

Emma stood back whilst Jill made the telephone call. She marvelled at some of the large ancient stonework statues. She guessed they must be several thousand years old.

"Mrs. Caxton."

Emma turned back to face Jill.

"Mr. Giles will be with you in a few moments."

"Thank you," said Emma. "Should I wait here?"

"Yes, just at the side there is fine."

Emma moved away slightly to let the next person have access to the reception desk. A few minutes later she saw a young man striding towards her carrying an envelope. Emma smiled to herself. She thought he looked about 20 years old!

"Mrs. Caxton?" asked the man.

Emma smiled. "Yes, you must be John Giles." She put the bag containing the two bottles of wine on the floor and held out her hand.

John smiled, nodded and they both shook hands.

"It's so good of you to see me, John. Please call me Emma."

John gave her a nervous smile back. "This is your envelope, Emma. It contains photocopies of all the information you wanted."

Emma took the envelope and had a quick glance inside. There were five sheets of A4 paper and Emma was pleased they listed everything she had asked for.

"You have been so kind and helpful, John. Please accept this little gift by way of a thank you." Emma removed the gift-wrapped package containing the two bottles of wine from her bag and handed it to him.

John accepted the present with a smile. He was very surprised. "Thank you very much. I'm really pleased I was able to help. Have you been to the Ashmolean Museum before?"

"No, and actually, this is my first time visiting Oxford. I intend to bring my family for a few days' holiday. I definitely want to have a full day here in the museum."

"It really is a fascinating place to work. I started here two years ago, after university. I still get lost here sometimes."

They both laughed.

"Thank you again, John. I'd better go before the traffic gets too busy."

They shook hands and said their goodbyes.

Emma walked back in the direction of the 'Park & Ride' bus stop. The earlier sunshine had long gone and the night was already drawing in. Emma shivered. There was just a hint of snow and the air temperature had certainly dropped. She hoped to get home before there was a serious snowfall.

After a disappointing start to her day in Oxford, Emma was now thinking how successful and exciting the rest of her day had turned out to be.

When Ian arrived home from his meeting with Charles, he'd only time for a quick sandwich before he left the house to collect Robert from school. Now, as he was driving his car, his mind was contemplating 'what next?' He knew Emma's efforts were progressing nicely towards a satisfactory conclusion for the 'Mademoiselle Chad' painting and he was hopeful there would be a similar positive conclusion with Charles's collection. They might both be achieved over the next few months. So then what? What are we going to do next?

Ian was still pondering this as he approached the school gates. Two minutes later he'd parked in the school's car park and waited for Robert to come out.

Whilst he was sitting quietly, he reflected on the fact that he and his family were financially secure and his parents were now settled in their new home. Here I am, at 43 years of age, he thought, do I really want to carry on in the art world – be like Andrei, and never see the full benefit of all my efforts and good fortune? When was the last time we went to Monaco? Ian tried to think back. Was it nine months, a year, more? He couldn't remember exactly. To make matters worse, it had just started to snow. Ian hated the snow. He hated cold weather. Why am I still living in this country and not enjoying myself in the warm sunshine? Millions of people would give their right arm to be in my family's position. He looked through the gradually steaming-up windscreen and watched as the first few children ran towards the car park. It was already much darker and the snow was falling like small white feathers onto the car's bonnet. He decided it was definitely time to have another conversation with Emma.

Chapter 8

Ian went to the freezer and removed the casserole Emma had prepared for tonight's meal, before putting it in the oven. All he had to do now was to cook the rice when Emma returned from her trip to Oxford.

"Dad, can you help me with my homework?" asked Robert. He was sitting at Emma's desk in the home office.

Ian walked through to join his son. "Where's the please?"

"Sorry," replied Robert, with a sheepish expression. "Please, Dad."

"What's the subject?" Ian pulled up a chair to the opposite side of the desk.

"It's maths. I'm not very good at letters. Numbers are fine, but it's the letters I don't understand."

"Do you mean algebra?"

"Yes, that's right."

"Maths was not my strongest subject at school… especially algebra. That's really your mother's area. She shouldn't be too long. Can you do some of your other homework first?"

"Okay. Can you tell Mum when she comes in… please?"

Ian smiled. "Okay. Do you want anything to drink before dinner?"

"No, I had a glass of water earlier. I'll have something

with my dinner." Robert moved his maths books to one side and removed two other books from his rucksack.

"I'll be in the kitchen. Dinner should be about an hour."

"Okay", replied Robert. His focus was now on geography and an ongoing project about the Grand Canyon in the USA.

It was about 20 minutes later when Emma arrived home. The snow was now covering the front garden. She was relieved to be home in one piece. Ian heard the car arrive in the driveway and went to the front door. Emma locked the driver's side door and made a dash to where Ian was waiting.

"Come in quick. I see you've got the paperwork," said Ian, holding the door open.

Emma pushed past Ian and into the hallway. She handed the envelope to him and sat on the stairs to remove her boots. "Yes, mission accomplished."

Emma stood up and kissed Ian.

"Welcome home. Did you enjoy Oxford?"

Emma put on her slippers and placed her coat on the side of the stairs. "Yes, Oxford's an interesting place. I think we ought to make time for a long weekend visit. Maybe Robert will be inspired."

Ian smiled and walked towards the kitchen. "Dinner will be ready soon. Robert would like you to help him with his maths homework. He's sitting at your desk in the office."

"Okay," called out Emma. "I'll see him in a minute. I just want to go upstairs first."

Later that evening, Emma was sitting at the breakfast bar whilst Ian was washing the dirty dinner crockery. They both updated each other about their day's events. Afterwards, as Ian was drying his hands, he said, "By the way, I've managed to speak to Gillian, at Sotheby's, about your painting. She suggested we contact James Marshall. I don't know him but, apparently, he's quite experienced and knowledgeable when it comes to Seurat's work. She thinks that if we can convince Mr. Marshall, then it'll put us in a much stronger position going forward. Then it'll be the turn of the main experts, the critical people who'll make the final decision."

"Who's Gillian? I've never heard you mention her name before," responded Emma, with a little unease in her voice.

"She joined Sotheby's just after I left. She works with Penny. It was Penny who recommended her. Apparently, she used to work at Christie's and specialises in 19th and 20th century French post-impressionist, neo-impressionist and pointillist artists."

"Oh, okay," replied Emma, somewhat mystified. "So, when do we contact this Mr. Marshall?"

"Gillian said she'd ring him first and advise him that we'll be contacting him early next week. Between now and then we need to put together a very professional presentation of all the provenance findings."

"I can start on that tomorrow, but I'll need your help."

"You have a go first. Then I'll cast my eye over your draft."

Emma nodded and made a large yawn. "I think it's bedtime. We've both had long and busy days."

Ian looked through the kitchen window and noticed the outside security light had come on. He spotted the bushy red tail of a scuttling fox as it disappeared into the hedgerow. "I've got a feeling there'll be three of us at home tomorrow. Look outside, the snow's falling heavily."

Emma looked through the same window. "Oh well, at least we're warm in here. Let's go to bed."

Ian thought about talking to Emma about their future, but decided it was much too late tonight and… well, maybe, it could wait a while longer.

At 8.20am the next morning, Emma made a telephone call to Robert's school saying that due to the weather and the length of the journey, Robert would be staying at home today.

"Was that you on the phone?" asked Ian, as he entered the kitchen.

"Yes. I've told the school that, because of the weather, Robert will be staying at home today. Apparently, a number of the teachers and some of the other day pupils have already telephoned with the same message."

"Okay," said Ian, with a small smile on his face. "Maybe I'll help Robert build a snowman."

Emma smiled back. "I'm sure he'll enjoy that. Can you pop up and tell him please, Ian. I'm preparing breakfast."

Later that morning Emma was in the office trying to concentrate on summarising the provenance report for the meeting with Mr. Marshall. However, she'd now become distracted by the shouts and laughs from outside in the front garden. She could see a half-completed snowman, but also snowballs being hurled by both Ian and Robert at each other. She smiled and was pleased that, despite missing one day at school, Robert was able to have a little bit of fun, 'dad time', with Ian. Something Ian certainly wouldn't have been able to do whilst working at Sotheby's.

Eventually the snowman was completed and it stood in the middle of the front lawn. Emma made hot tomato soup for lunch and called 'the builders' in, saying it was time to dry out and eat. As Ian and Robert cleaned themselves up, ready for their food, Emma reflected on how happy and lucky they all were as a family.

It was four days later when Ian telephoned James Marshall. After the usual introductions and a brief discussion about the 'Mademoiselle Chad' painting, James agreed to meet them both at his New Bond Street gallery, in seven days' time.

Emma was sitting opposite Ian in the office whilst he made the telephone call. "Is he going to see us?" she asked, with just an edge of concern in her voice.

"Next Tuesday at 1pm," responded Ian. "That's when it's going to get very interesting."

"Excellent!" responded Emma, before briefly clapping her hands. She was relieved they were going to get an independent, expert opinion. "What do we need to do until then?"

"I'm going to speak to a colleague at the Courtauld Institute. I'm certainly happy with the very professional provenance report you've put together, but it might make all the difference if we can get some scientific support as well. I know they keep records of various profiles of the chemicals used in old paints, so hopefully they'll have profiles for Seurat's paintings. What we want is a comparable profile against an authenticated Seurat painting completed about the same time as your picture was painted."

"Will your colleague be able to do that before we see James Marshall?"

"Hopefully, yes," replied Ian, "But it's not critical at this stage. All we want from James Marshall is his opinion as to whether your painting 'could' be a work by Seurat. If he's in any way doubtful, or rejects it outright… well that puts a totally different perspective on the matter."

Emma smiled. She was excited but still anxious. She knew she'd have this mixture of feelings until an answer, one way or another, was finally decided.

"Remember," continued Ian, "It's the final experts who we've got to convince… the people who put together the official catalogue raisonné. They're the people who are putting their reputation on the line. It's always a safer choice to reject a picture than to say 'yes'. When we finally meet them, we need to be absolutely certain we're giving them our very best shot."

Chapter 9

Although it was a number of years since Ian had attended the Courtauld Institute of Art as a postgraduate student, he knew two people who still worked there. One was Simon Lyle. When Ian telephoned, Simon told him he was very busy and was even working this coming Saturday morning. Nevertheless, as a favour to a friend, he suggested that if Ian brought the painting in on Saturday, about lunch time, he'd see what he could do.

On Saturday, just after 12.45pm, Ian and Emma were walking along The Strand in London. After passing by the famous Somerset House building, they arrived outside the North Wing entrance of the Courtauld Institute. Ian pushed open the door. Emma followed, carrying her picture in Ian's special canvas transporting bag.

They entered the reception area and Ian asked at the front desk for Simon Lyle. Ten minutes later Simon joined them.

"Hello, Ian. Long time no see. I see you're keeping well," said Simon, shaking Ian's hand. He was taller than Ian, with grey wavy hair and just a hint of a Scottish accent. Emma guessed he must be about 60.

"Thanks for seeing us, Simon. This is my wife, Emma," replied Ian, introducing his wife.

"Hello," said Emma

"Hello, Emma. It's nice to meet you. Come on, let's get to work."

Emma and Ian followed Simon along various corridors, all still familiar to Ian.

"So, you think you've found a Georges Seurat picture… painted about 1889," commented Simon, as they walked together.

"We hope so," said Emma, holding tight on the canvas bag.

"Emma's been able to establish a good provenance," added Ian.

"Okay. Here we are." Simon opened the door to his laboratory-cum-office. Ian and Emma both walked through the doorway into a smallish room. It contained a number of cameras, laptop computers, monitors and various other types of electronic equipment.

Ian smiled. "You have lots of tech gear in here, Simon."

"Yes, you need it. There's such a demand for scientific analysis and technical support for paintings nowadays. About 60% of the pictures we see are forgeries. Some are so good that, without our scientific evidence, they could easily pass as the real thing."

Oh dear, thought Emma.

"Right," continued Simon, "Let's have a look at what you've got."

Emma put the canvas bag on the nearby table. She unbuckled the three straps and pulled out the painting. It was covered in loose plastic bubble-wrap. Slowly unfolded the protective packing and handed the painting to Simon.

Simon held the picture directly under a nearby table lamp. "Mmm, looks very good. Let's see what the science tells us."

Simon gently placed the painting on a nearby easel

and fixed it into a vertical position. He then went over to a laptop computer and typed in some commands. "Look here," he said.

Ian and Emma moved closer to the laptop and looked at the screen. They were looking at what appeared to be a graph showing a number of different spikes, each varying in height and colour. Along the bottom were listed the names of different chemicals, some of which Emma had heard of... but most of which she hadn't.

"This graph is a record of the chemical paint profile Georges Seurat used when he painted the 'Models', or, as the picture is sometimes referred to, 'Les Poseuses'. It was painted about the same time as your picture. It's been fully authenticated and now resides with the Barnes Foundation in Philadelphia. Okay, let's see if we can get a similar match with your painting."

Whilst Simon walked over to the far side of the room to collect what Emma thought looked like a sophisticated hair dryer, Ian explained, "What we're hoping to see is a similar pigment profile. That will then prove if both pictures were painted with the same, or very similar, paints. Simon knows the paints commonly used by Seurat. What we certainly don't want to see is a profile that includes paints not even in existence until the 20th century."

Simon returned with Emma's look-a-like 'hair dryer' in his hand. He plugged the attached cable into the electric mains socket and explained to Emma, "This is a special camera that takes a series of infrared and ultraviolet light photos. It identifies the data of your painting. If you look at the computer screen, you'll see the profile gradually being built up."

Although Ian had seen this process in action before, it was all new to Emma. She leaned closer to the computer's screen which showed a similar base graph but with no coloured data spikes.

Simon pointed the camera closely to the painting and slowly moved it across and down until he'd covered the whole of the canvas. After a few minutes, he stopped and switched off the camera. "Okay. Let's have a look at the results."

Emma stood back to let Simon get closer to the screen. He pressed several keys on the keyboard and new coloured spikes slowly appeared.

"It's looking good," said Ian.

Once all the spikes had appeared, Simon leaned forward and again pressed a number of the computer's keys. "Now, let's see how the two graphs compare."

As if by magic, the original graph was now superimposed on top of the data from Emma's picture.

"Wow!" exclaimed Emma. "They're very similar, almost identical."

Simon peered closer. "Yes, that's not bad. There's an odd colour difference here," he said pointing at the screen, "but a significant amount of the data does confirm that the paint from both pictures probably came from the same palette."

"Does that confirm our picture was painted by Seurat then?" asked Emma, hopefully.

"Not quite yet," replied Ian. "It's a significant step. It says that the paints used on your picture were similar to those being used by Seurat in the 1880s. It still doesn't confirm, absolutely, that it was by the hand of Georges Seurat. It could still have been completed by an associate or an apprentice of Seurat's, using the same studio paints. The reality is, we'll never know for certain. We are talking of a time span of over 130 years ago. The good news, though, at least to me, is that it has all the hallmarks of Seurat's personal style."

"I agree," responded Simon. "Sometimes it's very difficult to be 100% certain, but from what I can see, you've got a good chance. Assuming your provenance stacks up, of course."

"I'm happy with the provenance, Simon," said Ian. "Emma has done a fabulous investigative job there."

Emma blushed at Ian's praise.

"I'll just print you copies of the graphs." Simon tapped the keys again and walked over to the printer and switched it on. After the printer had warmed up, it produced three prints. Simon signed and dated all three copies.

"There you are, Emma," said Simon, handing over the three signed A4 printed sheets.

Ian held out his hand towards Simon. "Simon, it's been good to meet up with you again and many thanks for giving up part of your Saturday afternoon for us."

Simon shook Ian's hand and then Emma's. "It's been really good to meet you both. You have an interesting painting there, Emma. Hopefully you'll find success with it too. Let me know how it all goes."

Emma smiled and said, "We certainly will." She then repacked the painting into the protective bubble-wrap and placed it into Ian's canvas bag, complete with Simon's three signed graph reports. Her nervousness had now disappeared and was replaced with a tingle of excitement and anticipation.

Next stop, Mr. Marshall's gallery.

Chapter 10

Ian and Emma were back in London again the following Tuesday. They were walking along New Bond Street and heading towards James Marshall's gallery. Emma was carrying her painting, once again in Ian's canvas bag, whilst Ian carried the provenance report and Simon's three printed graphs.

They were early for their appointment so were walking slowly and window shopping at the same time. They stopped outside several galleries, but Emma also wanted to look at the displays in two of the jewellery shop windows.

At 12.55pm they arrived at their destination. Ian pushed open the door. A ringing bell announced their arrival. The gallery was typical of the art galleries along New Bond Street. It immediately felt expensive and the limited number of paintings on show were perfectly displayed. Spotlights aimed subtle lighting at each picture, achieving the best possible effect.

Emma glanced at an oil-painted landscape scene. A very romantic view of old England, she thought. It reminded her of a John Constable. However, when she saw the advertised price, she wondered whether it was, indeed, a genuine Constable.

"Good afternoon, sir… and madam. Can I help you?"

The voice came from a middle-aged man who had appeared from behind some of the displays. He was smartly dressed in a blue pinstriped suit and had a large, welcoming smile. He walked over to where Ian was standing.

"Hello," said Ian, "We have an appointment with Mr. Marshall at 1pm."

"Ah, Mr. and Mrs. Caxton. Yes, Mr. Marshall is expecting you. I'll just go and tell him you have arrived." The man turned and walked away, exiting between a pair of dark blue satin curtains at the rear of the gallery.

Emma pointed to the painting she had just been looking at and whispered to Ian, "Is that the right price?"

Ian smiled and just whispered back, by way of an explanation, "This is Bond Street, Emma."

"Mr. and Mrs. Caxton. Hello. I'm James Marshall." A portly gentleman, with a well-groomed head of grey hair, approached them. "My niece asked me to look at one of your pictures. A Georges Seurat painting, I understand."

Ian was a little surprised. "Gillian is your niece?"

"Yes, yes," replied Mr. Marshall. "Nice girl, isn't she? Knows her art. Is that the painting?" He pointed at the bag Emma was carrying.

"Yes," replied Emma. "It's called 'Mademoiselle Chad'."

"Good, good. Let's go through to the studio. We can examine it properly there. Are you looking to sell?" asked Mr. Marshall, as he led the way to the rear of the gallery. Once through the curtains, he turned immediately to his right into a small but perfectly lit room. It was professionally set up for viewing and displaying individual paintings.

"Probably not at the moment," said Ian, looking across at Emma for her reaction. They joined Mr. Marshall opposite an empty easel. "The painting's not in the current catalogue raisonné. We're hoping to convince the authors of our new find."

"I see," responded a slightly dejected Mr. Marshall. "Oh well, let's see if you've managed to uncover a new masterpiece."

Emma put the bag on a nearby table and unbuckled the straps. She then removed the wrapped picture.

"You have it well protected," said Mr. Marshall, watching Emma as she carefully removed the bubble-wrap.

Emma smiled and then handed the painting to Mr. Marshall.

"Okay. First looks are good. Let's pop it on the easel."

Here we go, thought Emma.

Mr. Marshall adjusted one of the three hanging spotlights fractionally and stood back. He then walked further backwards and side to side, never averting his eyes from the painting. He walked up to the picture again and looked at it very closely, this time with the aid of a small torch. He then turned the picture over and reviewed the details on the back, before returning the painting to its original position.

"Give me a minute would you," he said and then disappeared back through the door.

Emma looked at Ian with a surprised look on her face. Ian just shrugged his shoulders. Moments later Mr. Marshall reappeared, followed by the man who had welcomed Ian and Emma to the gallery. The man smiled at them before concentrating on the painting. He too looked at it from different angles, and then lifted it off the easel. Both men inspected the details on the back of the frame and whispered to each other. The painting was then returned and secured back onto the easel.

It was Mr. Marshall who broke the silence. "This is Mr. Jacobs. You've already met." Ian, Emma and Mr. Jacobs all smiled again. "I wanted to show him your painting, and get his opinion."

Mr. Jacobs now spoke whilst looking directly at the

picture. "It's a nice painting. The style is certainly similar to Seurat's. It's not a composition that I recognise, but very similar to some of his other works. Mind, his style is so easy to fake nowadays."

"If it is a fake," interrupted Mr. Marshall, "then it's a damn good one." He turned to face Ian and said, "What about provenance?"

Ian summarised the work Emma had done and offered Mr. Marshall a copy of Emma's report. He also produced the three graphs that Simon had printed and explained their results.

"This is all very impressive," said Mr. Marshall, gently waving the paperwork now in his hands. "Can I keep these copies and read them in my own time?"

"Of course," replied Ian. He looked at Emma, who smiled and nodded her agreement. After all, they had several paper copies at home and it was on Emma's computer digitally.

It was three days later when Mr. Marshall's letter arrived. It was addressed to Mr. and Mrs. Caxton. Emma anxiously opened the envelope and read the letter's contents:

Dear Mr. and Mrs. Caxton,

It was a pleasure to meet you both yesterday in my gallery and I thank you for bringing your painting to my attention.

My opinion of the 'Mademoiselle Chad' picture is that it could well be a piece of work by the hand of Georges Seurat. So much so, that I'm prepared to offer a purchase price for the painting today, without the full authentication by the artist's catalogue raisonné authors, of £2.2 million.

I look forward to hearing from you in due course.

Yours Sincerely,

James Marshall. MA.

London.

Once Emma had finished reading the letter, she realised that her heart was pounding and she'd started to perspire. Reading the letter again, she wanted to make sure she hadn't made a mistake. Yes, it was true. Mr. Marshall was offering 2.2 million! No further questions asked. Wow!

Emma immediately texted Ian and five minutes later Ian telephoned home. "Hi, Emma. Great news. What do you want to do?"

"I don't know. What do you think the painting could actually be worth?" asked Emma. Her heart was still bumping against her ribcage and she was struggling a little to breathe.

"Well, that's the big unknown and depends on what the catalogue raisonné experts decide. If they say 'no', well it could be about 20,000 pounds, but if they said 'yes', well maybe…" Ian pondered for a few seconds. "Possibly as high as six to ten million. Seurat's picture, 'Island of the Grand Jatte' painted about 1884, sold for US$35 million in 1999. But that was in the USA and the market has changed quite a bit since those heady days."

"We always said not to be greedy," said Emma.

"A bird in the hand and all that," responded Ian. "2.2 million pounds is a good offer, but James Marshall is definitely no fool. He knows the odds. I've checked him out. He's a very successful art dealer… and extremely wealthy. He also knows his Georges Seurat paintings."

"Can we talk about it more when you get home?" asked Emma. She really didn't want to make a snap decision.

"Of course. See you later." The line went dead. Emma sat down next to the breakfast bar. She picked up the letter and read it for the third time. What do I do now? She thought.

Chapter 11

That evening Ian and Emma went through all the possible pros and cons of selling or keeping the 'Mademoiselle Chad' painting. One minute Emma had decided to sell it, then she changed her mind and decided to keep it, in the hope that Ian could persuade the catalogue raisonné experts of its true authenticity.

Ian, however, had a fair idea of what Emma would finally decide. She would agree to sell it to James Marshall. But he wanted her to examine all the options for herself before she made that decision.

"I'm going to sleep on it, Ian," was Emma's final statement. She stood up and headed towards the door.

Ian finished the last of his coffee, smiled and gently shook his head from side to side. He knew it was a big decision for Emma. £2.2 million was a serious amount of money. If she kept the picture and it turned out not to be accepted, he knew Emma would be devastated, especially after all the hard work she'd put in. However, if she did sell it and the painting was eventually accepted as part of Seurat's work and sold for about £6 million, yes, she would be sad, but certainly not as devastated.

"Ian. Ian, wake up."

"What? What time is it? What's the matter?" replied Ian, still half asleep. It looked very dark outside.

"I've decided," said Emma, she was wide awake and sitting up in bed.

"Fine, but why have you woken me up in the middle of the night?"

"I'm going to sell!"

"Okay. Well done. Now let's go back to sleep." Ian rolled over and pulled the duvet back under his chin.

"Don't you want to know why and how I'm going to spend some of the money?"

Ian pushed the duvet back and pulled himself up into a sitting position. He was awake now, so decided to concede to his wife's wishes. "Okay, now you have my undivided attention."

"Well, the final thing that convinced me was that I want to reward the people who helped me complete the provenance history. Without them I wouldn't be in this fortunate position. Some helped me significantly more than others so they'll get a bigger share."

"That's very generous of you. How much are you going to give?"

"I've not worked that out yet, but probably 5,000 pounds for the main contributors."

"They will be pleased. Now can we get some sleep? I've just spotted the clock – it's ten past four."

Six hours later, Ian telephoned James Marshall. Emma stood at his side and listened to the conversation. Ian clarified a few points with Mr. Marshall over the potential sale and then told him he had a deal. Mr. Marshall was really pleased and told Ian to bring the painting to his gallery, sometime in the next few days, where he would have a banker's draft waiting for him. Both parties were happy with the arrangements and Ian ended the call.

"That's all agreed then?" asked Emma, excitedly.

"Yes, the money will be waiting for us when we take the painting back to the gallery. No regrets?"

"No. I've made my decision. If Mr. Marshall eventually sells the painting for six, seven or whatever, millions of pounds, well good luck to him. Everybody will be happy… and a winner."

"Well done you. Not a bad return on… what? A 50-pound investment!?"

"Plus all my time and hard work."

Ian laughed.

"And, of course, not forgetting, all the help you gave me," continued Emma. "I couldn't have achieved any of this without it." She then gave Ian a big kiss.

Ian was at home on his own when the telephone rang. "Ian Caxton," he answered.

"Ian? It's Charles. Charles Owen."

"Hello, Charles. How are you?"

"Good thanks. I've only got a minute, but I thought I'd let you know my accountants have just told me my grandfather's paperwork has been sent for probate. So, fingers crossed it's all going to work."

"If your accountants are happy, I'm sure the probate and tax people will be too."

"Let's hope so. I've got a lot riding on all this."

"Yes, I know," replied Ian. He crossed his fingers. "Have you any idea how long it will take?"

"My accountants say about two to four weeks. I'll let you know as soon as I get any news."

"Okay, Charles. Good luck."

"Let's hope I'll not need it. Must go. Cheers."

Ian put the telephone down. He still wished Charles good luck. However, in his experience, dealing with government departments was rarely simple and straightforward.

Chapter 12

It was two days later when Ian and Emma delivered the 'Mademoiselle Chad' painting to James Marshall's gallery. They left 30 minutes later with a banker's draft to the value of £2.2 million. The banker's draft, unfortunately, was made payable to Ian's name, which annoyed Emma, but then Ian reminded her that it might raise some eyebrows at her personal HSBC bank if that amount of money was paid straight into her account. He also suggested that the draft should be paid into his Swiss bank account and he would then arrange for smaller instalments to be transferred to her account, as and when she wanted the money.

Emma thought about Ian's suggestions and, on reflection, decided that what he was saying did make sense. "Okay," she said a little reluctantly.

"We'll talk about how you want this money when we get home this evening," replied Ian. He knew his offer was the best option, but he was determined not to deflate Emma's excitement.

Emma nodded her agreement, but suddenly felt the chill of the cold early March air.

Ian put his arm around her shoulders and squeezed gently. "Right, my dear, I've booked a table at a nice restaurant near Covent Garden for lunch. Let's call it a celebration."

Emma looked at Ian and gave him a smile. "You know, Ian Caxton, I'm enjoying the art world."

"Also, I'd like to have a chat about a few other things."

"That sounds ominous," responded Emma. "What 'few things' do you want to chat about?"

"Let's wait until we get to the restaurant. It's much too cold to discuss out here."

"Okay," said Emma. She gazed at Ian with a little concern whilst he hailed an approaching taxi.

They both climbed in and Ian announced, "Lobster and Crab Kitchen, please, Henrietta Street, Covent Garden."

"Okay, guv," replied the taxi driver.

Ian sat back in his seat next to Emma.

"Come on, Ian, tell me what you're thinking," said Emma. She was anxious to know what he wanted to say.

"Okay," Ian replied, adjusting his position to face Emma. "Well, firstly, when I collected Robert from school the other day, he told me his two main friends, Richard and Arthur, were boarding at the school. One was a week-dayer, Monday to Friday I think it is, and the other is full time. They apparently told him they have a great time in the evenings and it would be even better if Robert was there too. Robert was asking me if he could join them, to be a boarder as well. I told him I'd have to discuss it with you."

"Oh," was Emma's first reaction. "I didn't think you approved of Robert being a boarder."

"Well, I'm not keen, but Robert's a bit older now and he wants to do it. It's not as though we're forcing him."

Emma looked out of the side window, not really focusing on anything, just thinking. Suddenly she turned back to face Ian. "Does he want to board full time or just during the week?"

"We didn't get that far into the conversation. I didn't tell you about this earlier because we were sidetracked by James Marshall's offer."

59

"We need to speak to him and, of course, his headmistress. There might not be any vacancies at the moment."

"Good point," responded Ian. Why hadn't he thought of that? "Ah, here's the restaurant, we'll carry on the conversation over our meal."

The taxi pulled up outside the restaurant. Ian leaned over and paid the fare, adding a nice tip.

"Thanks, guv."

Ian and Emma got out and the taxi was driven away.

"This looks nice," said Emma, looking at the large window display. "Have you eaten here before?"

"Just once, a few years ago. The seafood was wonderful then and they still have good reviews, so hopefully, it'll be fine."

Ian pushed open the door and let Emma through. The maître d' walked over and welcomed them. A few minutes later they were sitting at a table in a cosy alcove.

"This is nice, Ian, a good choice," said Emma, looking around.

A waiter attended their table and offered two large menus. After discussing the wine options with the waiter, Ian thought a nice bottle of Chablis would go well with the seafood. Emma nodded her agreement.

They both started to read their menus, but were interrupted when the wine arrived in a bucket of ice. Ian nodded when he was shown the label and the waiter poured a sample for Ian to taste. Again, Ian nodded and said the wine was good. Two glasses were poured and the waiter walked away.

Emma was the first to speak. She read straight from the menu. "I think I'll have the crab bisque with charred sweetcorn, and for the main course, the cod served on a chestnut puree with spinach oil accompanied by charred Brussels sprouts and bacon."

"Mmm, sounds good. I think I'm going for the clams and mussels and then the lobster."

The waiter reappeared and Ian gave the order. He then picked up his glass and offered a toast. "To Emma, the new star in the world of art dealers."

Emma smiled and picked up her glass, touching it against Ian's. "I've got a long way to go yet."

Ian laughed and after sipping his wine asked, "So, coming back to Robert, what are your thoughts?"

"It'll be strange and quiet in the house without him. Maybe we could consider the week-day option to start with... if it's available."

"So you're not against the move, in principle?"

"No, as you say, he's growing up and it might do him some good. Make him appreciate what he has at home. It would also save us having to ferry him to and from school every day."

"I'm surprised. I thought you'd give me a fight."

"No, I agree with you. It's not us forcing him to board. He wants to do it, so let's give it a try. If he doesn't like it, well, we can always move him back to day attendance."

"Right," said Ian. He was really surprised with his wife's reaction. "Do you want me to ring the headmistress, Miss Wardley, tomorrow?"

"No, I think I'll do that. Even if they do have a place available, I still want to see where Robert would be sleeping and the general boarding conditions before we agree."

"Ah, here come our starters." Ian had spotted two waiters walking towards their table.

When the first courses had been consumed, Emma decided to challenge Ian on his earlier comment. "Ian, you said you had 'a few things' to discuss?"

"Oh yes." Ian pushed his bowl of empty clam and mussel shells aside. "That was bigger than I was expecting. I also wanted to talk about the apartment in Monaco. It's been a long time since we were there."

"I know," said Emma. "I thought about it the other week. I never thought I'd say this, Ian, but I've missed going there. We must try and get back before winter is over."

"Me too. I've still got to finalise the work on Charles Owen's paintings but, other than that, we ought to go, especially if Robert's going to be boarding."

Just as Emma was about to speak, a waiter arrived and collected their empty dishes. She waited until he'd gone before saying, "Even if Robert's just a week-day boarder, I'm sure our parents would love to have him for a couple of weekends."

"Right, we have a plan of action," announced Ian. "You're going to speak to Miss Wardley and I'll see what flights are available."

Chapter 13

Emma telephoned Miss Wardley and discovered there were two vacancies available in the dormitories; one was in the same dormitory as Robert's friends, Richard and Arthur.

A week later, she and Ian visited Brookfield School where they were given the 'parents tour' of the dormitories. On the way home they both agreed that the rooms were reasonably modern, clean and tidy. The general supervision and organisation also appeared to be very good. On the following Monday morning, not only did Robert have his usual academic school bags, but two full suitcases as well. Initially Robert would be starting as a week-day boarder, but during the Easter break, Emma, Ian and Robert would sit down together to discuss any changes to these arrangements.

Meanwhile, Ian had booked two first-class flight tickets to Nice and had also advised 'Harbour Heights' of their plans. Reception confirmed they would have the apartment fully prepared for their arrival. Now, thought Ian, all I have to do is wait on Charles to see whether probate has been granted.

Ian didn't have to wait too long. It was a day later at 4.30pm when he heard his mobile phone ringing. "Hello, Ian Caxton," he answered.

"Ian, hi," announced an excited Charles Owen. "Great,

great news! My accountants have confirmed that probate has been granted, but of course, I've still got the inheritance tax bill to pay. Just been on to my bank and have agreed a temporary loan, so we're all go, go, go."

Since his conversations with Andrei all those years ago, Ian was now always careful with his words when responding about delicate money matters on the telephone. "So, are you happy with everything?"

"I certainly am. Look out for a letter in your post. Will chat again shortly. Must go. Cheers!"

Before Ian could say goodbye, Charles had rung off. Well, thought Ian to himself, he's certainly a happy chap. I wonder what he meant about a letter in the post?

Emma was feeling a little strange and under-employed now she was not involved with any business activity. Over recent weeks, much of her time had been consumed with her investigations, trying to put together the provenance history for the 'Mademoiselle Chad' painting. In addition, with Robert now boarding at school, she didn't need to allocate time to take and collect him each day. She couldn't remember the last time she hadn't been busy, juggling different demands on her time. She wandered into the office where Ian was on his computer and surrounded by some of his books. "Do you want a cup of coffee?"

"Er, no. I'm okay at the moment, thanks. I had one not long ago," replied Ian, with his mind largely on what he was reading.

Emma sauntered over to her desk but remembered she'd tidied it up only yesterday. She turned around and approached Ian's desk. "Is there anything you want me to do?"

"Mmm?" replied Ian, only half listening. "No, I don't think so."

"Oh."

Now, giving Emma his full attention, he asked, "Do I sense you're at a loose end, a bit bored?"

"Yes, I am. It's so long since I've actually had nothing to do."

"Well, we're going to Monaco in a few days' time so you could start to think about the clothes you're going to take."

"I've largely done that already."

Ian laughed. "I thought housewives always had lots of jobs to do."

"Very funny."

"You could see if we've had any mail this morning."

Emma walked out of the office and into the kitchen where she collected the key to open the outside letterbox. She removed four items of mail, relocked the letterbox and returned indoors. "Two bills, one circular and one addressed to you," she announced when she'd returned to the office. She held out the envelope addressed to Ian.

"Can you open it, please? I'm in the middle of doing something here."

Emma duly opened the letter and removed a cheque. She looked inside the envelope for an accompanying letter, but there wasn't one. She then read the cheque's details. "My goodness!" she suddenly exclaimed. "This is a cheque for one million pounds!"

"What!" Ian jumped up from his seat and walked around to Emma. He read the details and noted it was signed by Charles Owen.

"Charles told me to watch out for a letter in the post, but… wow."

"So, what have you done to earn this?" asked Emma, gently waving the cheque.

"Nothing really, I just helped him with his inheritance tax problem. Remember? I told you all about it."

"Yes, but you didn't tell me about this." Emma pushed the cheque towards Ian.

"I didn't know myself, until now. I thought he'd pay me something if we got his painting authenticated sometime in the future. That's what I'm working on now."

"Maybe the inheritance tax bill is a lot less than he was anticipating. This is your reward."

"Some reward," replied Ian, "Maybe he's expecting a lot more from me in the future."

"Well, you have promised him you'd get his painting authenticated."

"Not exactly promised. But I'm convinced his painting is the genuine version. My main task now is to prove the French one is a copy."

Emma wondered why Ian was so convinced that Charles's painting was the real version. "What are you doing now?" she asked, looking at the books on Ian's desk.

"I'm trying to establish why the French feel so adamant that their copy is the real work of Paul Gauguin."

"What if there are actually two pictures of the same subject painted by Paul Gauguin? Didn't some artists paint sketches and sort of first drafts before the main painting?"

"That's a very good point! More reason for me to establish what their painting's provenance is."

"Can't you just ask the French museum that it's in?" Emma couldn't see why Ian hadn't done this when he'd visited a few weeks ago.

"It's not that easy. I want to find out for myself. I certainly don't want to alert them to my investigations, not at this stage."

"I can see that," responded Emma, "So, are you sure you don't need my help?"

"Okay, two pairs of eyes and all that …"

For the rest of that day, both Ian and Emma explored

the internet and scrutinised Ian's books. Emma thought they were making some progress, but Ian felt there was still much more to explore and double check. However, Emma's question of whether there might be two very similar pictures painted by Gauguin was spooking Ian a little.

What if she's actually right and I'm wrong!

Chapter 14

It was late in the afternoon when Ian and Emma arrived at 'Harbour Heights'. Their aeroplane had left London Heathrow airport at 11.45am, with the air temperature just above freezing. Now, as they got out of the taxi, Emma could feel the warm late winter sunshine on her face. She knew that the weather in Monaco in March could sometimes be a bit of a lottery but, at the same time, it was usually a lot warmer than in the UK.

Ian paid the taxi fare and they entered the reception area pulling their suitcases behind them. Ian wondered how long it had been since they were last here. He couldn't remember exactly, but knew it was over 12 months ago.

"Welcome back to 'Harbour Heights', Mr. Caxton… Mrs. Caxton," said the pleasant receptionist as they approached the reception desk.

"Thank you," responded Ian.

"The Penthouse Suite is all ready. I hope you have a lovely stay. Do you want any assistance with your luggage?"

"No, no. We're fine, thank you," replied Ian.

Emma smiled and they both walked towards the elevator where a uniformed lady was waiting for them. Ian immediately recognised Louise.

"Welcome back, Mr. Caxton, Mrs. Caxton. Please…"

said Louise, moving aside and allowing Ian and Emma to enter first.

"Thank you, Louise. We've been away for quite some time. I hope you've been keeping well," said Ian.

Once Ian, Emma and their baggage were inside, Louise followed and pressed the 'Close' button for the doors. She then pressed the top floor button. It had its own personal name, 'Penthouse Suite'. "I'm keeping very well. Thank you for asking. Nothing has really changed whilst you've been away. Your suite has been prepared to your requirements, but if you need anything else just telephone reception."

The elevator swiftly and silently ascended, arriving at the top floor in a matter of moments. The doors then opened, Louise stepped aside and Ian and Emma exited pulling their suitcases.

"Thank you," said Ian. He gave Louise a smile. They pulled the two suitcases the short distance to the double doors to their suite. The sign 'Penthouse' was sited just above the metal security plate.

Ian placed his right hand on the metal plate and heard the click as the door unlocked and moved slightly ajar. Emma pushed the door and walked in first. Ian followed, pulling Emma's suitcase. He then collected his own and closed the door. Emma wandered across the lounge towards the large patio doors leading onto the balcony.

"It all looks okay," said Ian, glancing around the room.

"I thought it would smell musty, but it's nice and fresh," responded Emma, walking back to join Ian.

"It's all part of the preparation they do. Have a look in the bathrooms and kitchen. They'll all have been restocked, probably this morning."

Emma smiled. "A little bit of luxury, isn't it?"

Ian put his arms around Emma and kissed her. "All thanks to Andrei. We're so lucky."

"I know I originally said that I didn't like the idea of inheriting this apartment from Andrei," replied Emma, looking into Ian's eyes, "but it really is growing on me. We need to come here more often."

"With Robert now boarding, we're not restricted to school holiday times anymore."

"That's true, but I'd still like to bring Robert here occasionally, maybe Easter and late summertime."

Ian nodded and walked back to the suitcases. One at a time, he pulled them into the main bedroom.

Emma went back to the patio doors, unlocked them and stepped outside onto the balcony. She walked across to the railings and looked down into the harbour area. There she watched the usual comings and goings of yachts and boats and people strolling along the esplanade. Some of the early evening lights were shining and reflecting on the water. She took two deep breaths, sucking in the fresh sea air. Suddenly goosebumps appeared on her arms. The breeze had picked up and the sun would soon be disappearing for another day. Smiling to herself, she definitely felt very happy.

After a couple of minutes Ian joined her. He had two glasses of cold Chablis in his hands. He handed one of the glasses to Emma and proposed a toast. "Here's to a relaxing and enjoyable few days."

"Cheers, Ian," replied Emma, and they both chinked their glasses. "Isn't this just a spectacular view?"

They both stood next to the railings, gazing into the harbour and then out to sea. The sun was about to disappear, but the sea still had the last few minutes of its golden glow. Ian also loved this view and they both pointed and discussed what was happening below. After about ten minutes, they sat down on the two balcony chairs and put their glasses on the small wooden table. Over the horizon the sun had now disappeared. Unfortunately, there were only a few wispy clouds so there wasn't going to be a lovely sunset but, nevertheless, they sat back quietly and watched the colour of the sea slowly change from its dark golden hue to an inky blue, whilst a silky white glow from the moon's reflections appeared.

Next morning, Ian was awake early. He quietly crept out of bed trying not to wake Emma. He got dressed and walked into the kitchen and made himself a mug of tea. After a few sips, he went back into the bedroom and opened the private safe in the bottom of the wardrobe. The safe was only large enough for small items and a few documents. He removed the security keycard required to enter the security vaults in the lower basement. The plastic card was approximately the same size as an ordinary bank card, but, as well as being personalised with all the security information, it had a photo of Ian's face.

He closed the safe and quietly walked back into the kitchen area. In the better light he looked at the card and smiled. He still thought his photograph was not overly flattering. He tried to remember all the security information that Bates, one of the security guards, had told him. He decided he still had a good idea of most of the requirements, but also knew that if he'd forgotten anything, the security guards would help him out.

Ian picked up a small notepad and pen and put them in his rear pocket. He then exited the apartment, walked towards the elevator and pressed the request button. He only had to wait a few seconds for the elevator to arrive. Louise was not on duty, but another uniformed lady that he'd not met before smiled and stepped aside to let Ian enter. "Good morning," said Ian.

"Good morning, Mr. Caxton, my name is Adele," said the petite lady. She was pleasantly attractive and had a strong

French accent to her English pronunciations. "Which floor do you require?"

"Lower basement floor please, Adele," stated Ian. He stood back and watched Adele press the button to close the door, then the button for the lower basement floor. Ian remembered that whenever the lower basement floor button was pressed, the security team in the vault area were notified that a keyholder was shortly arriving.

The elevator descended straight to the lower basement. Once they'd arrived, Adele opened the door. Ian stepped out and said, "thank you." He was immediately confronted by two uniformed guards. Ian knew he wouldn't be allowed to go any further until he'd produced his personalised keycard. He smiled and showed the card to the large guard on his right-hand side. The guard took the card, looked at the photograph and waved Ian forward.

All three men walked to a desk where a computer was located. The guard inserted Ian's card into a small electronic device and looked at the computer's screen. Ian knew his card would automatically link with the main computer in the security office. He also remembered Bates saying that this procedure has to be followed every time. All activity is recorded 24 hours a day via several hidden security cameras.

Ian looked into the corridor with the 12 strongroom doors along each side. There were no windows, but the air was still cool and fresh, just as he remembered it.

The guard, now satisfied, handed the security card back to Ian. "Thank you for your patience, Mr. Caxton, please go ahead."

"Thank you," said Ian and the guards both nodded.

One, however, followed two paces behind Ian as he walked along the corridor. He stopped outside the door numbered 14. There were no handles on the door, just a metal plate and a small horizontal slot above. Ian inserted his card into the slot. Immediately, a green light flashed above the door. Ian smiled. He put his left palm on the metal plate and stood aside when the green light flashed again. The guard stepped forward and placed his hand on the metal plate. The green light flashed for a third time and then a few seconds later the door made a clicking noise and slowly began to move. As the door opened, three internal lights automatically came on. The guard then walked away, back towards his desk.

Ian entered the vault and stared around the room. Then after closing the door he placed his notepad and pen on the small table in the middle of the room. He then went over to where his six paintings were being stored. Selecting the first one he placed it on the table and started to make his notes.

Chapter 15

It had been just over six months since Oscar had kissed and waved goodbye to May Ling at the VC Bird International Airport. They had since kept in regular contact via emails and video conferences, but they both admitted they were missing each other and neither had the same energy for work as previously. Something had to change.

Eventually Oscar picked up the courage and, during one emotional video conference, asked May to marry him. They both thought how strange this situation was, proposing over the internet, but May said yes! Over the next week, May set about selling her businesses in Hong Kong and Beijing. With the Chinese government's more aggressive political interference in the area, many people in Hong Kong were becoming worried and already a number of the wealthy had either left, or were currently looking for their way out. The main impact for May was that her businesses had reduced in value. Nevertheless, she did eventually get buyers for both her businesses and her two personally owned apartments. Then, very quickly after the sales had been completed, she moved all the money from her two Hong Kong bank accounts to her existing bank accounts in Switzerland. Also, as soon as the sale of her Hong Kong island apartment was completed, she moved into rental accommodation close to the former airport at Kai Tak. Each day she was becoming more and more anxious about living in her home country. So much so that, over the next few days, she arranged for all her favourite personal possessions and some expensive paintings to be packaged up and shipped to her brother's home in Singapore.

The following few days were spent tidying up the last few loose ends. Then, after watching on television several clashes occurring between the Chinese authorities and protesting Hong Kong residents, she gave her landlord one month's notice on her rented apartment. However, she had no intention of seeing out that month because two days later she was on an aeroplane heading towards Singapore.

Oscar had become more worried by the day about May. He'd watched, via the internet, some of the demonstrations in Hong Kong and hardly recognised the country he had grown up in. Both he and May had agreed to temporarily halt communications whilst May tried to cut all her ties in China and Hong Kong. She'd told Oscar the less the government knew about her plans, the better.

It was not until Oscar received an email from May, telling him she had now safely arrived in Singapore, that he was finally able to relax. She told him she was temporarily staying with her brother and his family and still had a few things to sort out in Singapore. However, she pleased Oscar immensely when she told him she'd already booked her flights. First to Los Angeles and then to Antigua, where she would arrive on the 21st. Oscar checked his calendar; the 21st was in ten days' time!

In England, Viktor and Penny were building on their positions in the art world. Viktor was successfully dealing with Alexander, mostly on his own now, and Penny was becoming a very important cog at Sotheby's in the growing domain of her boss, Jonathan Northgate. She'd now decided that his style was much more ambitious than Ian's and more adventurous than the former MD. Some of his decisions did cause her stressful moments but, all in all, she knew life had become much more exciting.

Ian had encouraged Viktor to take more personal charge in their dealings and relationship with Alexander. He wanted to slowly inch his way out, but still keep his relationship with Viktor. So far this was working okay and Viktor was continuing to use Ian's experience and expertise, especially where he felt he needed a second opinion.

Viktor was also keen to know how Ian was progressing with his attempts to achieve authentication of the painting, 'Fête Gloanec'. Would he really be able to overturn the authorised version currently displayed in the Musée des Beaux-Arts d'Orléans? He knew Ian had a sort of sixth sense, but would he ever be able to convince the French… even if the facts eventually proved indisputable?

When Ian arrived back in the apartment, Emma was sitting at the breakfast bar. She was drinking tea and reading emails on her laptop.

"You were up early," said Emma. "Where have you been?"

"I was awake at six o'clock, so I went for a walk. Have you been up long? Had breakfast?" asked Ian, trying to change the subject.

"No, I was just about to have a shower," replied Emma, shutting down her computer. She was still wearing her lilac-coloured silk dressing gown.

"Do you fancy scrambled eggs? There are six in the fridge."

"Okay. Give me 20 minutes and I'll be back," said Emma, before disappearing into the bedroom.

Ian removed four eggs from the refrigerator and placed

them in a small bowl. He hoped they'd be a little warmer by the time they were going to be cooked. He then walked across to the office area and opened up his own laptop. He wanted to send an email to Viktor. Once the computer had booted up he referred to his notepad and typed all the details of the six paintings he'd looked at in the vaults. He also asked Viktor if he would investigate the background of each of these paintings and promised he'd make it worth his while.

Over breakfast Emma suggested that she'd like to meet up with Zoe again. Ian thought it was a good idea and told her he would telephone Bob and see if they could meet for dinner one evening. Ian had not been in touch with Bob for quite some time, certainly not since Viktor and Penny's wedding. He wanted to know how their art gallery business was performing.

After they'd finished breakfast, Ian picked up his mobile phone and dialled Bob Taylor's number.

Bob was surprised and pleased to hear from Ian. "Great to hear from you after all this time, Ian. How's things?"

"Good thanks, Bob. And you and Zoe?"

"Yeah, we're fine too. Business could be better, but winter's not a great time for us."

"Bob, Emma and I are over in Monaco for a few days. Emma says she'd love to meet up with Zoe again. I was wondering if you were both free for dinner one evening?"

"How long are you over for?" responded Bob.

"We fly back a week on Friday."

"Okay, that gives us plenty of options. We're free most evenings but the only snag is we'll have to get someone to stay with the children. Zoe has a couple of contacts so I'll get back to you tomorrow."

"Yes, that's fine. I'm looking forward to hearing all about your business empire."

Bob laughed. "Not sure about the empire bit but, as I say, we're okay. I'll ring you tomorrow, probably in the morning."

"Okay. Bye for now."

Emma was standing next to Ian and waited to hear a summary of his conversation.

"They're free most evenings but Zoe will need to get a babysitter in, so Bob will telephone tomorrow.

"Hardly babies nowadays," replied Emma, "but I guess they're still not old enough to be left on their own."

"The next question is," said Ian, laying his phone down on the breakfast bar, "do we entertain them here or take them to a restaurant?"

"Restaurant I think," responded Emma. "I want to be able to have a proper conversation. It's far easier when someone else is doing all the cooking. We could go back to that seafood restaurant we both enjoyed last time. 'Blue something', wasn't it called?"

"I remember, The 'Blue Marlin'. I'll book a table once we know which evening it's going to be."

Ian and Emma spent the rest of the day walking around the harbour and then the shopping area for extra food and provisions. The weather was lovely for the time of the year, although the locals were all wrapped up in their overcoats and furs. However, coming from the UK, Ian and Emma were comfortable just wearing lightweight summer clothes.

As part of their food shopping, Ian had spotted a fishmonger's and they decided to buy some prawns and scallops for dinner that evening. Emma thought it would be fun as they rarely cooked more than snacks in the apartment. For most dinners, they ate at the local restaurants.

After their meal they were sitting in the lounge with glasses of Chablis. The dinner had worked out well. Emma had cooked the prawns and scallops in salted water and then finished them off by frying in a little garlic and herb butter. Ian had prepared a salad and poured the wine.

"I enjoyed that," said Ian, sipping his chilled wine.

"Yes, it was good wasn't it," continued Emma. "I could get used to this sort of life."

"Do you know, Emma," responded Ian, more seriously now. He sat up and put his wine glass on the small table in front of him. "I was thinking about Andrei the other day. In particular, the fact that he kept working full time despite financially not needing to do so. He told me once that he'd only spent about one third of his time each year in this apartment… and this was his home. It was only when his health began to deteriorate that he finally stopped working and decided to see some of the world as a tourist. But by then it was almost too late. I don't want that to happen to us. I want us to enjoy the fruits of our success before we get to our parents' ages. Thanks to both Andrei's generosity and our good fortune, over the last few years, we could comfortably retire now and maybe just dabble a little in buying and selling the odd painting."

Emma also put her glass on the table and looked directly at Ian. "I don't want to travel the world, Ian, like Andrei did. Holiday breaks, yes, we ought to reserve more time for those, but not for months on end. We've still got Robert to consider."

"I know," responded Ian. "But I still think we ought to slow down workwise."

"And do what instead? I don't want to be on holiday all the time."

"I don't know, but I think we should both start to think about it."

Chapter 16

It was on the fourth evening of their stay in Monaco that Ian and Emma met up with Bob and Zoe at the 'Blue Marlin'. As it was a seafood restaurant, Ian and Emma remembered the fishing and oceanic ambience. The walls were covered in old distempered timber boards, painted in faded tones of blue and yellow. Old fishing equipment and a number of framed photographs, recounting memorable catches of blue marlins, all added to the intended maritime mood and character of the place.

As they were led towards their table, Ian guessed the restaurant was about half full. Their table was next to a large glass window, the perfect location to view the colourful night lights and all the activity across the harbour.

"This is a great table, Ian. You must have paid the maître d' a nice tip for this spot," said Bob, as they looked out at the picturesque view before sitting down.

Ian smiled. "Luck of the draw, but it is nice. So's the restaurant's ambience. Have you eaten here before?"

It was Zoe's turn to speak. "I remember coming here just once, but that was before the children were born." She looked at Bob for his support.

"Mmm. Is it that long? Anyway, the food must still be

good because the restaurant is still in existence after all these years."

"We ate here the last time we came to Monaco, didn't we, Ian?" said Emma. "The food was excellent then."

Ian nodded. "Right, what does everyone fancy to drink?"

A minute later a waiter came to their table and handed them each a menu. Ian gave him their drinks order and they then concentrated on the different meal options. When the waiter returned with their drinks, each gave him their food orders.

Bob picked up his glass. "Well, it's great to see you both again and thanks for the invitation to dinner. Here's to you both. Cheers."

Ian, Emma and Zoe chinked their glasses with Bob's. "Cheers to you both too," replied Ian. "Let's hope we have many more evenings like this."

They spent the rest of the evening chatting, eating and drinking. Their conversations centred mainly on their children, schools, Monaco, the art world and their businesses.

After the dessert course, Emma stood up and asked to be excused. Zoe decided to join her. The two men sat drinking their wine until Ian spoke, "I may have some business to put your way shortly, Bob."

"Okay," responded Bob. "Tell me more."

Ian explained the details of his six paintings. However, he didn't mention that he'd inherited them from Andrei or that they were currently residing in the vaults at 'Harbour Heights'.

"I'm in the process of investigating their background and provenance but, once I'm satisfied with their authenticity, would you be interested in selling them for me?"

"Of course, old buddy." Bob knew that, if Ian rated the pictures, they would be good quality paintings.

"Good. I don't want you to commit money for them. I'd be prepared to take, say, 70% of the selling price."

"That's very generous, Ian. Let me know when you're ready."

"I will. Ah, the ladies are returning."

When Emma and Zoe arrived back at the table they didn't sit down. Zoe reminded Bob that their childminder was due to leave in 20 minutes, so they ought to be leaving.

Ian paid the bill, adding a good tip, and they all left together. Outside, the air temperature was chillier now, so they walked briskly along the esplanade. Ian noticed the silhouette of 'Harbour Heights' in the distance. It was brightly lit up and standing noticeably higher than the surrounding properties.

At the corner of the next street, they all said their goodbyes and Ian and Emma picked up the pace again. Ten minutes later they walked into the reception area, which was noticeably warmer than outside. Louise was standing next to the doors of the elevator and stepped further aside so they both could enter.

"I hope you had a lovely evening," said Louise, pressing the 'Penthouse' button.

"Yes, thank you, Louise. It was very nice. We met up with some local friends and had a lovely seafood meal," responded Ian.

Louise smiled. "Here we are," she said, as the elevator stopped at the top floor. The doors opened and Ian and Emma stepped out. The three of them said "good night" and Louise returned to the elevator and took it back to the ground floor.

Ian put his hand on the metal plate at the side of their door and heard the usual click. Slowly the door opened and they both walked through.

"That was a really nice evening," announced Emma, placing her handbag on the breakfast bar. "Good food and nice company. I really like Zoe."

"Yes, I like them both. Mind, I'm a little concerned that Bob wasn't quite as bubbly as he normally is… about their business, I mean."

"He did say winter was usually a quiet period."

"I know. Even so," responded Ian. He hoped Vic would get some positive news about his six paintings. He knew they were the type of pictures that could sell well in Monaco. That would certainly give Bob and Zoe's business a nice boost.

Two days later, and, after reading Ian's email, Viktor set about investigating Ian's six paintings. However, he did wonder why Ian was not working on them himself.

After two hours of exploring, Viktor noticed a common theme was beginning to emerge. The titles of the paintings and the artist names were ringing a bell. Was it an alarm bell?

Chapter 17

In Antigua, a very nervous Oscar was waiting in the 'Arrivals' building at VC Bird International Airport. It was early morning and May Ling's flight was one of the earliest planes due to land. Oscar kept scanning the 'Flight Arrivals' board for signs against her flight number saying 'landed'. Three other flights, due in slightly later than May's, already had their 'landed' signs illuminated. Not only was Oscar nervous, but he was also now worried.

To try and calm his nerves, Oscar walked over to a kiosk and bought a cup of coffee. When he returned to his position, he glanced again at the 'Flight Arrivals' board. He was both relieved and elated that the word 'landed' had finally appeared against May's flight number.

He sipped his coffee and cursed as it was still very hot. However, deciding he couldn't really greet May with a cup of coffee in hand, he placed it in a nearby bin and walked back to his viewing spot to resume watching the passengers arriving through the far double doors.

"Hello, Oscar," said a female voice from behind him.

Oscar turned in surprise and looked straight into May's face. "How did you get here!?" he exclaimed.

"By aeroplane," retorted May, surprised and somewhat confused. "I've just this minute walked through those doors."

"Sorry, I was just getting rid of my coffee cup."

"Aren't you going to give me a kiss?"

"Oh, yes. Sorry," blurted Oscar. This was certainly not the sort of greeting he'd planned. He leaned forward, wrapped his arms around his wife-to-be and gave her a long and intimate kiss.

When he gently pulled away, May smiled and said, "That's better. Come on, take me home."

Oscar took charge of May's two suitcases which, fortunately, were on wheels, and they headed towards the 'exit' sign. As they walked across the small concourse May was carrying her cabin bag in one hand and had placed her free arm through Oscar's.

When they'd exited the air-conditioned building and walked out into the open air, May noticed the warmer temperature, despite the early hour. "The temperature feels similar to Singapore," she announced.

Oscar smiled. "This time of the year it's not as humid. Much nicer. That's my car over there."

"I see you've still got your little open-top car."

"I like to feel the warm breeze as I drive along. You don't mind, do you?"

May laughed. "It will ruin my hair, but it's great fun."

About 30 minutes later Oscar drove his jeep onto his driveway. He was just about to get out of the car when he noticed May was sitting still. She was looking straight ahead with a smile on her face.

"Why are you smiling? What's so funny?" he enquired.

"I'm just thinking, Oscar. Just thinking how lucky I am." May turned her head and faced Oscar. She then leaned across and gave him a kiss. "Come on you, I'm desperate for my swim in the Caribbean Sea."

Ian and Emma's holiday in Monaco had come to an end and they were now boarding the aeroplane back to London. Once they'd found their first-class seats, Emma sat down whilst Ian placed their cabin bags in the overhead lockers. When he'd sat down himself, he could hear Emma giggling to herself.

"Okay, what's so funny?"

Emma tried to stop giggling, but now started to snigger. "I was just fastening my safety belt when I remembered the time I was pregnant and had to ask for an extension. I felt like I was the size of an elephant."

Ian also smiled as he remembered the incident. "You certainly don't need one of those now. You've got a lovely figure," responded Ian, still smiling.

Emma blushed a little, but enjoyed the complement.

"Can I offer you a glass of champagne or orange juice?" said the stewardess, standing next to them and holding a silver tray of drinks.

"Champagne for me please," said Emma.

"The same for me," replied Ian. He accepted the glass and leaned towards his wife. "I think we ought to have a toast. To Monaco and many more visits."

Emma placed her glass gently against Ian's. "Yes. Cheers." She smiled. "Lots more."

Ian sat back and secured his own safety belt. He then watched Emma as she put her champagne glass down and picked up a magazine. He was really pleased with Emma's transformation. Initially she'd shown little interest in the apartment but, now, well, she seemed to have even more enthusiasm for it than he did. He decided he must put a little more pressure on her to convince her that work was not the be all and end all. He was determined they should see more of the world as tourists and travellers. He was also thinking they should return to Monaco on a much more regular basis. After all, they were going to have much more free time soon, as Robert had already told him he was keen to be a full-time boarder from the start of the new term.

The aeroplane began to ease backwards. The stewardess collected their empty glasses and, from his window, Ian watched the activity on the ground below. The earlier sunshine had now disappeared and a few spots of rain had started to fall. An early reminder, he thought, they were heading back to England.

About ten minutes later the plane was accelerating down the runway. Resting his head against the back of the seat he closed his eyes. His mind soon began to refocus on the ongoing challenge back in the UK. Resolving the problem of two paintings, both having the same name, 'Fête Gloanec'.

Chapter 18

Penny had just left the apartment for work and Viktor was now alone. He'd decided his main task for today was to find out if his hunch about Ian's six paintings was correct. He removed a large plastic box from a cupboard in one of the bedrooms and carried it into the lounge. There he placed it in the middle of the floor and lifted off its lid. Inside were a number of old copy files and reports he'd saved from his days at Sotheby's. In particular, he was looking for a copy of the first report he'd produced for Ian. He remembered being asked to research paintings that had disappeared during the Second World War.

Eventually he found what he was looking for... and, still sitting on the floor, he started to read.

During the Second World War, the German Nazis were responsible for one of the largest acts of art theft in the century. During the late 1930s and the first half of the 1940s, they plundered and confiscated well over 500,000 paintings from private collections, churches and museums across Europe. It was highly organised and supported by Hitler.

It is estimated that there are well over 100,000 stolen paintings still not accounted for but, in reality, nobody knows for certain the exact total. Some reports say it could be twice this figure. What is more certain is that many of these paintings are still residing in Russia. When the Soviets left Germany, it is widely thought that Stalin ordered many of these paintings to be recovered but, once they'd arrived in the Soviet Union, they were never repatriated. Similarly, in America and other places where art is bought and sold, paintings from this era are, even to this day, hanging on the walls of private collectors or just lost in the basements of museums and art galleries.

Viktor stopped reading and decided to move and sit on the settee where he hoped he'd be more comfortable. Once settled, he continued to read.

In many cases, records of the original owners have disappeared and provenances have been falsified and rewritten. Existing provenances, some easier to fake than others, were obliterated. Labels on the back of paintings were changed. A network of opportunists, dealers and so-called experts appeared and they provided new authentication – critical for all paintings' valuations.

In 1999, the 'Commission for Looted Art in Europe' was established with the prime aim of recovering and achieving restitution of all lost and stolen artwork. It has had some success, recovering more than 3,000 items. However, for any organisation or individual to be successful in claiming back their stolen painting, it is necessary for the Commission to firstly authenticate the painting by establishing its correct provenance and then be satisfied that the claimant is in fact fully entitled to it.

There are many thousands of paintings that are still unaccounted for and, even if they did come to light, the original owners may well have died by now and their families, if they had any, could be completely unaware of their potential inheritance. The really valuable paintings, however, are well known within the industry so there would still be records of some sort.

Viktor stopped reading and thought back. He remembered Ian telling him about cases where Sotheby's, because of their thorough and detailed archive records, had been asked to help with some restitution cases. He also remembered seeing some of the older auction files showing who bought what painting and for what price. Invaluable information when trying to backtrack on ownership, true provenance and providing insurance valuations.

Concentrating on the report once again, he now flicked through to the end, where he remembered he'd listed all the missing paintings he'd managed to identify. However, he was quickly disappointed when the listing was no longer attached. Now where can it be? he asked himself. He knew it wouldn't have been destroyed, but had it been misplaced or attached to a different report?

Slowly Viktor's memory reminded him that he had been involved with another report. It was to do with a client's painting collection. He closed his eyes and tried to think back. Gradually it all came back to him. John McLaren! Yes, that was the case.

Viktor returned to the box and searched through the files until he came across a brown folder with the name 'John McLaren' written on the front cover.

Removing the file, he returned to the settee and started to look through it. One of Penny's cases. Yes, that's right, I went with her to the house in Mayfair. Strange people. Viktor skimmed through the file picking out highlights. All 18th and 19th century paintings inherited from the grandfather. The family were moving to Florida and wanted to sell the collection. It turned out that all ten paintings were listed on the website of the 'Commission for Looted Art in Europe'. That's right, that's when I downloaded the Commission's latest 18th and 19th century listing. Now that's got to be in this file. Viktor flicked to the end of the report. Yes, here we are.

He removed the listing from the McLaren file.

Now, he thought, all I have to do is check Ian's six paintings against this listing… and hope that I'm wrong.

May was settling into, and savouring her time, living in Oscar's villa. She was enjoying her new, more relaxed lifestyle and especially Oscar's company. Oscar had been proudly introducing her to more of his friends and colleagues that she hadn't met on her first visit. Those that she had met before were pleased to see her back again and wished her well.

Garfield and his wife, Ella, Oscar's next door neighbours, had, within two days of May's arrival, invited them both to one of their barbecues. There May had been introduced to other people but she knew she wouldn't be able to remember everyone's name. It was all a new cultural experience for her, people being so warm and friendly. She couldn't remember smiling and laughing so much for many a year.

Oscar had chauffeured May into St. John's several times for shopping and they'd also visited the 'Shell Gallery' again. Wesley welcomed her back to Antigua and hoped she'd enjoy her permanent move to the island. May found Wesley an interesting character and loved the colour and vibrancy of the paintings on display. She decided that, once she'd properly settled down, she'd contact some of her former Hong Kong colleagues to discuss the possibility of establishing a new market for this colourful and unusual type of work.

Oscar, meanwhile, was thoroughly enjoying his new life with May. He'd never really been lonely since arriving in Antigua, but occasionally he did feel alone, especially after Gladstone had moved to Jamaica to live closer to his son and family. May's arrival had totally changed his life.

May was enjoying the warm evenings and the private

time they were now able to share together, especially sitting on the patio for dinner and cocktails. Tonight was a similar experience. The air temperature was warm and a cooling breeze was gently whispering through the palm trees. A lovely full moon was lucent in an otherwise black and cloudless sky. They'd both just finished their meal and were now relaxing, enjoying the peace and tranquillity. The only noise came from the tree frogs and the intermittent soft crash of the waves as they rolled over and lapped up onto the beach.

"What's that noise, Oscar? I hear it every evening," asked May.

"Noise? Oh, do you mean the frogs?"

"Frogs! I thought they might be crickets."

"That 'koo-keeeee' sound is synonymous with the Caribbean. The locals say they get so used to it they never hear it. I must admit it wasn't until you mentioned it just now that I realised it was there. It's the tiny Caribbean Tree Frog. There are lots of them about, but strangely I've never seen one."

"It's a little hypnotic. Very relaxing somehow."

"I think it's the males trying to attract females."

May laughed. "You don't make that noise."

Oscar smiled. "I would if I was a tree frog and spotted you!"

May got up from her seat, leaned over and gave Oscar a kiss. "You're an old romantic," she said, picking up her glass, "Come on, let's go for a walk on the beach. There's a lovely full moon… and I want to discuss something with you."

Chapter 19

Viktor was aware that Ian was back home from his trip to Monaco, so sent him a short email suggesting they meet. 'Not something to put in an email or advise on the phone' was how he concluded his message.

Ian was curious after he'd read Viktor's vague communication. He assumed Vic had found out something unpleasant about his paintings… but he wasn't totally surprised. After all, these six pictures had been left to him by Andrei, and Andrei's dealings had not always been above board. Certainly, one or more of the paintings could well have something of a chequered history.

Ian telephoned Viktor's mobile. "Hi, Vic. Thanks for your email."

"Hi, Ian. Did you have a nice time in Monaco?"

"Yes, it was lovely. We had dinner with Bob and Zoe. Bob sends his regards, by the way."

Viktor smiled. "Thanks. I've checked out your six paintings so I think we ought to meet."

"Fine," responded Ian. "When are you free?"

"Tuesday and Thursday are best for me."

"I'm coming to London on Thursday. I already have an appointment at 2.30, so should we meet in the morning?"

"That's good with me. Come to the apartment at about

eleven o'clock. I'll make us some lunch for later. You've not been here yet, have you? I'll email you my address and directions."

"Thanks, Vic. See you then. I'm looking forward to seeing your palatial pad," replied Ian, ending the call. He entered the appointment into his diary and then prepared a mug of coffee. He was on his own in the house as Emma had arranged to meet up with her sister for lunch and some 'retail therapy'.

As he switched the kettle on to boil, the telephone began to ring. "Hello, Ian Caxton," he answered.

"Hi, Ian, Oscar."

Ian looked at the clock. "Can't you sleep? It must be five o'clock over there."

Oscar laughed. "Actually, it's just after six. I'm usually up at this time. Great time for a swim."

"So how are you and May getting on? She's not walked out on you yet, I hope," joked Ian.

"No. Not yet anyway. She's great, Ian. We're getting on really well. She's adapting to life here… and me, very quickly."

Ian smiled. "That's good. Pass on my regards. So, what can I do for you?"

"It's about May, well both of us, actually. We're planning to get married."

"Hey, that's great news. Emma will be pleased too. When's the date?"

"We've not got that far just yet. Lots to sort out. However, I'd love it if you would be my best man."

"Of course, Oscar. I would be honoured. Is the wedding going to be in Antigua?"

"That's what we're thinking. I hope that's not going to be a problem?"

"Certainly not. Emma and I will make it into a lovely

holiday. Let me know the full details when you've sorted them all out."

"Will do… and thanks. Must go. May's waiting to go for our usual early morning dip in the sea."

"Okay, Oscar. Great chatting… and congratulations!"

Ian finished making his coffee and looked out of the window. The morning frost had nearly gone, but the large grey clouds still looked threatening. Ian shook his head and said to himself, this is definitely not the Caribbean.

When Emma arrived home in the early evening, she put her shopping bags down in the hallway and walked into the kitchen. Ian was cooking their evening meal.

"Hi," he said, slightly surprised. "I didn't hear you come in. Did you have a good day?"

"Yes, exhausting, but fun." Emma walked over and kissed Ian. "Jane was in good form, as usual. She sends her love."

"That's nice. No bags?"

"A woman cannot go shopping and not buy anything," responded Emma. "There's five bags in the hallway. I'll take them upstairs in a few minutes. How long before dinner? I'd like a quick shower, if that's possible."

"I'm preparing a chilli. I've not cooked the rice yet. How long do you want?"

"About 30 minutes." Emma walked back towards the hallway.

"Okay. By the way, Oscar called. I'll tell you the details over dinner," said Ian. He turned the heat down under the saucepan and topped up his glass of wine.

When Emma arrived back in the kitchen, Ian was just dishing up their meal. "I've poured your wine."

"Thanks," she said, picking up her glass and taking a sip. "That's better. So, you began to mention Oscar. How are he and May getting on?"

Ian picked up the two plates and carried them over to the breakfast bar. "Getting on really well, I guess. They're getting married!"

"Oh, that's lovely news. When's the big day?" Emma asked as they sat down to eat.

They've not decided yet, but… Oscar has asked me if I'll be his best man."

"That's great, Ian. How lovely. What did you tell him?"

"Of course I told him yes. I feel really honoured. Oscar says the wedding is going to be in Antigua so we could make it into a lovely holiday."

"Yes, we could. That sounds just perfect."

Chapter 20

On the following Thursday, Ian travelled on the train to London for his two meetings. The first was with Viktor and he'd planned to see Charles Owen in the afternoon.

When the train arrived at Waterloo station, Ian got off and headed towards the taxi rank. It was 10.25am, the queue was relatively short and it only took a few minutes before he'd boarded his taxi. He read out Viktor's address to the driver and sat back as the taxi headed towards the Docklands district. Ian checked Viktor's instructions again and told the taxi driver where he wanted to be dropped off.

It was just before eleven o'clock when Ian stepped out of the taxi. He rechecked Viktor's instructions and started to amble along the 'pedestrians only' walkway. Two minutes later he'd arrived outside one of the tallest of the many modern Docklands residential skyscrapers. He doublechecked the address and then entered through the large glass entrance doors.

Viktor was waiting for him in the reception area.

"Hi, Vic. Wow, this is something special," said Ian, looking all around him at the vast glass and steel construction.

They shook hands and Vic asked, "Did you have any problems finding us?"

"No. The taxi driver seemed to know the area and then I just followed your instructions on foot."

"Good. We just need to get you a temporary security pass. Then I'll fly you to the moon!" Viktor laughed and led Ian towards the security desk.

Five minutes later they entered the elevator. Viktor pressed the button next to the number 29, which Ian noticed was the top floor. The doors closed and the elevator quickly, but very smoothly and silently, accelerated upwards. Ian could feel the speed of the ascent through his legs. After three floors the subtle blue lighting suddenly changed and daylight appeared. Ian turned around and realised it was a glass-sided elevator. He looked out at the panoramic view of the neighbouring Dockland buildings. As the elevator rose higher, the River Thames became visible. In the distance he spotted the 'Shard' and a number of the tall skyscrapers located in the city's financial area.

"This is quite something, Vic. I can see why you and Penny chose it."

Viktor smiled.

The elevator slowed down and then stopped. The doors opened and Viktor led the way along a brightly decorated corridor until they came to a door displaying the number '29d'.

"This is us," said Viktor. He unlocked and pushed open the door. Ian was led across the hallway and into the lounge area.

"Wow, this is fabulous, Vic." Ian walked over to the large pair of windows to take in the view. "You can see for miles."

"Each of the four apartments on this floor also has access to the shared roof garden. There you get the full 360-degree views. It's great up there in the summer, but cold and windy this time of year."

"You and Penny must be really pleased."

"Yes, we are. My father contributed to the purchase as part of our wedding present, but most of the money came from a loan against my inheritance from Andrei. There's no way we could afford this sort of property otherwise."

Ian smiled and thought of Andrei and his generosity to both Viktor and himself.

"I've brewed a pot of coffee," said Viktor, as he walked back towards the hallway. Ian followed. They walked into the kitchen area which was large, modern and pristine. A tray, containing a cafetiere of coffee, two mugs and a plate of biscuits, was sitting on the breakfast bar. Viktor walked over to the large American-style fridge-freezer and removed a small jug containing milk. He then added this to the tray.

"This kitchen is really nice too. It still looks brand new," said Ian, surveying the cooker, hob and worktops.

"That's Penny. She insists on everything being spotless."

Ian smiled. He remembered her desk at work that was always tidy and well organised.

Viktor picked up the tray. "We'll go into the dining room. Mind, it's mainly used as an office. We usually eat in here."

They both walked back into the hallway and then first left into the dining room. It was next to the lounge so had similar views.

Viktor placed the tray next to a laptop, some folders and files that were already on the table. They both sat down, Viktor poured the coffees and Ian helped himself to milk.

"Right," announced Viktor, picking up one of the files which had slips of paper sticking out of the top. "I've researched the six paintings you emailed me about and, in summary, four are listed on the 'Commission for Looted Art in Europe' website. That's why I thought it would be better if we met, rather than putting this sort of information in an email."

Ian flicked through the file. "I'm not surprised about

this, Vic. These six paintings were left to me by Andrei. You know the sort of art world he lived in. The question is, what do I do now?"

Viktor had a couple of answers, but let Ian ponder the problem first. After a few seconds, Viktor continued, "The good news, however, is that the other two paintings seem fine; they don't appear on this listing. They still could, of course, be copies or fakes, unless you have the up-to-date provenances. The research I did only took them up to 1938."

"No. Andrei only left the paintings," replied Ian, despondently. "There's no paperwork in Monaco, at least not that I could find. However, it does make you wonder how Andrei acquired them."

"Tricky," replied Viktor.

After Ian left Viktor's apartment, he caught the Docklands Light Railway into the city and then the Underground to Embankment station. From there he walked the short distance along Northumberland Avenue to Trafalgar Square. There he met Charles Owen.

As the two men strolled around the square and passed by the two fountains, Ian updated Charles with his recent findings about the French museum's version of 'Fête Gloanec'. Charles was intrigued with Ian's discovery and even more so once he'd heard about Ian's new idea.

Charles suddenly stopped walking and looked directly at Ian. Slowly, a broad grin appeared on his face and he rubbed his hands together. He then patted Ian on the shoulder and quietly announced, "What a great idea."

Chapter 21

Oscar and May were slowly progressing with the various preparations necessary for their wedding day. They had decided on a nearby five-star hotel for the ceremony and reception, but still hadn't finalised a date. The hotel had given them a list of five options and they were just waiting on Ian, and May's brother, to confirm their availability and which were the best dates for them. In the meantime, they had started to list who else they wanted to attend the wedding. In addition to Ian, Oscar had suggested, amongst others, Wesley, Garfield and Gladstone. May also wanted three of her best friends from Hong Kong.

After days of more discussion, Oscar was beginning to wonder if they'd made the right choice to have a big wedding. May, too, was also having second thoughts about her decision not to have a traditional wedding in Hong Kong. She really wanted her mother to attend but had to accept that this was not going to happen, even if it did take place in Hong Kong. Her mother was suffering from Alzheimer's disease and far too frail to travel from the Kowloon nursing home.

Besides, David, May's brother, had made it clear that he was definitely not going to go back to Hong Kong ever again even, eventually, for his mother's funeral. May was also worried that her mother's death could well be very soon but, hopefully, not before the wedding day.

David Ling was five years older than May and after their father had died, when May was only four years of age, David had become more than just the big brother. May desperately wanted David to 'give her away' but, although David said he would, he also told her it was doubtful his wife would join him, due to looking after the children. Even when May said she would pay for the whole family's expenses, David told her it was more to do with the practicality than the cost. There was the children's schooling and college to consider.

May was not very pleased.

Ian was sitting in his office and pondering on the six paintings still residing in the vault at 'Harbour Heights'. He was trying to remember what he'd originally found when he'd been through all the drawers and cupboards in Andrei's old office. He'd found some stationery items, but couldn't remember seeing any documents relating to these pictures. Also, the apartment's small safe was empty. So, what about the vault? He remembered looking in most of the small safes there, but they were empty too. Had he looked inside all of them? He was certain none were locked, as the doors had been left slightly ajar. Had he missed something there? He couldn't think of any other possibility. Andrei had been far too organised not to have had documentation for each painting.

"Ian," shouted Emma from the kitchen, "Lunch is ready."

"Okay. Coming," replied Ian. He left his desk and ambled into the kitchen.

"I've used up all the old vegetables and made a soup."

"Sounds good," replied Ian. "I could do with something warming."

They sat down at the breakfast bar and Emma started

the conversation. "Have you heard whether Oscar and May have decided on a date for their wedding yet?"

"No. I emailed Oscar our preferred dates but, I now gather from his last email, he wishes they were just having a simple ceremony," replied Ian. Privately he could understand Oscar's feelings.

"I'm sure that's not what May is thinking about," replied Emma.

"They'll sort it all out eventually." Ian realised he was treading on dangerous ground, so tried to change the subject. "Have you thought about how long a holiday you'd like to have in Antigua?"

"It depends on the date they finally decide on. It might clash with Robert's school holiday. Ideally, I'd like to go for about two to three weeks."

"My guess is they'll decide on sometime in January or February. They're the two months we've been given. It's hurricane season from about late May to November."

"Let's hope it's late January or February. It would mean we'd miss some of our winter. Why don't you drop the hint?"

Ian laughed. "What would you have thought if someone had suggested a date for our wedding?"

"They did if you remember – you! You were in Hong Kong at the time and drove my mother up the wall."

"Me!" exclaimed Ian, with total surprise. "I left it to you, your mother and father to sort it all out. I was thousands of miles away, if you remember?"

"Exactly!"

There was a pause in the conversation whilst they ate their soup. Ian didn't know what Emma's comment meant, but decided the best option was to change the subject. "I might be flying out to France for a day next week. Charles Owen has got to sort out a day's holiday from work first. We're going to the Musée des Beaux-Arts d'Orléans."

"For the 'Fête Gloanec' painting again?"

"Yes. I've not been able to find out the full provenance details for the museum's picture. I've got an idea and Charles has agreed to carry it out."

Ian explained his plan whilst Emma finished her soup.

Emma briefly laughed. "Do you really think it's going to work?" she asked, although privately she thought it was a clever idea.

"I'm not sure we have any other alternatives. Charles thinks it should be fun!"

It was six days later when Ian and Charles's private charter plane took off from Gatwick airport. Charles ran through the script Ian had provided but Ian then suggested a couple of slight amendments. After two more run-throughs, Charles was more or less word perfect.

Chapter 22

Ian wandered around the Musée des Beaux-Arts d'Orléans whilst Charles was attending his appointment. He hoped all the information he had given Charles about the life and work of Paul Gauguin would work.

Ian briefly stopped and noticed he was standing in front of a large oil painting depicting a battle in the snow between Napoleon's army and the Russians. He looked at his watch. Charles had been gone for over an hour. Either he's been arrested or his meeting has gone very well. Hopefully the latter, he thought.

Then, out of the corner of his eye, Ian spotted Charles walking along the corridor accompanied by a young lady. At the top of the stairs they both stopped, chatted and finally shook hands. The lady walked away and Charles, carrying his briefcase, began to descend the stairs. Ian gave him a minute, then followed.

Charles followed the 'exit' directions and finally walked out of the building. He crossed the Rue Fernand Rabier and headed towards the Place du Campo Santo. Ian followed behind but at a reasonable distance so that any onlookers would never guess they were together. Ian finally caught up with Charles when he found him standing near the spectacular 15th and 16th century archways. They were now both well out of sight of the museum.

"How did it go?" asked Ian, eagerly. He'd just arrived and stood next to his colleague.

Charles gave Ian a big grin. "It went brilliantly! Camille was really helpful. I'm not sure she was totally convinced that I was a mature art student, but she was more than happy to talk about their Gauguin collection. I also think she fancied me a bit."

Ian laughed. "But did you get the provenance details?" He was still eager to see what Charles had obtained.

Charles opened his briefcase and showed Ian a collection of papers. "Photocopies of the whole history of their Gauguin collection. Thought it would be useful to you."

"Excellent! Well done." Ian was certainly relieved. "Right, we now need to get a taxi. Our flight is booked to leave in two hours. It will cost us a lot more money and time if we're late. I'll read all those papers once we get on the plane."

They eventually boarded their private plane with 20 minutes to spare. Directly behind them the stewardess closed and secured the door. The engines were switched on and the pilot made his usual checks. Ten minutes later their plane joined a short queue of two other planes waiting for clearance.

Both men were now strapped into their seats. Charles removed the paperwork from his briefcase and handed it over to Ian. Ian quickly thumbed through the pages until he got to the 'Fête Gloanec' file. As he was about to start reading, the plane began to accelerate along the runway. He put the papers down onto his lap, looked out of the window and waited for the plane to take off. It was only a few seconds later that the front of the plane began to lift. There was an extra roar from the two engines as the plane rose into the air, Ian gave a deep sigh and picked up the papers again.

After a few minutes the plane began to level out and Charles asked, "I hope that's what you wanted."

Ian put the papers down on his lap again and slowly turned towards Charles. "Yes," he said, hesitantly. "But unfortunately, we now have another problem."

"Would you gentlemen like some champagne?" asked the stewardess, now standing next to them.

"Well, I think I have something to celebrate," announced Charles to the stewardess. "I'm not sure about my colleague here though."

After Charles was served with his drink, Ian decided to join him and thanked the stewardess.

Charles took a sip of his champagne and leaned closer to Ian. "So, what's the problem now?"

Ian put his drink down and leaned closer to Charles. In a low voice he said, "The provenance looks too good. It seems to stack up."

"So, you think the museum's picture is the real 'Fête Gloanec' now!?"

Ian was confused. "No. I'm still sure yours is the real painting, but this provenance is going to be more difficult to dispute. I was hoping to spot an obvious flaw."

Charles looked away and started to think. Eventually he said, "Could there be two genuine 'Fête Gloanec' paintings?"

Ian smiled. "My wife asked me the same question. It's not impossible. One could have been a first attempt, rejected for some reason by Gauguin, and a newer version subsequently painted. Either way, our case is going to be a bit more difficult to prove."

"Okay. So, what do we do next?"

"I've got some work to do," replied Ian. "I need to find something to question in this French provenance. I've got to find something that proves, categorically, it is not the real 'Fête Gloanec'. The only route I see at the moment is to obtain scientific evidence for both pictures."

"The French are not going to agree to that!"

"No, I know," said Ian, somewhat frustrated. "As I say, I've got a lot more work still to do."

Viktor was following up on Alexander's latest telephone call. He'd just arrived outside two large wooden gates. It was 8.45am. These gates were the main entrance to a substantial red brick house, located on the edge of St. John's Wood. This was a district in London that Viktor had visited several times before. He knew it was one of London's most upmarket residential locations. Consisting of elegant villa-style housing sweeping along the side of Regent's Park, it also included the picturesque Little Venice area and part of Swiss Cottage. One of the most popular areas to live in London – for those that can afford the several-million-pound price tag!

Viktor pushed through the partially opened gates, strolled across the tarmac driveway and looked up at the house's ornate facade. Two of Alexander's vehicles had already arrived and were parked much closer to the house. When Viktor arrived outside the front door, he noticed it was already wide open. He walked straight through and into the hallway, but quickly stepped to one side as two men were carrying an Edwardian chest of drawers in his direction. The man at the rear was Billy, the foreman. As the two men squeezed past him, Viktor asked Billy, "Has Alexander arrived yet?"

The two men carried on walking but Billy shouted back, "He left about 'arf 'our ago. Said for you to carry on as usual. We ain't touched any of the pictures yet."

"Okay. Thanks." Viktor entered the room immediately on his right and removed a notepad and pen from his briefcase. He looked around the room. It was quite spacious, probably the lounge, but appeared very old-fashionably decorated. It had already been stripped of most of the furniture but there were four oil and two watercolour paintings still hanging on the walls. Viktor went over to the first picture and started to make his notes.

About an hour later, Viktor was leaning on the breakfast bar in the kitchen. He was writing up the last of his observations and findings.

"Okay to pack the pictures now, Vic?" It was Billy who'd arrived in the kitchen. "That's all there's left to pack."

"Yes, fine. I've finished myself." Viktor put his notepad and pen back into his briefcase.

"Nice 'ouse ain't it?" said Billy, walking with Viktor back into the hallway.

"Very nice," replied Viktor. "A bit dated, but still must be worth about three million pounds, if not a bit more."

"Really! Wow. The furniture's worth a few bob too. All going into store for the mo."

The two men walked out of the building and onto the driveway.

"Come on, you slackers," Billy shouted to his team. "Tea break's over. Johnny, bring the packing materials for the pictures."

"I'll be on my way then, Billy. I'm done here."

"Yeah, okay Vic. Look after yourself, mate."

Viktor strolled past the two large vans and back through the two open gates. He then turned right and followed the route back towards the Underground station. He was still considering the painting collection he'd just viewed. A bit of investigation required, he thought but, all in all, a productive and hopefully very profitable morning's work. He was sure Alexander would be pleased. However, one particular picture had caught his eye and he wondered if Alexander would be agreeable to a deal.

Chapter 23

Ian decided to email Bob Taylor to advise him that the six paintings he'd previously mentioned, would not now be available... at least for the time being. He explained that more research work was necessary to clarify some queries relating to the provenances. He also said that once these issues were resolved, he would contact him again.

Bob replied thanking Ian for keeping him up to date with the situation.

Right, thought Ian. Now that I've cleared my desk, I can concentrate on the Musée des Beaux-Arts d'Orléans version of the provenance for the 'Fête Gloanec'. He went over to his bookcase and selected a large volume containing many pictures and lots of information about Paul Gauguin's paintings. He took the book back to his desk and flicked through it until he came to the section titled 'Fête Gloanec'. He then compared the museum's report of the same painting with the book's information.

After about 40 minutes, Ian decided he was getting nowhere. The only additional information worth further exploration, was an investigation carried out by a Parisian art museum in 1935. Unfortunately, there was no mention of the museum's name or the result of the investigation.

Ian was frustrated and more than a little concerned. He'd assured Charles that his painting was probably worth many millions of pounds and now… well, he was beginning to question not only his own belief, but also his professional judgement.

He decided to take a break and make himself a mug of coffee. Whilst he was waiting for the kettle to boil, he suddenly had a flash of inspiration! Of course, he thought, but firstly I must ask my old friend Albert.

Albert Badeaux has been working at the famous Musée D'Orsay in Paris for over 20 years. Ian had first met him when Albert was seeking the help of Sotheby's with regards to two paintings that were causing a major issue in France. Ian was able to assist Albert and subsequently they became good friends. They had kept in touch periodically by email, or when both were in Paris or London.

Ian carried his mug of coffee back to his office and switched on his computer. He found Albert's last email address and hoped it was still current. It was an outside chance, but he was confident that Albert would at least agree to give it a try.

Ian typed the following email:

Bonjour Albert,

I hope you and your family are well. We are fine.

I am researching a painting for a client that is currently on display in the Musée des Beaux-Arts d'Orléans. It is titled 'Fête Gloanec'. The artist is 'Madeleine B' (Paul Gauguin).

I have details of the painting's provenance provided by the museum. The provenance states that, in 1935, an investigation was carried out by a Parisian museum. Unfortunately, it doesn't mention the museum's name. I was wondering if you could check the Musée D'Orsay's records to see if it was your museum that completed this examination.

We must meet up again soon. Are you coming to London in the near future?
Best wishes,
Ian.

Whilst Ian waited on Albert's reply, he decided it was time to get Charles's version of 'Fête Gloanec' forensically examined. This exercise would be expensive, but he knew he couldn't go much further without these scientific reports. Only at that point would he and Charles know for certain if their painting still had a sporting chance of being authenticated… or not.

That same evening, Ian telephoned Charles and explained the situation. Charles immediately agreed to both the scientific investigation and to a date and time when he could hand over the painting to Ian. What Ian needed to do now was speak with Simon Lyle at the Courtauld Institute. Then, depending upon Simon's findings, possibly talk to Penny's relative at the Tate Museum.

Within two days of Ian's request, Albert had emailed him with a holding message.

Hello Ian,
So good to hear from you again.
I will investigate our records to see if we have any information about 'Fête Gloanec'. It's not one that I immediately recognise.
I am away for six days, partly visiting some clients and partly on a short holiday. I will email you as soon as I can. I also need to speak to a colleague about your picture.
Your good friend,
Albert.

It was five days later when Ian delivered Charles's painting to Simon Lyle. After a brief chat, Ian left the picture for the scientific examination. Simon said he would telephone Ian within the week with the results.

Two days later Ian received another email from Albert that read:

Hello again, Ian,

I am sorry to tell you, but we have no records of the 'Fête Gloanec' having been inspected at the Musée D'Orsay.

I have spoken with a colleague at a separate museum. He's an expert on Gauguin's life and work. He thinks his museum might well have completed the investigation in 1935. He is going to check.

I will contact you again soon.

Your good friend,

Albert.

Ian was pondering on this email when the telephone rang. "Hello, Ian Caxton," he answered.

"Ian, hi. Simon Lyle. I've examined your picture and can confirm the pigment and chemical paint profile is very similar to our records of paintings already authenticated to Gauguin work during the 1880s."

"That's great news, Simon," replied Ian, enthusiastically.

"I knew you'd be pleased. I'll email you copies of the three graphs… along with my invoice of course!" said Simon, laughing. "Incidentally, the blue oil paint Gauguin used is interesting because that particular paint was not produced after 1910."

"Excellent. Can I assume, therefore, we can potentially rule out a modern copy?"

"I think so, unless a supply of this old blue paint was found again after 120 years," joked Simon.

"Thanks, Simon. That's very helpful. I'll arrange for the owner of the painting, Charles Owen, to collect it later in the week. Is that okay?"

"Yes, that's fine. I'll have it packaged up ready for him. Good luck."

Ian said goodbye and closed the call. He was delighted with Simon's findings and eager to see the graphs for himself. Nevertheless, whilst this was definitely a significant step forward, he also knew that the battle was definitely not over yet. Simon's report would only state that the paints used on Charles's picture of 'Fête Gloanec' were similar to those Gauguin was using about 1888. On its own, this does not confirm, absolutely, that Charles's picture was painted by Gauguin. It could still have been completed by an associate or colleague of Gauguin using the same studio paints. However, on a more positive note, accepted records of Gauguin, when he was living in Pont Aven, state he was usually painting on his own. So hopefully, thought Ian, only Gauguin would have been using this full palette of paints at that time.

That same evening, Charles telephoned Ian. He was eager to be updated on any developments. Ian told him the good news about Simon's report, but also emphasised that there was still a long way to go.

"Okay," said Charles. "I guess we're in for the long haul. By the way, I received some great news today. I've got a buyer for 'Dexter's End'!"

"That's wonderful news, Charles. I hope the buyer's not a developer," He knew the property needed a lot of money spent on it to bring it into the 21st century, but still hoped someone would respect its character and not just bulldoze it.

"I don't know. I've left all those details to the agent. After all, I'm paying him a small fortune."

Ian smiled at Charles's comment. "Good luck. By the way, I told Simon you would collect the painting from Courtauld's. When can you do that?"

"That's okay. I'll do that. Probably Thursday, about 5pm."

"I'll tell Simon for you," responded Ian.

Chapter 24

Despite Ian's suggestion to Emma that they should slowly reduce their time involved in the art world, she felt she was only just starting! It was still a very new and exciting time for her. She'd achieved some success and was keen to search for more bargains. With Robert now a full-time boarder at school, she knew she had lots more time to be able to explore the internet, antique shops, auction houses and the occasional second-hand dealer. Her mother had even stopped criticising her change of career when Emma told her they had sold the 'Mademoiselle Chad' painting for £2.2 million!

Nevertheless, she did agree with Ian that they should allocate more time for holidays and visits to the apartment in Monaco. It was a dilemma. It was not solely the money that excited her. It was the intrigue and challenge, the buzz, the provenance search, uncovering historical facts and finding new vital information, plus… achieving success and making a profit for all her efforts. Definitely much more fun than accountancy.

When her sister Jane suggested a shopping trip to Brighton, Emma's immediate thought was 'The Lanes'. This was the area she knew also contained art galleries, as well as antiques and bric-a-brac shops.

As Jane lived closer to Brighton than Emma, Emma suggested they go in her car. On the agreed day, she left home just after 9am and collected Jane some 35 minutes later. They arrived in Brighton just after 11am and were sitting in a cafe drinking their morning coffee at 11.30.

"Is there anything special you're looking for?" asked Emma. She knew her sister mainly liked to look in the clothes shops, both for herself and her children.

Jane put down her coffee cup. "No, not really. I mainly want to look in some of the clothes shops. There's always something unusual in these independent shops. What about you?"

"I'll have a look at the clothes too, but I would like to pop into some of the galleries and bric-a-brac shops. I might find an interesting painting… maybe a bargain!"

"You've really got the bug for paintings now. Is that Ian's influence?"

"I suppose, partly, but it's also great fun. You just don't know what you're going to find. Mostly it's, well, rubbish really, but occasionally you find something that others have missed. It's a fascinating challenge trying to establish a picture's provenance."

"Time consuming, I bet, but you've made some money too."

Emma smiled. "I'm still learning from Ian. He has a real 'nose' for finding winners."

Jane nodded and drank the rest of her coffee. "Well, we'd better get moving. There are a lot of shops here for us to visit."

Emma had already finished her drink, so they both stood up and left the cafe.

Right, thought Emma, let's see what little gem I can find today.

Viktor had submitted his valuation report on the St. John's Wood paintings to Alexander. At the end of the report, he also mentioned that he'd like to buy one of the paintings for himself.

Three days later Viktor was working in the dining room at home. He was currently researching one particular painting for a client when he was interrupted by his mobile phone ringing.

"Hello?" enquired Viktor tentatively. He didn't immediately recognise the number.

"Vic, hi. Alexander."

"Hello, Alexander, I didn't recognise your number, sorry."

"Not your fault. I'm using my wife's mobile. Mine's just charging up."

"Are you okay with my report?"

"Yes, that's fine. It's the painting you want to buy that I was ringing about. I hope you've not deliberately undervalued it in your report," said Alexander, but he was only teasing Viktor.

Viktor was surprised and a little embarrassed. "I would never do that. I have my reputation to consider."

Alexander laughed. "Just a joke, Vic. What I was about to say is you can have the painting instead of your commission."

"Are you sure? You'll be losing your 50% share on the sale-price profit. I'm happy to pay you for your share."

"I know. Let's just say it's a thank-you gift from me. I know I'm not being ripped off any more. You've earned it over the last few months."

"Thanks," replied Viktor. "It's going to be a birthday present for my wife."

"Tell her Alexander sends his greetings too."

"Okay. I'll do that."

"Got your diary to hand? A week on Tuesday, we've got a new valuation in Wimbledon. Are you okay?"

Viktor quickly checked his diary, but was pretty sure it would be fine. "Yes, I can do that."

"I'll email you the details. Cheers."

"Thanks," replied Viktor. "Bye."

Viktor switched off his phone and made a provisional note in his diary, 'Wimbledon valuation'. He was enjoying his relationship with Alexander. He was a fair man and Viktor was determined to show the same level of respect. Even more so now that Ian had largely stepped away from the original agreement. He definitely felt far more confident and encouraged, too, by most of his valuations being accepted in the fine art world. When he had an unusual painting, though, he would telephone Ian with the picture's details and his own thoughts on the value. So far, Ian had backed his judgement every time.

Viktor sat back in his chair and put his feet up on his waste paper bin. Slowly a small smile appeared on his face. He was feeling happy and generally pleased with himself. With Alexander, he was now doing something that he thoroughly enjoyed and felt more like he was his own boss. One area, however, that was still niggling him, was that he didn't yet feel his time was being fully employed. Working with Alexander and his small client base was only occupying about 50% of his business time. He still wanted to do something with a little more adventure... or even daring! Something that would be stimulating and get the heart pumping. He was missing Ian's 'partnership' adventures and the inspiring 12 months when he'd been working with Ian and Penny at Sotheby's. They were the best and most exciting times. He wanted to get those exhilarating moments back.

Chapter 25

When Emma arrived home, Ian was preparing their evening meal. He heard her arrive in the hallway and place, what sounded like, several large bags of shopping on the floor.

Emma walked into the kitchen and kissed him.

"Did you have a good day?" asked Ian, whilst he was stirring a sauce.

"Yes, but I feel like I've been walking for hours."

Ian smiled. "I heard the noise in the hallway. It sounds like you've been spending your money."

"I bought two tops and three pairs of trousers. I'll take them upstairs shortly."

"By the way, I received an email from Oscar. He and May have finally agreed on a date for their wedding."

"Excellent. When is it?"

"28th January. Five months' time."

"Five months!" exclaimed Emma. "I'll need to check my wardrobe."

Ian shook his head from side to side. "Dinner should be ready in about half an hour."

"In that case I'll have a quick shower and freshen up," said Emma, pouring herself a glass of Chablis and topping up Ian's. She then walked into the hallway and picked up her bags. "By the way," she shouted, "I bought an unusual cartoon picture as well. I thought it would look nice in the office."

Over dinner, Ian and Emma were sitting at the breakfast bar and chatting about each other's day. The cartoon picture Emma had bought was on her right-hand side, still in its paper bag. At the end of their meal, Emma picked up the bag and removed the picture. She handed it to Ian and asked, "What do you think?"

Ian lifted the picture to study it properly. He noted it was a caricature. Drawn using black ink on a white cardboard background, it was mounted in a simple black wooden frame. About 30 x 20 centimetres in size, the picture depicted a side view of a male figure stretching out his right arm and pointing a paint brush towards a canvas set on an easel. The artist appeared to be painting a large green '$' sign. It was signed 'Jacob Bliss, 2009'.

Ian smiled. "I like it. It's fun."

"I thought so too," replied Emma. "It looks like somebody was trying to make a sort of political statement. Maybe, 'art equals money'."

"I've never heard of this Jacob Bliss. He's a new one on me."

"Neither have I. I bought it because I thought it was just a fun picture. Sums up our business world."

Ian laughed. "Do you think so? Maybe you've become as cynical as this Mr. Bliss."

"I'm going to put it up on the wall behind my desk. Anyway, it only cost 25 pounds."

"Certainly worth 25 pounds."

"By the way, how are you getting along with Charles's picture?"

Ian's expression suddenly changed from a smile to more of a scowl. He was still finding progress frustrating. "I've had a positive reply from Simon's investigation."

Emma nodded.

"So that's a step forward, but I'm still waiting for a reply from Albert in France. I'm hoping he'll come up with some good news."

"What are you hoping for?"

"The French museum's provenance states that, in 1935, an investigation was carried out by a Parisian museum. Unfortunately, it doesn't state which museum. Albert has already told me the Musée D'Orsay's records don't help, but he's been in touch with a colleague, someone who's more au fait with Gauguin's work and his life. I'm waiting for his answer."

"What do you hope this colleague will say?"

"1935 was such a long time ago and, as far as I can establish, the French haven't carried out any more investigations since. I'm hoping Albert's colleague will report some sort of error or something inconclusive about the French museum's painting's provenance. Something that with modern technology could possibly be challenged. I know I'm clutching at straws… but…"

"Do you still think Charles's painting is the real one?"

Ian took a deep breath. "Yes," he said, unconvincingly. "But you might be right. There could still be two 'Fête Gloanec' pictures, both painted by Gauguin. But… and this is my main problem, I just 'felt' Charles's copy was the real version. When Vic and I saw the other one in France… well, it didn't give me the same feeling."

"Feelings are not facts," said Emma, stating the obvious.

"I know… and that's the issue," pleaded Ian. "I don't always get an itchy scalp, or a sweaty hand, when I see an original work of art but, when I do, I'm rarely wrong."

Emma laughed. "Only RARELY wrong?"

"Okay then, NEVER wrong! That's why I'm exploring every factual avenue to prove my point."

"In the meantime is there anything else we can do together?"

"I'm not sure. What I want to do is build up so much evidence that it forces the French museum to agree to a forensic examination. I can't see from their records that a scientific examination has ever been done... and obviously technology has moved on massively since 1935."

"Do you want any more wine?" asked Emma, standing up after noticing Ian's glass was empty.

"I think I need some. Thanks."

Emma removed the half-full bottle of Chablis from the fridge and refilled Ian's glass. She also half-filled her own. "What if you discussed your thoughts with the catalogue raisonné people for Gauguin? Would they be prepared to help?"

"I don't know. At the moment, they're convinced that the French museum's painting is the real work of art. They probably don't know Charles's version even exists. Without a lot more evidence to the contrary, I'm sure they wouldn't be interested in my comments. They'll just deem Charles's picture to be a fake or a copy. Besides, they may then decide to speak to the Musée des Beaux-Arts d'Orléans and I certainly don't want the museum to know about us being a possible competitor. At some stage I might just want some more information from them. Talking of which, how's your French?"

"It's okay enough to have sensible conversations with Zoe in Monaco and with some of the other locals there, but far from fluent. Why?"

"Well, if I need to go back to the French museum, I can't really take Charles again. They already know him as a 'mature student' and I still want to keep a low profile... You did say you wanted to help."

Emma laughed. "It all depends on what you want me to do!"

Chapter 26

The final details of Oscar and May's wedding were now in place and the big day was approaching very fast. The ceremony and reception would be taking place in the grounds of a nearby five-star hotel. Invitations had been sent out and most of the acceptance replies had been received. Ian and Emma had booked a suite for two weeks, in the same hotel as the wedding. David Ling, May's brother, was due to arrive two days before the wedding. He was staying at Oscar's villa for three days and he'd be travelling on his own.

Oscar was especially pleased to receive a nice acceptance letter from Gladstone. Gladstone had arranged to stay with old friends on the island for three days. Wesley and Garfield had both confirmed they'd be attending with their wives.

Two of May's three invitees from Hong Kong, Linda and Sylvia, had also confirmed they would be coming and were travelling together with their husbands. Both families would be staying in the same hotel where the wedding was taking place. They also intended to extend their stay to include a holiday break.

"Well, May, just six weeks to go," said Oscar. They were both sitting on loungers on the patio, drinking their regular evening cocktails. They were watching the sun go down over the garden hedge and relaxing after another hectic day.

"I know," responded May. "I'm so nervous, even now. I don't know what I'll be like on the wedding day."

Oscar smiled. "You'll be fine. We'll be surrounded by our friends and have a wonderful day. It's going to be so special getting married next to the Caribbean Sea."

"It's sad, Oscar, that you have no relatives coming."

"As you know, I was an only child and my mother died some time ago. Dad has never travelled outside Hong Kong and he's far too old to start now. He'll be here in spirit. Besides, I'll have all my friends around me."

"You might not see your father again."

"I know. Before I moved here, I visited him and told him of my plans. He said he was really pleased for me and advised not to return to Hong Kong. He's also concerned about what's been happening since the Chinese took back control. Mind, he also said he was surrounded by good friends and would be fine."

"I know you still keep in touch with him."

"I promised him I would. He can use email, but he doesn't want to use video conferencing. He says when he sees himself on screen, he looks very old."

May laughed. "You still email him once a week?"

"Yes. I have a lot more to tell him now you're here. He wishes us well and says I'm a very lucky man."

"And so you are," replied May, with a large smile and twinkle in her eyes. "Come on, let's have a walk along the beach before it gets too dark."

The day before the wedding, all the travelling guests had arrived in Antigua. May had temporarily moved out of the villa and was sharing a room with Emma in the hotel. Ian had joined Oscar and David at the villa where he was staying for just one night. Later that evening they were going to be joined by Wesley and Gladstone. The plans then were for all the men to congregate at Garfield's villa for a barbeque. Oscar had told everyone that he didn't want a traditional stag evening, and when Garfield had suggested the barbeque, he thought it was a brilliant idea. Oscar volunteered to bring two bottles of rum and some champagne.

Meanwhile, the ladies were all gathered around the hotel's pool bar in their swimwear. It was Linda and Sylvia's idea. They'd arranged for this venue to be at the centre of May's hen night. Initially the champagne and cocktails began to flow and then the calypso music and dancing started. Finally, May was thrown into the pool. Linda and Sylvia both voluntarily jumped in to join her. Emma stood at the pool side videoing the events on her mobile phone.

At the rear of Garfield's villa, the beer was flowing, the conversation was loud and barbeque ribs and steaks were devoured with relish. Rum cocktails and Champagne were being consumed and glasses constantly refilled.

Just before midnight, the ladies staggered to their rooms and the men began to quieten down. Wesley and Gladstone disappeared in a taxi and Ian and David helped Oscar back to his villa.

Everyone slept soundly until, early the next morning, Emma gently nudged May, who was almost falling out of the side of her bed. May woke up very slowly and wondered where she was. She was also curious to know who was hammering on her head.

"Good morning," announced Emma.

"What time is it?" burbled May, trying to rearrange the rest of her body back into the bed.

"It's just after eight o'clock. Breakfast should be arriving shortly."

"I need to be sick," announced May. She threw the cotton sheet off her body and dashed towards the ensuite bathroom.

Over in Oscar's villa, David and Ian were awake and drinking black coffees in the kitchen. There was no sign of Oscar. Both Ian and David had been awake for about an hour and had occupied their time discussing Hong Kong, London and Singapore.

Ian looked at his watch. "It's just after eight o'clock. Do you think we should wake the groom?"

"Let's give him a little longer. We've got plenty of time. The wedding's not until 3.30. I told May I'd arrive at the hotel at about two o'clock."

"Are you excited to be giving your sister away?"

"Strange, isn't it? I was looking forward to my daughter's wedding, but having this rehearsal… well it's just so strange."

Ian told David about when he'd been Penny's 'temporary father' at her wedding. He explained how honoured and proud he'd felt when he walked his former PA down the aisle.

"Is there any coffee?" The question came from Oscar, slowly shuffling across the kitchen floor. His hair was dishevelled and his dressing gown barely hanging onto his shoulders.

"Just freshly brewed," announced David. He stood up and removed a mug from the cupboard. "Black?"

"Very black," said Oscar, sitting in David's seat. His eyes were barely open. "What's the time?"

"Just after eight," stated Ian. "You've got plenty of time to sober up."

"Funny," mumbled Oscar. He sipped the coffee David had passed to him and grimaced. "God, that tastes horrible."

Both Ian and David smiled at Oscar's pained expression.

"We'll get you back into the land of the living once you've had a long, cold shower," Ian said.

Oscar tried to look at him, but his eyes wouldn't fully open.

By late morning Oscar and May had both sobered up. May had taken a long shower and nibbled some of the breakfast delivered by room service. She felt more refreshed but, because she was sober again, her nerves started to remind her it was less than three hours to the ceremony. Emma reminded her about the appointment with the hairdresser and then there was a knock on the door. Linda and Sylvia had arrived to give added moral support.

Ian and David were preparing a light salad. Nothing too substantial as the reception meal was planned for late afternoon. Oscar had shaved and showered, and eaten one round of toast for his late breakfast. Whilst he was feeling much better, his nerves were also starting to remind him what day it was.

Ian was in control of the day's plans. After the light lunch, he was going to borrow Oscar's jeep and transport David to the hotel. He would then drive back to the villa to supervise Oscar and, between the two of them, they would clean and tidy the villa. As part of the hotel's wedding package, Oscar and May would occupy one of the two hotel bridal suites for their first night together as 'man and wife'. Ian didn't need to worry about the meal or seating arrangements. These had already been chosen by May – with a little help from Oscar. Just before three o'clock, Oscar and Ian would travel to the hotel in Oscar's jeep. There they would mingle with some of the early guests before taking their positions at the wedding location.

At 3.28pm, everything had worked to plan. Oscar kept asking Ian if he still had the wedding ring and, for the umpteenth time, Ian removed it from the same pocket to show Oscar it was still there. Oscar, full of nervousness, turned around and looked at the familiar faces. Garfield and his wife, Ella: she gave him an encouraging smile. He smiled back. Gladstone: Oscar had never seen him look so smart.

Wesley and his wife Witney: Witney in her colourful floral dress and large matching hat. He watched Emma sit down and then May's two friends joined their husbands who were already seated.

Oscar turned back, looked up at the minister and took a deep breath.

Ian smiled and leaned towards him. "Are you okay?"

"No," whispered Oscar, and took another deep breath. He was feeling very warm, or was it just nerves?

Oscar and all the guests were on the beach, but sheltered from the hot Caribbean sunshine by a large, white canopy, which slowly rippled in the gentle sea breeze.

Ian turned around and smiled at Emma. He then spotted May leaving the hotel building and being escorted by her brother. Ian nudged Oscar and whispered, "Here she comes."

Ian, Oscar and all the guests stood up. Oscar turned around again and watched his wife-to-be walking towards him. He smiled and decided she looked unbelievably gorgeous.

May was dressed in a pale yellow traditional Chinese Wedding Qipao. The dress had been designed by May herself, so it had a cooler fitting for a Caribbean-climate wedding.

May and David joined Oscar and Ian. May looked at Oscar and gave him a gentle smile.

Oscar smiled back and whispered, "You look fabulous."

They both then looked up at the minister and he started to speak.

Chapter 27

On the same day, in England, it was Penny's birthday. She had to leave home early for a business meeting but promised Viktor she'd be home early to open her cards and presents. Viktor reminded her about the birthday meal he'd specially organised at the local restaurant. Penny assured him she would be home in plenty of time to have a shower and a change of clothes.

At 5.45pm Penny arrived back at the apartment and after kissing Viktor she started to open her birthday cards and presents. They'd been on the dining room table all day.

She'd decided to leave Viktor's card and present until last. Finally, she opened his card, giggled at the cartoon on the front and read the words inside. She smiled and gave Viktor a kiss. "Thank you," she said. "That's really nice."

"I hope you like your present too," replied Viktor.

Penny picked up the parcel and ripped apart the coloured wrapping paper. She removed the painting and stared at the picture, eyes wide open. "Oh wow, Vic. This is superb! It must have cost a fortune." She leaned over again and gave him a long and affectionate kiss.

Viktor kissed her in return and after they released each other from their loving embrace, he said, "As soon as I saw it, I thought of you. I hoped you would like it."

"Oh, I do, Vic. It's wonderful. We must find a special place on the wall."

Viktor looked at his watch. "We'd better do that tomorrow. If you're going to get changed you'd better start now or we're going to be late for our meal."

"Okay." Penny lay the painting on top of the discarded wrapping paper still on the table. "I'll have a quick shower first." She then disappeared from the room.

Viktor picked up the painting and inspected all its details once again. Yes, he thought, and placed it back where Penny had left it. That went down really well.

Later that evening, after Penny and Viktor had finished their main course, Penny ordered a dessert, but Viktor declined in favour of a latte coffee.

"This is a lovely birthday, Vic. I've had a great day."

"What? And at work as well?"

"Yes. Jonathan Northgate remembered too. He wished me a happy birthday after the business meeting this morning. He also told me to leave work early so I'd get home in time for this meal."

"He sounds okay," said Viktor, sipping the last of his wine. "I don't think Ian liked him very much."

"I know. There was a big issue when they were working for Sotheby's in New York. He never did tell me what it was about."

"That's a long time to still be holding a grudge."

"I know, but Jonathan has always been good to me."

"So, you're still enjoying work?"

"'Enjoying' is probably a bit too strong. It's interesting and challenging and I certainly feel a lot more confident than when I first stepped into Ian's role. Do you think I've changed since then?"

Viktor pondered on Penny's question. "The big difference

is your confidence. You've always had the ability and potential; Ian saw that. That's why he wanted you to take over when he left. But gradually, your self-belief has increased as your reliance on Ian has diminished. Obviously, Northgate has noticed that too."

"You've not really answered my question."

"Didn't I?" said Viktor, hoping he had. "Yes, I think you've changed. You're stronger now, more likely to argue and impose your opinion into our discussions. Previously you tended to just agree with me."

"Oh," said Penny, somewhat surprised. "Do you think I've become too arrogant?"

Viktor laughed. "No, no I don't. I like you even more when you have an opinion and fight your corner but, at the same time, you're still prepared to listen to my suggestions. I've learnt a lot from you since we've been married."

Penny smiled.

At that moment, Penny's dessert and Viktor's coffee arrived.

When Penny had finished her dessert, she looked across at Viktor and said, "I know it's my birthday, but we've really only talked about me this evening. You haven't told me too much about your own business life recently."

Viktor placed his empty coffee cup on its saucer and thought for a few seconds. "No, we've not, but generally, things are okay."

"Just okay," interrupted Penny.

"Yes. My work with Alexander is good, but very part time. So is the buying and selling I do for my small group of clients. It was far more exciting when I was part of Ian's partnership and, also, during the last 12 months with you and Ian at Sotheby's. Now, as I say, it's… well, it's okay."

"I've been so wrapped up with my own work… I didn't know."

Viktor shrugged his shoulders. "It's not a problem, just that the adventure part, which is what I really enjoy, has somehow disappeared. When I went to France with Ian a few months ago to look at the museum's 'Fête Gloanec' painting, it was just like the old days. I don't seem to be able to develop those types of adventures on my own. Ian does, and Andrei was able to, but not me."

"I think you're being a little hard on yourself. I'm sure things will get better when you're more experienced. With art, everyone is always learning something new… more or less every day. Besides, after what you told me about Andrei and his shady deals, I'm not sure I want you to be that kind of adventurous."

Viktor smiled. "Maybe. I did some research work for Ian the other day on his six pictures. I discovered that four have a possible involvement with the 'Commission for Looted Art in Europe'. Again, that got my 'juices flowing' – is that the correct English phrase?"

It was Penny's turn to laugh. "I think I know what you mean. I also think we could both do with a holiday – somewhere hot and sunny."

Viktor's eyes lit up. "What a great idea. We could go back to the Maldives."

"I think we should leave that until a special anniversary. Our honeymoon was so memorable there and I want to keep that memory as fresh as I can. No, I was thinking of somewhere else…maybe the Caribbean."

"That sounds good to me."

"We'll have to look at our diaries… and I'll speak to Jonathan."

Viktor pondered on Penny's last comment. He knew exactly what his own diary contained without even having to check it.

Chapter 28

It was two days after the wedding when Ian received another email from France. He and Emma had just started the second week of their two-week stay in Antigua.

Ian opened up the email on his mobile phone. It read:

Hello Ian,

Some good news this time. See attached: an email I received from Claude Dupont.

Keep in touch,
Your good friend,
Albert.

Ian opened up the attachment and read:

Hello Albert,

Good to hear from you again. I hope you and the family are keeping well.

I have checked our records and can confirm it was our museum that carried out the inspection of the 'Fête Gloanec' painting in 1935. Apparently, the Musée des Beaux-Arts d'Orléans were concerned because they had received a letter suggesting their painting was a copy, not the original. Naturally they were concerned and asked us for our help.

Our report is very brief, but we confirmed that the picture had all the hallmarks of the original painting. The authors of Gauguin's catalogue raisonné also stated they had no reason for doubting its authenticity and it would remain in their future publications.

As far as I know, no further investigations have been carried out on the painting since 1935.

I hope this information is useful.
Kind regards,
Claude.

"Well, well, well," said Ian to himself. "Now we're getting somewhere."

"Talking to yourself now, are you?" It was Emma, who had just walked into their hotel bedroom from the balcony. She'd decided it was getting too hot despite it only being 9am.

"I've received an email from Albert in France. His colleague, Claude, has given me some good news."

"What sort of news?"

"Here, read the email." Ian handed Emma his mobile phone.

She read the email. "But this doesn't say anything that you didn't know already."

"Oh yes it does! It raises a lot of questions. Look here." Ian pointed to the screen. "Who sent this letter? What did it say and why was it sent? Why was the Musée des Beaux-Arts d'Orléans so concerned about this particular piece of correspondence? They probably get crank letters all the time, but why did they take this particular letter so seriously? Had it come from someone who really knew a lot about Gauguin's work? Why were the authors of Gauguin's catalogue raisonné so quickly convinced that the museum's painting wasn't a copy? Remember, in those days there wasn't the same level of scientific equipment available as today. The judgements made in 1935 were very subjective – and often made to protect self-interests!"

Emma was quite stunned by Ian's outburst. "Wow, you really think their painting's a fake, don't you?"

Ian smiled. He was still a little pumped up. "I told you. Charles's painting is the real 'Fête Gloanec' – and I'm definitely going to damn well prove it!"

That same evening in the UK, Charles Owen arrived back at his home just before midnight. He was shattered and felt very hungry, but when he looked inside the refrigerator, he cursed. He'd forgotten to visit the 24-hour supermarket. Except for about half a pint of milk and some cheese that had a green furry coat, it was bare. He slammed the door closed in frustration and walked over to the food cupboard. He knew he still had a few tins of beans, soups and fruit. He removed a tin of tomato soup and poured the contents into a bowl. He then placed this into the microwave and switched on the power. In his bread bin he discovered the end crust of the loaf he'd purchased some days ago. The crust felt hard. Oh well, he thought, it will soften up in the hot soup.

Next, he poured himself a large glass of California shiraz red wine and took a sizeable gulp. He placed the glass on the nearby kitchen table. The ping of the microwave told him his soup was ready. He put the bread on a plate and placed it next to his wine. Finally, he removed the steaming bowl of hot soup and tentatively carried it over to a table, where he sat down.

Slowly stirring the soup with his spoon, he casually looked out through the large picture window in front of him. Most of the view was initially in darkness, but slowly his eyes adjusted to the lack of light and he could now see fully across the River Thames. On the far embankment, a few solitary street lights illuminated the small areas immediately under each light. In the distance there was a yellow and red glow seemingly floating just above the London skyline. On the river, a single cargo boat slowly drifted downstream, Its four lights reflecting on the sombre flowing river directly below his apartment. He ripped some pieces of the almost stale bread and dipped them into his soup. Five minutes later, the bowl was empty and the bread was gone. He sipped more wine, pulled over his laptop and turned it on. He stared at the screen waiting for it to fully power up.

Just five more weeks, he thought. Just five more weeks of this demoralising lifestyle. Then I'll be free. My grandfather's house will be sold, finally. He prayed this new buyer would be more reliable than the last. The valuable bits of the house contents will also have been auctioned. His paintings? I'll keep them. They'll be my pension – except the 'Fête Gloanec', which, Ian says, will be worth tens of millions! That, I'll definitely sell. I'll be wealthy and able to travel the world and… Suddenly, his laptop sprang into life. He accessed his emails, flicking through and deleting what he called the 'dross'. His eyes lit up when he saw Ian's message. He quickly opened it, eager to read the contents:

Hi Charles,

I've got some good news. We'll talk about the details when I'm back in the UK.

*A little job for you in the meantime. Can you look through your grandfather's old papers for **anything** to do with 'our' painting that is dated about 1935. I'm looking particularly for **any** correspondence with French museums and art galleries around that time.*

Very, very important!

Cheers for now,

Ian.

Chapter 29

It was two days after Charles had received Ian's email that he was searching through all his grandfather's old papers trying to find any correspondence dated around 1935. It was 7.30 on a Sunday morning. He'd ignored the one opportunity a week to have a lie in as Ian had said how important it was. Sorting through all his grandfather's old files was one of the jobs he'd planned to do once he'd finished working. He had temporarily stored the two cardboard boxes and the three plastic containers in his third bedroom. This room really was too small to be of any real use as a proper bedroom so Charles used it as a home office. However, since his grandfather's death, it had become a temporary storage and general dumping area for his grandfather's papers and the rest of the possessions that weren't going to be sold to Alexander's company. Also stored here were all the paintings he'd inherited.

To begin with, Charles hadn't really known where to start. The files containing the more valuable papers such as the deeds, bank details, insurance documents and copy provenance files, he'd properly organised and stored in his safe. However, the rest of the paperwork was now being looked at for the first time and it wasn't filed in date order… or indeed, any sort of order that he could understand.

After two hours, he'd only gone through one cardboard box so, after a break for coffee, he was now carrying the second box into the dining area where he placed it on the table. He initially removed all the files and papers and, after a brief scan, he placed each sheet and document into separate piles, sorted by topic and date order. Over the next hour he realised the task was taking far longer than he'd anticipated. At one o'clock, he decided to have another break and make himself a cheese and ham sandwich.

Whilst he ate his lunch, Charles pondered on what he had found so far. The only interesting find, he decided, was a small photograph album. The pictures meant nothing to him, but each photo had been carefully annotated underneath with the names of the people in the picture, where it had been taken and, more importantly, the date. The pictures were all black and white prints and the dates ranged from 1924 to 1951. He assumed these pictures were of his great-grandparents and maybe even great-great-grandparents. He hoped that the contents of the plastic containers would include similarly old papers and documents as well.

After lunch he completed the search and refilled the box in the order of the piles on the table. Finally, on a blank piece of A4 paper, he wrote a list of all the documents and files and placed this sheet on the top before folding the lid back down. He carried the box back to the small bedroom, returning with the first of the plastic containers and repeated the exercise again.

By four o'clock he was bored and had achieved very little, certainly not unearthing any documents relating to 1935 or the 1930s in general. He'd found two old life assurance policies dating back to 1929 and 1933 and decided to investigate these further to see whether there was a death benefit still to be paid.

He returned the plastic container back to the bedroom,

collected the second one and placed it on the table. Tired and somewhat frustrated he decided it was time for another mug of coffee.

Ten minutes later he opened the plastic container and decided, one way or another, this would be the last one for today. Again, he lifted files and papers out and gave each document a cursory glance before placing each sheet and document into separate piles, sorted by topic and date order.

He was nearly half way down the box when suddenly he came across an old dark brown file which had '*George Owen – fine art correspondence*' written on the front.

Oh wow, said Charles to himself. George? That was my great-grandfather!

Charles carefully opened the old folder and found a collection of carbon copy sheets of typed letters. George Owen's name was typed at the end of each letter. Also filed were a number of original letters, all addressed to George. Again, none of these papers were in date order. If George had employed a secretary, thought Charles, it was probably only for her looks and typing skills.

He read each sheet slowly, and with increased enthusiasm noted the date of each piece of correspondence. It gradually became clear to him that Great-grandfather George had not only been a keen buyer and seller of fine art, but had been very successful at it too. He'd obviously had a keen eye for a bargain.

Charles sorted each letter and sheet into date order, and where it was obvious the correspondence related to another letter, he attached them together. Finally, now sorted into a sensible order, he flicked back through to a carbon copy letter dated 5th May 1935. It was addressed to the Musée des Beaux-Arts d'Orléans in France and went into considerable detail about the painting titled 'Fête Gloanec'. Charles then read the attached reply from the museum. It was addressed personally to George, written in French, short in content, but very curt in manner.

Charles immediately left the dining room and walked over to the kitchen area where his laptop was lying on the breakfast table. He composed the following email to Ian:

Ian, hi.

Hope you are having a great time in Antigua. The weather here is the pits.

Great news! I've found the correspondence you were looking for. It was filed with my grandfather Peter's papers – an old file in my great-grandfather George's name! I'll photocopy and give you a copy when we next meet up. Champagne has now been put on ice!

Charles.

Charles read through the email again and then pressed the 'send' button. He looked back at the dining table. I suppose I'd better tidy up all this mess.

Ian didn't pick up Charles's email until the following day. After reading it, he gave a jubilant shout!

Emma heard him while sitting at the dressing table doing her make-up. "You made me jump, you idiot. What's the matter?"

"Sorry, Emma, but Charles has found the letters!"

"What letters?"

"The letters I told you about the other day. Written in 1935."

"Oh those. So what does that mean?"

"It means, my dear, that I think we are really getting somewhere. Charles says his grandfather's paperwork also contained some of his great-grandfather's papers too!"

"But this doesn't prove his painting is the real one, surely."

"No, not on its own. I need to understand what the

correspondence was all about. I won't be able to do that until I see all the papers."

Emma was puzzled. "Can't Charles just send you a copy attached to an email?"

Ian smiled. "Of course he can, but emails aren't secure so we're always careful with what and how much we actually write. I learnt that from Andrei."

"So, is it time for a celebration this evening? We've only got two days left of this holiday."

"We shouldn't celebrate the painting just yet. We've got a long way still to go. But, yes, I do think we should celebrate a lovely holiday. I've really enjoyed it. Haven't you?"

"It's been wonderful, Ian. A lovely wedding and a fabulous break from our usual routine. Where are you going to take me to next time?"

Ian was thinking of something else whilst Emma asked the question. Then he suddenly asked, "How do you fancy a few days in Paris?"

Chapter 30

Viktor had spent several hours on the internet looking at possible hotels and villas on a number of different Caribbean islands. Penny had suggested this part of the world for their next holiday, so he was determined not to let the idea just drift.

Gradually he reduced the possibilities down to a short list of three. A five-star hotel on the platinum west coast of Barbados, a luxurious villa in St. Lucia or a part-hotel, part-cruise package. He was not sure about the cruise, although the ship did visit a number of the smaller Caribbean islands. He wanted Penny to see his suggestions before considering booking anything.

Over dinner that evening, Viktor explained his findings and Penny immediately decided that the St. Lucia villa option was her preferred choice. She thought it would be quieter and more intimate and relaxing. Also, they wouldn't be constrained by hotel meal times and would have their own private swimming pool.

"That's great," responded Viktor. "What dates are we looking at?"

"I had a chat with Jonathan earlier today and told him I wanted to take a holiday. He was quite relaxed about dates, so let's see what holidays are available and we can take it from there. Two weeks isn't going to cause any problems."

"Okay, I'll see what I can sort out," replied Viktor, enthusiastically.

Forty-eight hours after he and Emma had returned home from Antigua, Ian was travelling on a train heading towards London. He'd made an appointment to meet up with Charles as he'd now worked out a few ideas about the next steps to take with regards to the 'Fête Gloanec' painting. However, which one he took would largely depend on what Charles's great-grandfather had said in his correspondence with the Musée des Beaux-Arts d'Orléans.

The train was on time and, as it was a sunny but raw chilly day, Ian decided to walk the short distance to their usual meeting place, the 'Hind's Head' public house. After just a few minutes, however, he regretted this decision, as this was most certainly not Antiguan weather.

As Ian entered the main bar, he immediately felt the benefit of the warm room. Spotting Charles ordering his drink, he walked over to join him.

"Hi, Ian," greeted Charles. He'd noticed Ian as he approached. "What would you like to drink?"

"I'll have a pint like you, please."

Charles ordered the second drink. "Did you have a good time in Antigua? A wedding, wasn't it?"

The barman handed Ian his drink and Charles paid.

"Cheers," said Ian, sipping his beer. "It was excellent, thanks. The weather was perfect. The wedding went really well. It's the first wedding I've ever attended on a Caribbean beach."

Charles briefly laughed and led Ian over to a table in the far corner, where they both sat down.

"Good call of yours to get me to look at my grandfather's papers," said Charles after he'd taken a sip of his beer. "I'd planned to sort through those papers when I'd finished working, but your email sounded urgent."

"Finished working?" asked Ian. What was all this about? he wondered.

"Yes. Didn't I tell you?"

"No. What happened?"

"Well, after we had our last chat, I started to think seriously about what I'd told you, and also my future. I knew I was wasting my life and, now that my grandfather's inheritance has largely been sorted, I've decided the extra money from work just isn't worth the mental and physical stress anymore. I don't want to be the richest man in the graveyard."

Ian smiled. His own thinking was in total accord with what Charles was saying.

"Anyway, I had a chat with my boss and, in summary, I will leave at the end of March."

"Okay. So, what are your plans? What are you going to do after that?"

"I'm not really sure. Largely depends on the result of my 'Fête Gloanec'. I want to have a long break and go travelling. I need a rest and a change of scenery. Might even look for a property in Portugal."

"That's a sudden change."

"Not really. I think I told you that 'burnout' is part and parcel of my occupation. If I stay on much longer I know I'm going to have serious problems. They may have to carry me out in a wooden box. My grandfather's inheritance has just given me the extra push I needed."

"Good luck… with whatever you eventually decide," said Ian, with meaning. "So, you'll have more time to concentrate on 'Fête Gloanec'?"

"Talking of which, here are the photocopies I promised." Charles passed a green cardboard folder to Ian. "This is all turning out to be quite a thriller. Maybe I should consider writing a book!"

Ian laughed and took the photocopies. He quickly read the letter from Great-grandfather George addressed to the museum, and then the museum's reply.

"This is really useful and interesting stuff." Ian picked up his glass of beer and had a long drink. "I think we're definitely getting somewhere. There's also some more information you need to be aware of."

Ian told Charles of the extra details he'd obtained following the email correspondence with Albert and Claude in France.

"That all ties in nicely with George's correspondence," said Charles. "No wonder you were eager for me to search through my grandfather's old papers."

"Yes. You mentioned at 'Dexter's End' that you had several boxes of papers to sort through, so I just hoped something might be in them. A shot in the dark really."

"Inspired! So, what's our next step?" asked Charles eagerly.

"I've promised Emma a trip to Paris."

Charles smiled and looked quizzically at Ian.

Ian continued. "Needless to say, I've got more plans than just sightseeing." He then explained his strategy.

"Ian! That's just brilliant."

Chapter 31

Ian was sitting in his office, pondering on the words he was going to use in his email to his colleague, Albert, in Paris. Eventually he began to type:

Hello Albert,

Many thanks for your email and please thank Claude Dupont for his message as well. The information he provided has been very useful.

Emma and I plan to visit Paris very soon and I was wondering if it was possible to meet up with you and Claude? There are some questions I would like to ask Claude and prefer to do this face to face.

Emma and I can fit our visit around yours and Claude's availability.

Maybe you and Camille would also like to join Emma and I for dinner one evening?

Best wishes,

Ian.

The Musée du Autry has a somewhat chequered history. Established on the Left Bank of the Seine in 1876, its intention was to be one of the finest art galleries, not only in Paris, but in the whole of France. It started well and visitors flocked to see its collection of 'great master' paintings. However, during the First World War the main building suffered considerable damage and much of the museum's historic art collection was 'temporarily' lent to other Parisian museums whilst the structure of the Musée du Autry's buildings was rebuilt. The paintings needed to be housed in high security establishments, to protect them against obvious potential damage caused by humidity and minimise general deterioration.

Immediately after the war, money was tight and it wasn't until the late 1920s that the museum was able to fully reopen its doors to the public. Unfortunately, by this time, the Musée du Autry had a poor management team and they failed to recover all of the museum's historic art collection. Both the Parisian public and foreign visitors gradually forgot all about the Musée du Autry and flocked instead to the Louvre and the Musée D'Orsay. It therefore struggled financially and then suffered further damage during the Second World War. Again it had to close for quite some time. Eventually a group of keen private investors and sponsors got together and decided to rebuild the museum and return it to its glory days. The buildings were sympathetically restored and, following persistent negotiations and threats of legal action, all their 'lost' art collection was finally retrieved and, once again, displayed in its rightful place.

Today, 'the Autry' has finally re-established itself as one of the leading exhibition spaces in Paris. The numerous visitors can now enjoy viewing masterpieces by Gauguin, Rubens, Van Dyck, Matisse, Botticelli, Raphaël, Titian, Arcimboldo and Modigliani.

For the last 15 years, the curator of the Musée du Autry has been Claude Dupont. Well respected in the European art world, Claude has managed the museum with enthusiasm and great business acumen. Exhibition and visitor numbers have tripled since the start of his stewardship.

After emailing Albert his answers to the queries about the 'Fête Gloanec', Claude decided to do some investigations of his own. After all, he had personal knowledge of the painting, having been employed for two years by the Musée des Beaux-Arts d'Orléans just after he'd left university. However, he couldn't remember anybody mentioning any controversy and he also knew the painting had been listed in the Paul Gauguin catalogue raisonné for as long as he could remember. As a result, he was wondering what had happened that was casting a shadow of doubt.

It was nearly two weeks later when Claude received a further email from Albert. This time Albert's email was suggesting a meeting with an Englishman called Ian Caxton to discuss the 'Fête Gloanec' painting. Albert had included a short resume of Ian's career and abilities and recommended they all meet up when Ian arrived in Paris.

After reading Albert's email, Claude smiled. His own recent investigations had now identified a potential flaw in the painting's provenance. Did this Monsieur Caxton have similar information? He immediately thought such a meeting could be very interesting, especially as he now knew Monsieur Caxton was a former senior employee of Sotheby's. He gave Albert some dates and signed off by saying 'he was looking forward to hearing what Monsieur Caxton had to say.'

After receiving Claude's email, Albert too was intrigued. He knew Ian would not be spending so much time on this picture unless he really felt there was a lot to be gained by doing so. He therefore sent his own email to Ian with the list of dates Claude had suggested. He also told Ian that he and Camille would love to meet him and Emma and enjoy their company over dinner.

"Emma," called Ian from his home office.

Emma had just come into the house from the garden. She washed her hands in the utility room and then joined Ian in the office. "You called, my lord," she said jokingly, still drying her hands on a towel.

Ian smiled and looked up from his computer. "How does the 3rd to the 8th of next month sound for our trip to Paris?"

"It sounds fine to me. Have you checked our calendar?"

"My diary's okay but I've not checked the calendar."

Emma walked into the kitchen and looked at the dates Ian had mentioned. "We've got a parent's evening at Robert's school on the 1st and we're all due at my parents on the 9th so, yes, those dates are fine. Will you book the hotel?" she said, coming back into the office.

"Yes. I think we should travel by Eurostar. It should be a lot quicker than flying."

"It's been some time since we've travelled to Paris by train. It should be fun."

"By the way, I've invited a French colleague, Albert, and his wife Camille to join us for dinner. You've not met either of them."

Emma was used to Ian springing these 'little surprises'. "That's booked already, is it?"

"No, no," replied Ian. "Albert and I used to meet up for lunch or dinner when either he was in London or I was in Paris. I just thought it would be nice to do it again, this time with our two wives."

"Okay," responded Emma. She was just about to walk away when Ian spoke again.

"I've also arranged to meet Monsieur Claude Dupont. He was the man who sent that email I showed you when we were in Antigua. He's an expert on Paul Gauguin's work. I think he'll be able to help with my investigations into Charles's painting."

149

"Are we actually going to have some sightseeing time together?"

"Of course we will. I thought you might like a morning free to do some shopping on your own."

"Mmm. Well, you can pay for any of the clothes I get."

"Remember you'll be limited to the suitcase you take out to France from home."

Emma walked away, but then, from the hallway, shouted, "I might just have to buy an extra suitcase as well then."

Chapter 32

At the 'Shell Gallery' in Antigua, Wesley, Oscar and May were sitting around the small table in Wesley's office. The air conditioning was only working sporadically as Wesley was still waiting for the engineer to arrive. In the mean-time, he had purchased two small electric fans and they were moving the warm air about but not really reducing the temperature.

"I'm sorry I can't open the windows," apologised Wesley. "That just encourages the hot air to come in."

"It's okay," said May. "We're used to the hot and humid summers in Hong Kong."

"If it gets too hot, we'll go over the road to the bar. Their aircon system works fine."

Oscar smiled. He thought back to the hours he had spent with Wesley, but more often with Gladstone, drinking at that bar.

May nodded and suggested they start the meeting and then see how it was in about half an hour's time.

"Okay, lady," said Wesley, sitting back in his chair, which immediately made its usual protesting creak. "Let's hear what you've got to say."

Oscar thought Wesley's weight had not changed during all the time he had known him and he couldn't understand how the chair still managed to support the whole of Wesley's large frame.

May spent the next 20 minutes outlining her ideas as to how she would use her contacts in Hong Kong, Beijing and, to a lesser extent, Singapore, to expand the market for Wesley's colourful West Indian paintings. She told him that, through Oscar's earlier dealings, she'd been able to develop a small amount of interest. However, she was convinced that the potential market was now much bigger and she wanted to try to push the pictures once again. She listed the galleries that had displayed these types of pictures in the past and told him that these same galleries had again confirmed their interest.

Wesley was impressed with May's ideas and liked her drive and ambition. The terms of their arrangement were discussed and agreed before, finally, Wesley drew the meeting to a close by saying, "Well, you two, we have a deal. I'm frying in this office, so let's call it a day and I'll buy you both cold beers across the road."

It was just after 3.30pm when Ian and Emma's Eurostar train arrived at the Gare du Nord railway station in Paris. They had enjoyed their journey in first class and were amazed at the speed the train had achieved whilst crossing the French countryside.

Stepping down from their carriage and onto the platform, Emma noticed it was an unusually hot and sultry early spring day. She began to wonder if she'd packed the right clothes.

As they walked along the platform pulling their suitcases, Ian looked around him. He guessed it was probably about five years since he'd last been here.

They passed through the ticket barrier and headed towards the overhead sign saying 'Taxis'. A short queue of people was quickly being reduced by the nose-to-tail flow of taxis. Five minutes later Ian and Emma sat down on the rear passenger seats of a red Peugeot car. Once their cases were loaded into the car's boot, Ian announced to the driver, "Ritz Paris hôtel, s'il vous plaît."

Ian had selected this hotel for its location and reputation. He hadn't stayed here before – Sotheby's didn't allow expenses to run higher than four-star hotels – but he wanted to treat Emma to something a little more special this time. He'd also arranged for them to occupy an executive suite.

The taxi joined the heavy flow of Parisian traffic and initially moved no faster than a walking pace. Ian smiled to himself and thought of Andrei. He and Emma were heading for the sort of hotel he had regularly frequented. Andrei would have approved.

The taxi pulled up outside the front of the hotel but, before he and Emma had a chance to move, Emma's door was whisked open by a smart blue-uniformed doorman who welcomed them to the Ritz Paris hotel. Ian paid the taxi fare and followed Emma and the doorman towards the reception desk. Their suitcases were collected by a porter who was walking directly behind them.

Ten minutes later they were in their room. Emma pulled back the curtains to take in the view.

"This is really nice, Ian, and a lovely view… and look, there's a stunning garden below," said Emma excitedly.

Ian wandered over, slipped his arms around Emma's waist and shared the view over her shoulder. He stared through the large picture window. "Pretty special isn't it? You deserve a bit of pampering… occasionally."

"Only occasionally," retorted Emma, with a big smile on her face.

Ian ignored the taunt. "This is a great central location. We're very close to the Seine, the Louvre and the Musée

D'Orsay. I think we ought to go to the D'Orsay tomorrow. It's my favourite museum in Paris. The Louvre is good but far too large to do it justice in only one day."

"When are we meeting your friend and his wife for dinner?"

"I've arranged it for tomorrow evening. The restaurant Albert recommended is only a five-minute walk from here."

Emma pulled away from Ian's embrace. "Okay. I think we'd better unpack. I also want to have a shower and change my clothes."

The following evening, Ian and Emma walked the short distance to the restaurant. Albert and Camille had already arrived and were waiting for them just inside the entrance doorway. After introductions and the familiar male 'French' embrace between Ian and Albert, they were escorted to their table.

The ladies chatted using a mixture of French and English. Emma guessed she and Camille were probably about the same age and they were soon speaking about each other's lives and children. Meanwhile, Albert, who was fluent in English, discussed the wine menu with Ian. Once the drinks had been decided on and ordered, Albert asked what Emma and Ian had been doing so far in Paris. Emma explained that they had arrived late yesterday afternoon and spent most of today at the Musée D'Orsay.

"I hope you liked my museum, Emma," said Albert.

Emma looked at him a little surprised and then quizzically at Ian.

"Err, sorry, Emma," said Ian, quickly coming to Emma's rescue. "I may not have mentioned that Albert is the deputy curator at the Musée D'Orsay."

Albert smiled, but Emma gave Ian one of her telling looks.

"Yes, Albert," replied Emma, returning her attention back to their guest, "Ian told me it was his favourite Parisian museum and it certainly lived up to all my expectations."

"Excellent!" announced Albert. "As you English say, 'another satisfied customer'!"

They all laughed but Emma had not forgotten the embarrassment Ian had caused her.

Their drinks and menus arrived together and each now considered the meal options. Emma queried two items on the menu and Camille explained. Finally, they had all selected their food and the waiter took their order.

Whilst Emma and Camille recommenced their discussions, Albert leaned a little closer to Ian and asked, "Tell me, Ian, what is this story about the 'Fête Gloanec' painting?"

Ian told him about Charles's inheritance, his own visit to 'Dexter's End' and then he summarised his earlier investigations.

"I can see now why you became excited about Claude's email."

"I'm hoping when we meet with Claude tomorrow, he'll be able to help with my additional queries. He may also have a few suggestions of his own."

"When I spoke to him yesterday, to confirm our arrangements, he told me he had some more interesting news for you."

Chapter 33

Next morning after breakfast, Emma and Ian split up for the day. Camille had volunteered to meet Emma in the hotel's reception area at 10.30am and take her on a tour of the best shops. Ian decided to have a walk along the banks of the Seine until it was time to meet with Albert and Claude at 11am.

Ian strolled along the Right Bank and enjoyed the lovely warm sunshine. He stopped briefly as two boats passed by. There were four rowers in each boat and behind them, in a small motor launch, a man was bellowing out instructions for the rowers. After another ten minutes, he checked his watch and decided it was time to head towards the Musée du Autry. At the next bridge, he crossed over the River Seine and continued to follow the route from his tourist map. At five minutes before eleven o'clock he walked through the large glass doors and into a modern, air-conditioned reception area. Above the reception desk was a large sign printed in bold black letters, '**Musée du Autry**'.

Ian and Albert spotted each other and Ian headed towards his colleague.

"Good morning, Ian," said Albert and they both shook hands.

"Bonjour, Albert. That was a lovely dinner last evening. A great suggestion."

"I hoped you and Emma would enjoy it. Camille and I often eat there when we're both in town."

"I gather Camille has volunteered to show Emma around some of the Parisian shops today. Brave lady."

"You think so?" queried Albert.

Ian realised that he had probably confused Albert. "Not literally." Ian smiled. "It's another English phrase. In this case I mean that Emma will probably want to go into every shop she sees."

Albert laughed. "I understand now. The ladies, they are going to be busy!"

"That's right."

Albert looked at his watch. "Claude should be joining us very shortly." He looked around. "Ah! Here he comes."

Ian saw a slim, middle-aged man, about Ian's build, walking towards them.

"Mr. Caxton, I presume." He held out his hand and Ian grasped it.

"Ian, this is my good friend, Claude Dupont," said Albert. "We were at university together, so we've known each other for many, many years."

"I'm very pleased to meet you, Monsieur Dupont… and thank you for your email. It proved to be very useful."

"Let's use first names, Ian. It makes life much easier and less formal," said Claude. He patted Albert on the shoulder. "Come. Let's go to my office. Fresh coffee should be waiting for us."

The three men walked towards a dark green door to the left of the reception desk. Claude led the way. He opened the door via a coded security pad and they all walked through. Within four steps they'd arrived at a small private elevator. Claude pressed the request button. The double doors immediately opened and the three men stepped in. Ian smiled when he saw the sign above the floor numbers that said 'maximum 4 persons only'. It was a tight squeeze with just the three of them.

Claude pressed floor number 7, which appeared to be the top floor. The doors closed and the elevator began to ascend. When the doors opened again, Ian looked into a spacious personal office. Claude led the group over to a meeting table where, placed in the middle, was a silver tray containing a cafetiere of coffee, three china cups and saucers, milk, sugar and a plate of biscuits. "Gentlemen," invited Claude with a wave of his hand. "Please sit down and help yourselves to the refreshments."

Claude opened the meeting. "Now, Ian, I gather you are interested in the 'Fête Gloanec' painting at the Musée des Beaux-Arts d'Orléans. Can I ask why you're so interested?"

Ian told Claude a similar story to the one he'd told Albert the previous evening.

"That's all very interesting, Ian, but I used to work at the Musée des Beaux-Arts d'Orléans. It was my first appointment after leaving university. There was never any mention that this painting could be a copy... or a fake. Indeed, the Gauguin catalogue raisonné people have listed it in all of their publications."

"But, as I mentioned earlier, George Owen, the great-grandfather of the current owner, wrote to the museum in 1935. He suggested then that the museum's painting was a copy. He said he owned the original and gave them a list of reasons why he was so adamant. The museum was alarmed enough to have the painting examined."

"And they found no evidence that supported Mr. Owen's claim," interrupted Claude.

Ian was beginning to wonder if this was going to be a wasted journey.

"With respect, Claude, the French are famous for 'protecting their own'. 'Closing ranks' as we say in England.

The museum and the catalogue raisonné had no incentive to 'believe' their painting was a copy. Today's level of scientific technology wasn't available. All judgements were subjective and it was certainly much easier just to rubbish Mr. Owen's claim. They knew it was just one man's opinion… an Englishman's opinion, of course." Ian was getting angry.

Claude laughed and Ian looked at Albert. Albert too was smiling. What the hell's going on? he thought. He was ready to get up and leave.

"Stop teasing him," said Albert to Claude.

"Ian," said Claude, after he had stopped laughing. "I just wanted to find out how strongly you believed in your case. I've done some investigations myself. I'm with your opinion."

"What?" exclaimed Ian. He was fed up with being messed about.

"Let me explain," replied Claude. "I've found out that, in 1915, there was an art gallery in Paris that was eventually proven to be a major copier and faker of paintings, particularly when it came to the French impressionists' work. This gallery, translated into English, was called the 'Normandy Gallery'. Before 1915, it was known to be a high-class gallery and sold many original works by the masters of the day. However, and we won't go into names, a very high-ranked politician in the French government purchased three paintings from the gallery. Two were allegedly painted by Gauguin and one by Monet. The brother-in-law of the same politician was a well-respected art historian and valuer. He looked at his brother's new purchases and declared the two Gauguins were forgeries! As a result, the politician and his brother-in-law informed a senior member of the Parisian police force. The chief inspector decided to investigate. He wanted to know how many other customers had been duped by the 'Normandy Gallery'. The answer, I'm afraid, was quite a few.

The case came to court late in 1915 and the three partners and two employees were sentenced to long terms of imprisonment. The 'Normandy Gallery' was also closed down."

"Okay," said Ian, eagerly. "So where does our particular painting come in?"

Claude continued, "During the police investigations they found several invoice books. In these books were listed pages of the original paintings that the gallery had bought and sold... plus a list of their fakes. I've seen one of these invoice books and..." Claude smiled and leaned forward a little towards Ian. "I found your 'Fête Gloanec'! The gallery's invoice book listed the original plus one copy."

"Oh, wow!" said Ian out loud. "Did this invoice show to whom the two paintings were sold?"

"Yes. Name, address, date and price paid by the customer."

Ian's eyes suddenly lit up. "So, can we check them against the provenances?"

"I already have... and the provenances all tie up. As we know, one of the paintings was bought by an English collector and one stayed in France."

Ian wondered how on earth Claude had obtained a copy of Charles's provenances, but decided to leave that for the moment.

"Now the bad news." It was Albert who had spoken this time.

Ian immediately looked at Albert, but it was Claude who spoke next. "We don't know from the paperwork which is the real painting and which is the copy."

But I do, thought Ian. However, I still have to prove it! He thought for a few more seconds and then replied, "Well, we need to get both paintings forensically and independently examined. However, I can't see the Musée des Beaux-Arts d'Orléans agreeing to that. As I said before, they have no incentive to do so."

Both Claude and Albert looked at each other and smiled again. It was Claude who was next to speak. "I think I know a way, Ian. Just leave it with me."

Chapter 34

When Ian returned to the Ritz hotel, he told Emma all the details of his meeting with Claude and Albert. He said he was really excited and eager to hear more from Claude.

"Are you going to tell Charles your news?" asked Emma.

"No, not yet. Not until I've heard more from Claude. The French may still insist their version is the original."

The next morning at 10.00am, Claude made a telephone call to the Musée des Beaux-Arts d'Orléans. He asked to be put through to the assistant curator, Anton Renaud.

"Claude! How nice to hear from you. How's your lovely Amélie?"

"She's very well, thank you for asking… and Charlotte?"

"Yes, yes. She still works too hard, but she won't listen to me. So, Claude, what can I do for you?"

"It's a little bit delicate to discuss on the telephone, Anton. Are you coming to the meeting in Paris next week?"

"Of course. It's at the Louvre this time. I shall definitely be there."

"Can we have dinner the night before? My treat. Just the two of us?"

"This sounds very 'cloak and dagger' Claude. Are you sure you don't want to say anything to me now?"

"Let's just say it's about one of your paintings. I really don't think you'd want me to say any more on the phone."

"Okay. I'll have to wait until our dinner then." Anton was now curious but also a little worried. Claude wasn't usually so serious.

As agreed, Claude and Anton met for dinner. After exchanging the usual greetings and ordering their meal, Anton couldn't wait any longer.

"Claude, you were very cagey during our telephone conversation last week. What is it you want to tell me?"

Claude took a sip of his red Burgundy wine and then recounted the meeting he'd had with Ian Caxton. He said Monsieur Caxton was investigating the 'Fête Gloanec' painting and had new information which threw some doubt on the authenticity of the picture residing at the Musée des Beaux-Arts d'Orléans. He also told Anton about Ian's background, his qualifications and his being previously employed with Sotheby's.

"But our painting has been fully authenticated," pleaded Anton. "None of our collection are fakes."

Claude then summarised the latest findings and the question raised from the invoice books of the 'Normandy Gallery' in 1915. He also emphasised that there was no record identifying which painting was the original and which was the copy.

"And you think our picture is the copy?" asked Anton, raising his voice in anguish.

"No, I'm not saying that, Anton. I don't know which is the original."

"But our painting has been in the catalogue raisonné for many years."

"Do you know when the last forensic investigation was carried out on this picture?"

163

"Well, no." Anton was becoming more and more concerned. "Not specifically with this painting, no. I would need to check our records. We tend to have research completed when there's a new addition to our collection... or if a client requests and is prepared to pay for it. We have no other reason to carry out such investigations, especially on paintings we've had for, what, sometimes over 100 years."

"Mr. Caxton tells me their painting has been authenticated by the Courtauld Institute in London."

Anton immediately raised his eyebrows. "I see. So, you think we should carry out a similar exercise on our painting?"

"It would need to be done independently of your museum."

"But we know what we are doing."

"If you don't agree to an independent scientific investigation, Mr. Caxton says he will take his case to the highest authority to force you. Think of the publicity."

"This is blackmail!"

Claude smiled. "Anton, you know full well this is **not** blackmail. All Mr. Caxton is requesting is an independent forensic evaluation of your picture. If yours is the original painting, as you are convinced it is, what have you got to worry about?"

Anton pondered on this point. He had a few extra seconds thinking time because their meals had arrived. Once the two waiters departed he said, "I'll need to speak to my colleagues."

"Of course you will. But I suggest you do it as soon as possible. Come on, eat up. Your duck looks wonderful."

Anton looked down at his food, but suddenly he'd lost his appetite.

Chapter 35

"Charles?" asked Ian when he heard the phone answered at the other end of the line.

"Hello," responded Charles. He sounded quite ill.

"Charles, it's Ian Caxton. Are you okay?"

"I feel horrible physically, but wonderful mentally… I think."

"What are you talking about?" Ian was worried. He'd never heard Charles speak like this before.

"Hangover. The guys took me on a pub crawl last night. Yesterday was my last day at work!"

"Oh, I see. You had me worried."

"You woke me up. What time is it?"

Ian looked at his watch. "11.30."

"Oh… okay. I'd better get up and have a shower."

"Yes, you had… and some food."

"You rang me."

Oh yes, thought Ian. He'd been put off by Charles's hangover response. "Things are moving on quickly now with your painting. I'm going back to Paris tomorrow. Do you want to come with me?"

"What time… and what for?"

"I'm catching the 10.20 Eurostar. Meeting Monsieur Claude Dupont. It's about the 'Fête Gloanec' painting."

"Okay. I'll be there," replied Charles. Suddenly the line went dead.

Ian smiled and switched off his own phone.

"What was that all about?" asked Emma. She was sitting at her own desk, opposite Ian.

Ian explained about Charles's hangover and it being his last day at work.

"Oh, I see. Your trip to Paris then, it's just for one day."

"Yes. I've only got the meeting with Claude. He sent an email telling me he's got some good news. That's why I thought I'd invite Charles."

"Well, good luck. I'm thinking of going back to Brighton, for the day, tomorrow. I want to investigate 'The Lanes' area more thoroughly. I didn't really have time to visit the antiques and art shops when I went there with Jane last time."

"In that case, good luck to you too."

After his brief and strange conversation with Charles earlier that morning, Ian telephoned him again in the evening. Charles said he was feeling much better and was looking forward to the trip to France. They agreed to meet at London's St. Pancras International station at 9.30 by the famous bronze statue of the late Sir John Betjeman, the former Poet Laureate.

At 9.25, Ian was standing next to the large statue waiting for his colleague. He was reading a sign that informed him the statue was erected as a reminder to travellers that Betjeman was one of a number of famous people who had battled to save the iconic station from demolition back in the 1960s.

Ian suddenly felt a tap on his shoulder. It was Charles.

"Hello," said Ian, "I hope you're fit enough to travel today."

Charles smiled. "I feel so much better and more refreshed today."

"You do look and sound much more alive."

"It makes such a big difference having the weight of work released from my shoulders. I'm raring to go!"

"Okay. Let's get on the train and I'll bring you up to date. This could be a very, very momentous day!"

On the train Ian explained what had happened since he'd last updated Charles on his investigations. However, he decided not to mention Claude's information about the 'Normandy Gallery'. He wanted to keep that story for later.

Charles listened with eager anticipation.

"Remember," continued Ian, "the main purpose of this meeting with Claude is to 'listen'. Certainly, we can ask him questions. However, today is not the day for making snap decisions."

Charles agreed and told Ian that he was quite happy for him to do all the talking as his own knowledge of French was limited.

Ian smiled and then revealed that Claude's English was perfect and it would be the language used today.

At ten minutes to three, Ian and Charles's taxi pulled up across the road from the Musée du Autry. Ian paid the fare and the two men crossed the road and entered the huge building. Charles immediately noticed the drop in temperature due to the air conditioning. They walked across to the reception desk where Ian informed the smiling receptionist they had an appointment with Monsieur Claude Dupont.

Five minutes later, Claude appeared through the green door next to the reception desk and joined them.

"Bonjour, Claude," said Ian and he and Claude shook hands. "Thank you for meeting me today. Please meet my colleague, Charles Owen. He's the owner of our 'Fête Gloanec'."

"Welcome, Charles." Claude and Charles shook hands. "Did you have a good journey?"

"Yes, it was really smooth and the train arrived five minutes early."

Claude led them in the direction of the green door.

Claude entered his code into the security pad and pulled the door open. The elevator doors were open and they stepped inside. Claude pressed the button for floor 7, the doors closed and the elevator ascended. Charles looked at Ian and made an expression that indicated he was impressed. After just a few seconds the elevator stopped and the doors opened. Charles looked across at the expensively appointed office.

The three men walked over to the table and sat down. Again, there was the coffee tray and Claude said for them to help themselves.

"Right, gentlemen, down to business. I have spoken to both the curator and his assistant at the Musée des Beaux-Arts d'Orléans and they have agreed to the independent forensic examination of their version of 'Fête Gloanec'."

"Well, that's brilliant, Claude," said Ian, with a big beaming smile. "You must have pulled a few strings." He looked at Charles. He was also smiling.

Claude continued, "However, they insist that you pay all the costs associated with the examination."

Ian looked at Charles again, but Charles made no objection. He just shrugged his shoulders. Ian turned back to Claude and asked, "Okay, is that their only condition?"

"No. They also insist on you taking out insurance to the value of 40 million euros for the period the painting is away from their premises."

Again, Charles just shrugged his shoulders.

"We want the painting to be examined by the Courtauld Institute in London," replied Ian. "Charles's painting has already been examined there."

"They anticipated that you would request Courtauld's and they have already agreed as long as you agree to pay the costs I've already mentioned."

"That's good," replied Ian. He was sure that Charles would be okay with this. "But, is there any chance they'll back out at any stage… before it's examined, I mean?"

"One can never say never, Ian, but I would recommend you demonstrate good faith and agree to their conditions as soon as possible."

"What if their painting is not authenticated? Will they want another body to examine it… a second, or third opinion, so to speak?"

"No, they say their painting is the original picture and they have every confidence that a competent examiner, like Courtauld's, will concur with their view."

Ian looked at Charles. "Do you have any questions, Charles?"

Charles leaned forward and faced Claude. He spoke for the first time. "Surely the museum already has its own insurance arrangements. I don't see why they want me to pay again."

"Normally museum's insurance policies cover their paintings only whilst they are on their own premises. When any picture is lent out, for an exhibition say, the exhibitor is usually responsible for insuring it. The same principle applies here."

Charles looked at Ian and Ian nodded his agreement.

Ian then waited to see whether Charles was going to ask any more questions. When Charles said nothing more, he looked back at Claude. "Well, thank you, Claude, for this information and, also, the time you've spent on our behalf. It's very much appreciated. We need to establish the costs you mentioned and get back to you very quickly with our decision."

Chapter 36

On the Eurostar train back to England, Ian and Charles discussed the meeting they'd just had with Claude.

"So, Charles, what are you thinking?"

"Claude's a nice guy and appears to be on our side, but I'm not sure why. What's in it for him?"

"I think, from what my colleague Albert told me, Claude left the Musée des Beaux-Arts d'Orléans under a bit of a cloud. I don't know the details, but maybe he'd like to get his revenge."

"This all sounds like an expensive exercise. The museum people appear to be very confident about their painting."

"I hope you're not getting cold feet at this late stage, Charles," said Ian. He was concerned about what Charles might say next.

"No, no," replied Charles, now trying to be reassuring. "We've come this far, I just hope we can get over this last hurdle. Are you still convinced my picture is the original painting?"

"Yes, I am... and the Courtauld Institute report says so too."

"But, could they be wrong?"

"That's extremely unlikely. They definitely know what they are doing."

"Any idea as to how much this is all going to cost me?"

"I've tried to work out some 'ballpark' figures in my head. Certainly, somewhere between one and two million pounds."

"That's a lot of money if my painting turns out to be the copy."

"That's the gamble. If your painting is proved to be the original, it will be worth somewhere between 25 and 30 million pounds."

"Okay. So, what do we do next?"

"The next step is to establish accurate costings. I can speak to Courtauld's and a specialist transport company…"

"I know a Lloyd's insurance broker," interrupted Charles. "He lives in the apartment next to me. Do you want me to ask him to get a quotation? He might be able to do me a good deal."

"Yes, do that. We need to work quickly. We don't want to give the museum any opportunity, or excuse, to back down. We're almost there."

The train was now speeding across the French countryside and both Ian and Charles stared out of the window. Suddenly Charles looked at Ian and asked, "Won't the French museum carry out their own forensic investigations in the meantime?"

Ian smiled and nodded his head. "Almost certainly, so they'll know the answer before Courtauld's do."

Two days later, Ian and Charles were talking on the telephone. Charles told Ian the quotation he'd received for the insurance policy and Ian added this figure to the quotations he'd already obtained from Courtauld's and the transport company.

"We are looking at a total bill of 1.43 million pounds, plus any packing costs by the museum. In the grand scheme of things that should be minimal," said Ian. "What's the period for the insurance cover?"

"Their quotation is based on the picture being away from the museum for 30 days. That's their minimum period. Is that enough, or should it be for longer?"

"It should be okay. Simon Lyle at Courtauld's says he'll need the painting for a maximum of five working days. So, Charles, the big question still remains. Should I inform Claude that we want to go ahead?"

"1.43 million pounds you say… plus packing… it's still a lot of money."

"Charles, I'm so confident your painting is the original that I'm prepared to go halves on the costs with you."

"You're that sure? Okay, give Claude the good news!"

After they had finished their telephone call, Ian drafted the following email:

Hello Claude,

*Thank you for meeting with Charles and myself to discuss the **Musée des Beaux-Arts d'Orléans'** (the museum) version of the painting '**Fête Gloanec**'.*

Charles Owen has agreed to the terms and conditions specified by the museum. Do you know if the museum is going to make an additional charge for their packing of the painting?

We have obtained costings for the following:

1. *'All Risks' insurance for a sum insured of 40 million Euros. This will be placed with a Lloyd's of London underwriter. A copy of the policy wording can be made available if requested.*
2. *Transportation costs by Brooklands, a well-respected international transport company. They specialise in*

transporting high-value paintings and have an excellent safety record.

3. *A comprehensive examination report by the Courtauld Institute of Art. A copy of this document will be sent to the museum.*

Can you please confirm when the painting will be made available for collection?

Many thanks,

Ian.

Ian checked his email draft for any errors. When he was finally satisfied, he added Charles's email address as a 'cc recipient'. The cursor was now hovering over the 'send' button. Ian took a deep breath and pressed the key.

Chapter 37

In Antigua, May and Oscar were eating breakfast. They'd just returned from their regular swim in the Caribbean Sea and now Oscar was pondering on the day ahead.

"Oscar, I've been thinking about this villa," said May. This comment quickly grabbed Oscar's attention. "It's in the perfect location, but now that my personal possessions have arrived from Singapore, they're cluttering up two of the bedrooms. I think we should consider more wardrobe space or even building an extension?"

"What sort of an extension?" asked Oscar, with some concern and trepidation. He thought his villa was ideal for just the two of them.

"At the moment, we only have one usable bedroom. The other two have my things in, and one, the front bedroom, is also used partly as our office. It's all a bit cramped and we don't have any space for guests."

Oscar thought about guests. "What guests? The only guest I've had staying overnight is you... other than your brother and Ian, and that was just for the wedding."

"Well, we may want to invite Ian and Emma over to stay, or my brother and his family, or friends from Hong Kong. Then there's new friends and relationships we want to develop here in Antigua. We'll need to be able to offer our guests nice accommodation so that they'll be able to stay overnight."

Oscar realised May was being serious. "Okay. What are you suggesting?"

"The villa has plenty of land. We could extend outwards into where the carport area is at the moment. Your car can then be parked on the driveway. It's a long enough driveway and could easily take three or four vehicles."

"What do you suggest should be erected instead of the carport?"

"We can have a proper office and a larger ensuite bedroom for our guests."

"Or, we could have a smaller extension instead, and convert the front bedroom into a double office for us," said Oscar. He was trying to be practical… and reduce the cost.

"Yes, that's a thought, but we still need to have more storage for all my clothes."

Oscar smiled. Yes, he'd noticed all May's clothes! "Alright, have a more detailed think about what you want and where you want it. Then we can have a chat and get a quotation from a builder."

May stood up from the breakfast table, kissed Oscar and said, "Ella says that the Charlie Daniels building company has a good reputation. I'll telephone them after breakfast!"

Viktor and Penny were enjoying their quiet and intimate holiday in St. Lucia. Their villa had three bedrooms and, because it was a late booking, Viktor had managed to negotiate a good price for just the two of them. Smaller villas had also been available but they didn't come with such a large swimming pool. Despite the beach and the Caribbean Sea being only a short stroll away, most of their time was spent around the villa's pool. They only left the property for evening walks along the beach, the occasional restaurant meal and for trips to the local supermarket. All in all, it appeared to be a lovely and relaxing time. However, appearances can always be deceptive. It was not a completely relaxing time for Viktor.

Five days into their two-week stay, Penny had been enjoying the opportunity to sunbathe, read books and swim in the pool. Viktor, however, whilst also enjoying some of these activities, was spending more of his time just thinking. He was considering the future, not only for him and Penny, but also his business ambitions. Financially he and Penny were secure and the need to earn money was not his number one ambition. He still wanted more adventure in his life. He remembered back to the conversation he'd had with Penny on her birthday and the disappointment he'd felt when Penny said she understood his frustrations but was not keen on him following Andrei's example. He didn't want to be involved in 'shady deals', but he did still want to be able to take more risks. Since marrying Penny, he knew that his motivation had changed. He was concentrating more on his relationship with Penny… trying to make her happy. But, by doing so, he'd now realised he was unhappy in himself. It was about getting the balance right between keeping Penny happy, because he wouldn't want to lose her, and satisfying his business desires. Penny has got the balance right, Ian has achieved it too, so why can't I do the same? he thought.

Now, from the shade of the balcony at the rear of the villa, Viktor watched Penny lying on the lounger next to the swimming pool. Her left foot was gently dipping in and out of the pool, making small ripples in the water. He thought she looked gorgeous in her white bikini and oversized straw hat, reading her book. Reading what? Was it her third or fourth book? She was obviously content and happy. Why aren't I?

It was a day later when he had a sudden moment of inspiration. He finally knew what he wanted to do. It was all going to be… different!

Chapter 38

Ian and Emma were sitting in their office discussing two paintings. Suddenly Ian heard the familiar ping from his mobile phone. He was still awaiting Claude's reply to his earlier email.

"Let me just check that, Emma. I'm hoping it's a message from Claude." Ian quickly moved towards his desk and picked up his mobile phone. His heart rate began to increase. He looked at the screen and, yes, it was an email from Claude. He read the message out loud for both his and Emma's benefit:

Hello Ian,

I passed the details of your last email on to the Musée des Beaux-Arts d'Orléans. They are satisfied with your proposed arrangements and confirm their painting, 'Fête Gloanec', will be ready for collection on or after the 21st June. They will only be carrying out preliminary packing of the painting and expect your transport company, under their supervision, to finish the packaging suitable for its transit. Only when the museum is satisfied that the correct and proper protection has been provided will they give Brooklands permission to remove the painting from their premises.

They have also confirmed they will not be making a charge for their preliminary packing.

Please let me know the date when the painting will be collected.
Kind regards,
Claude.

"Is that the reply you were hoping for?" asked Emma. She could see Ian was still thinking about the message.

Ian looked up and faced Emma. "Yes, largely. I thought they would have wanted to do the main packing themselves."

"That's not a problem, is it?"

"No, I guess not. After all, Claude says the museum will still supervise the final packing."

"The 21st of June," said Emma. She looked at her calendar. "That's in ten days' time."

"Right, I'd better find out when Brooklands can collect. They originally said they wanted at least five working days' notice. After that, I'll tell Charles he can arrange the insurance cover."

"Are you excited now? You don't look it."

"I think I'm missing something, Emma, and I'm not sure what it is!"

Later that same afternoon all the arrangements were in place to collect the painting on the 21st. Charles confirmed that the insurance would commence then and told Ian he was still feeling partly excited and partly very nervous. Ian didn't mention his own personal feelings.

Ian emailed Claude and told him everything was set for collection on the 21st June. Claude emailed back advising he had informed the museum.

"Ian! Dinner is ready." It was Emma calling him from the kitchen. Ian was sitting at his desk and was still wondering if he really had missed something.

Ian arrived in the kitchen. Both their pasta meals were

sitting on the breakfast bar. Emma was sitting in her usual place, sipping a glass of Chablis.

"Dinner looks good," said Ian sitting down next to Emma. He picked up his own glass and sipped the wine.

Emma started to eat her food and then asked, "Have you found out what you thought was missing?"

Ian put his glass down and picked up a fork. "No, and I'm now beginning to think I haven't missed anything after all."

Emma looked at him somewhat surprised. "You seemed so convinced earlier."

"I know, but maybe it was just a feeling, not a fact."

"So, what's the next step?"

"Brooklands are sending two men and a car over to France on the 20th. They plan to arrive at the museum at 9 o'clock on the 21st, finish the packing and aim to be on the evening Eurotunnel shuttle. They'll then deliver the painting to Simon Lyle at the Courtauld Institute on the 22nd."

"Sounds all very precise."

"I want Simon to examine the painting as soon as possible... and I don't want any slip-ups on the way. I won't be totally happy until the picture has arrived with Simon. In the meantime, the museum could still change their mind."

"Surely they've agreed. Given their word. Why would they change their mind?"

"People do change their minds, Emma. We still have seven days to sweat and hope they don't!"

Charles was standing in his apartment looking out through the large picture window. He was watching the activity below on the river. He was more relaxed than he could remember and enjoying the new freedom from his previous working life. He could now afford the time to lie in until seven o'clock. So much more civilised, he thought, than his previous 5.30am alarm-clock call. He'd spent the last few days sifting through the rest of his grandfather's old papers and had generally tidied up all his own domestic invoices, bills and other filing. Then he had gone through all the cupboards, sorting and throwing out everything that was out of date or that he considered surplus to requirements. Finally, he'd employed a team of two ladies to clean everything in the apartment from top to bottom. He was determined to make the apartment as presentable as possible for when the estate agents visited to do their valuations.

He'd also been spending quite a bit of time on the internet looking for potential homes abroad. The Algarve area in Portugal was still his favourite option, but he hadn't totally dismissed some other nice countries further afield. However, he knew he wouldn't be able to make any final decisions until he knew the outcome of his 'Fête Gloanec' painting. Everything now appeared to be stacking up in his favour, Ian's opinion, Courtauld's report, his great-grandfather's investigations and subsequent letter to the Musée des Beaux-Arts d'Orléans. Yes, everything seemed to be fine … so why was he still so nervous?

For the last five days, he'd tried desperately to put the picture out of his mind. He certainly knew he couldn't do any more for the time being – other than wait on Ian's next telephone call.

He wanted to catch up on the months and years he'd lost working 13, 14 and 15 hours a day with no time to develop a proper relationship – no woman would put up with an 'invisible' partner. He knew and accepted that whilst he was working those silly hours, nothing very serious was possible. He couldn't remember the last time he'd had a proper holiday, something more than a couple of days in Dorset or Cornwall at bank holidays. All this was going to change. He was determined to make sure it would. His plans for the next few years included a loving wife, maybe some children, a homely villa with far-reaching sea views, all in a warm climate – what more did a man need?

But first, Charles wanted one thing more than anything else. He wanted a cheque in his hands for £25 million for his painting 'Fête Gloanec'!

Ian Caxton, please don't let me down!

Chapter 39

At 9.50am on the 24th June, Ian received an unexpected telephone call. He was in the kitchen when he picked up the handset.

"Hello?" He didn't recognise the telephone number highlighted on his handset.

"Ian? Simon Lyle at the Courtauld Institute. How are you?"

"Oh, hello, Simon." Ian now recognised the voice. "Very good thanks, and you?"

"Yes, fine. I thought I'd give you a call. Brooklands delivered the French museum's painting two days ago. We're starting the investigation later this afternoon. It'll probably take a couple of days. I just thought you'd like to know."

"Thanks. Do you think you'll have the results on the 26th?"

"Maybe by the late afternoon. Do you want me to give you a ring?"

"That would be very kind. Yes, please."

"Okay. Must go. Cheers."

"Goodbye Simon... and thanks." Ian switched off the call.

"I gather that was Simon at Courtauld's. Good news?" asked Emma. She'd just walked into the kitchen and was standing a few feet away from Ian.

"Simon's starting the investigation this afternoon. He thinks we should have the result in two days' time."

"You've put a lot of time and effort into this one. Fingers crossed."

"The worst-case scenario is that Simon confirms the museum's picture was painted about the same time as Charles's. Both the museum and the catalogue raisonné people will then say their opinions have been vindicated and their painting will continue to be considered the true 'Fête Gloanec'."

"So, what would happen to Charles's picture?"

"I'm not sure. There are several possibilities, but none that would value his painting at the 25 million pounds he's looking for."

"But you still think the museum's picture is a copy, don't you?"

"Yes," Ian said hesitantly. "But of course, I'm not the final judge. The French will fight us all the way. Only an indisputable report from Simon is likely to make them reconsider their stance."

"I see. Difficult, isn't it?"

"As the saying goes, Emma, we might win a battle, but I'm sure the French won't surrender the war!"

The telephone rang again. Ian answered it and noticed it was Charles's number. "Hello, Charles."

"Hi, Ian. Any news from Courtauld's about my painting?"

Ian relayed his conversation with Simon.

"So, we've got another two days to wait?"

"I'm afraid so. Simon will do a thorough job."

"Yes, I guess so, but will he come up with the answer we want?"

"He's promised to ring me as soon as he's finished. I'll ring you straight after."

"Okay. I've got a lot of money riding on this one."

"I know, Charles, I know." Ian too was feeling the pressure.

It was a day later when Ian received another telephone call. It was from an excited Simon Lyle at the Courtauld Institute.

"Ian, hi. Some interesting news."

"Hello, Simon. You sound excited."

"We've not finished our investigations yet. There are a few tests we still have to do tomorrow. Anyway, I was thinking, do you and Charles want to come to the Institute tomorrow? Say two o'clock? We can chat through the whole of the report there and then."

Ian asked some questions, Simon gave some technical answers and Ian finished by saying he was looking forward to the meeting.

Ian switched off the call. He was keen to speak to Charles, but as the report was not fully conclusive, just yet, he didn't want to put any potential false hopes in his mind. He decided to appear as calm as he could in the circumstances. He dialled Charles's mobile.

"Hello, Ian? You've got some great news?" greeted Charles.

"Not yet, Charles, but Simon wants us to meet him tomorrow at Courtauld's. Are you free?"

"Free!" exclaimed Charles. "For this, I'm free every minute of the day. What time?"

"Simon has suggested two o'clock. I'll meet you at about 1.45 outside the main entrance. I'll then tell you about some of the testing they do so you know what to expect."

"Great, Ian. This is it. Sounds good. See you tomorrow."

Ian smiled after he'd switched off the call. These were the days he loved best. The excited clients. The tension before the result. Whether the painting was worth millions or just a few pounds. Modern technology had certainly, and dramatically, changed the art world. No longer were authentications just based upon the personal judgement of 'experts'… or, ill-judgement in many cases.

Chapter 40

It was exactly 1.45pm when Ian approached the North Wing of the famous Somerset House building that accommodated both the Courtauld Institute of Art and the Courtauld Gallery. He easily spotted Charles pacing backwards and forwards outside the entrance.

When Charles spotted Ian, he hurried towards him and shook his hand.

"Have you been waiting long?" asked Ian. The two men walked together towards the entrance door.

"I got here about ten minutes ago. I wasn't going to be late," said Charles. He was now more anxious than ever.

"Let's get inside and I'll tell you about this meeting."

The two men walked through the door and into the reception area. Ian pointed to a red leather double seat and they both sat down.

"What we are about to hear from Simon," explained Ian, "is the result of two days of intensive investigation. It is a much deeper investigation than he did with your painting because yours immediately showed compatible technical features to those existing in previously authenticated Paul Gauguin paintings."

Charles nodded and Ian continued.

"Simon is likely to mention some technological machinery

and techniques such as optical microscopy, x-ray fluorescence, infrared spectroscopy and possibly chromatography-mass spectrometry. It's not important that you know what they all do or produce. The important point is that these methods all contribute to the analysis and identification of the canvas and the picture's age, the paint pigment mixtures and what lies directly underneath the picture. For example, it will identify if there's another layer of painting or paintings between the canvas and the picture you see. Also, the x-rays will show if there is any useful information on the canvas that is currently invisible to the naked eye. Okay so far?"

Again, Charles nodded, but he had to admit some of this was far too technical for his brain.

"Don't worry, most of the technological science is above me too. However, I do know that the pigment mixtures are really important. The colour of an oil paint is derived from small particles of coloured pigments mixed with an oil, often linseed. Pigment types include mineral salts and individual chemicals derived from rocks, plants and the like. To complicate matters further, artists take bits of different pigments and mix them together. Therefore, those mixes are personalised to the individual artist and nobody else. So, you begin to see it's almost impossible to produce a scientifically accurate copy of a painting. Copies rarely consist of the same pigment mix or the exact same oils. Even if a copying artist is an excellent painter and the copy 'looks' like the original, modern technology can now show all these differences."

"Okay," said Charles, now with a little more confidence. "So, if the French museum's painting doesn't have the Paul Gauguin pigment mixes, then it's a copy, right?"

"Gauguin did occasionally change some of his pigments, as all artists do. Even in the 19th century, new pigments became available and artists switched to the new options. Sometimes they did this because their normal supply was not available. However, it would be most unusual for an artist's complete palette to dramatically change in such a short period as say one or two years. So, technology can measure all the salts and chemicals that make up any one individual pigment colour. Therefore today, for example, any alleged Gauguin picture said to have been painted in 1888 can have its pigment results compared with already authenticated pictures painted by Gauguin during that same period."

"Yes, I can see that," reflected Charles. "But obviously they couldn't do that a hundred years ago because they didn't have the same technology. A really good copy would, presumably, only be subject to the whims and judgement of the 'experts' of that time!"

"Exactly," said Ian, "And art history has shown that not all of these 'experts' were necessarily scrupulously honest and fair either."

"Well, that's what we're hoping for here, isn't it?"

"Yes… ah, here comes Simon."

Ian and Charles both stood up together.

Greetings and introductions were made and Simon suggested they go to a quiet room where coffee was waiting for them. The three men walked along several corridors until Simon pushed open the door to his laboratory-cum-office. Charles followed Simon through the door and then gazed around at an array of technical equipment, he had no idea what most of it was, or what it was used for.

Ian immediately recognised the room. It was where he and Emma had met with Simon when he'd investigated Emma's painting 'Mademoiselle Chad'.

Simon led them to a small desk where a coffee pot, mugs and milk had been placed.

"Please, gentlemen, sit down and help yourself to coffee."

Simon wandered over to a laboratory bench and collected some folders and papers. Charles spotted the museum's painting on the same bench. It was leaning against the back wall.

Before sitting down, Ian poured the coffee into three mugs.

Simon arrived back and sat down. "Gentlemen," he announced, "you will be pleased to know that the painting I have just examined was not painted by Gauguin!"

Ian smiled and breathed a sigh of relief. Charles raised his arms in the air and shouted out, "Yes!"

Simon continued. "These papers" – Simon lifted the small collection in front of him – "are copies of the report I'll be emailing to the French museum. You can take them away with you after this meeting. I assume you would like to hear a summary of my findings?"

"Yes, please, Simon," said Ian. Charles nodded his head furiously. His face had a huge beaming grin across it.

"Well, there are three key factors that you should be aware of. Firstly, the pigments used are not the same as those being used by Gauguin around 1888. It's more likely that most of the pigments on the museum's picture relate to paints being used in the decade 1910–20. You will remember from my report on your painting, Mr. Owen, that I said the blue oil paint used matched Gauguin's palette, but was not available after 1910."

Charles nodded. He remembered Ian saying something along those lines.

"Secondly, the x-ray photographs show that there was another painting sandwiched between the canvas and the painting you see today. Interestingly, this painting was signed by someone called 'P. S. Ager' and is dated 1905."

"That's not a name I recognise," said Ian.

"Thirdly," continued Simon, "the canvas itself produced

some interesting information. In the top right-hand corner, it had part of a printed name. It was 'erie Norma'. We're reasonably sure the 'erie' is the end of the first word and 'Norma' the beginning of the second word."

"Galerie Normandy," interrupted Ian. "Or translated into English, 'Normandy Gallery'."

Both Charles and Simon stared at Ian in surprise.

"That's what we think," said Simon. "We've seen similar canvases to this one before. In the early 1900s there were a number of good copies of post-impressionist-style paintings being sold and passed off as originals. The Galerie Normandy was just one company who provided the market with some excellent copies, until 1915, that is. That's when the gallery was finally exposed, and it does fit in nicely with the paints being used during the period 1910–20."

Ian then mentioned his earlier meeting with Claude Dupont at the Musée du Autry. He told them about Claude's story regarding the Normandy Gallery and how the three partners and two employees were eventually caught and sentenced to long periods in prison.

"Well, I guess I'm going to be a rich man now," said Charles, rubbing his hands with glee.

Ian looked at Simon and then to Charles, but Ian wasn't smiling when he said, "Unfortunately we're still not quite there. There's one more hurdle to clear and that's getting the author of Gauguin's catalogue raisonné to agree with all our findings. That, I'm afraid, is **not** going to be a very easy task!"

"Good luck, boys," said Simon, with a rueful smile. "You're going to need lots of it."

Chapter 41

When Ian and Charles left the meeting with Simon, Charles was not sure if he was elated or disappointed. He couldn't believe that, despite his painting now being scientifically proven to be the original, there were still more people to convince.

"Do you know, Ian," said Charles. They'd now exited Somerset House and were walking along The Strand, "I'm not sure if I'm pleased or frustrated. Despite all the scientific evidence from Simon's investigations, you're telling me this is still not enough. You know, Simon knows and I now know, my picture is the real deal. The real 'Fête Gloanec'!"

"I understand your frustrations, Charles, but this is the art market. Put yourself in the shoes of the French museum and especially the author of the catalogue raisonné. For over 100 years, everyone has believed the museum's painting was the original. Why would they believe differently? Imagine when we tell them their professional judgement is wrong… and has been for over 100 years. Think of the embarrassment and damage to their reputation. They're not going to give up on this struggle without a serious fight!"

"Okay, I take your point, but I can't see they've got a leg to stand on. If they want a fight, for 25 million, I can give them a 'real fight'! I'll expose them all over social media. How will that help their reputation?"

The two men had stopped and were waiting at a set of traffic lights. They'd joined a large group of pedestrians trying to cross the road.

"Look, there's a coffee shop across the road. It'll be much quieter and easier to talk in there."

When the red light stopped the traffic, they crossed the road and entered the coffee shop. Ian bought two cappuccinos and they sat down in a quiet corner. Charles had calmed down a little, but it was Ian who restarted the conversation. "The last thing any of us wants is for this matter to be bandied about on social media. It's to nobody's benefit. We want to win this war, not prolong it."

"Come on, Ian, the first sound of social media and they'll cave in."

"The art market doesn't work like that, Charles, believe me. Our aim is to get the best reward for your picture, not to embarrass everyone in sight! Remember, the museum and the catalogue raisonné authors are not yet aware of the results of Simon's work. They're going to be shocked, embarrassed and wonder how the hell they're going to get out of this mess without incurring lots of bad publicity."

"So, you think they'll pay me 25 million for my painting… and my silence?"

Ian smiled. "You've been reading too many thriller books! I don't know what their reaction's going to be… we need to speak to them."

"Ian, look, you know this art world, you know how it works. If I get involved, I might regret what I say. Will you speak to them? You'd be much better… more diplomatic than me."

"I think that's definitely the best approach. Just leave it with me, I've got a few ideas."

It was later that evening when Ian drafted a short email to Claude Dupont and Albert. He suggested another meeting in Paris, this time with the addition of the senior personnel of the Musée des Beaux-Arts d'Orléans. The only subject on the agenda was to be the two Courtauld's reports. Ian finished his email by stating that 'time is of the essence'. There could be legal consequences if there was any undue delay.

When Ian switched off his computer, he went directly upstairs to the bedroom. Emma was already in bed, reading a book. "So, who's had a busy day?" she asked, jokingly.

Ian looked at Emma and pulled off his jumper. "It's been quite a day. Charles is certainly a challenge... but in a nice way. I'm having to hold his hand through all this, but hopefully we're now on the final leg."

"Have you sent your email?"

"Yes, I'm sure Albert and Claude will be on the telephone to each other first thing tomorrow morning. They're not fools. They'll know from the urgency of my email that the Musée des Beaux-Arts d'Orléans have a serious problem. I'm expecting a reply probably tomorrow afternoon."

"Do you think the museum will accept Simon's reports?"

"I'm not sure. If I were them, I'd get their painting checked out for themselves, if they hadn't already before it went to Courtauld's. It should be back with them in a couple of days' time. They also know that Courtauld's has a world-renowned reputation, so it's very unlikely they'd think Simon's results are unsound."

"Tricky situation for them... and, of course, for the catalogue raisonné people as well."

"Yes. If this all becomes public knowledge, a number of reputations will be shattered. Owners of Gauguin paintings around the world are going to be wondering if their pictures are copies too!"

"Serious repercussions then."

Ian smiled. "You know, Emma, if Charles does decide to expose this situation on social media, it could well open a very large can of worms for the art world!"

"Yes, I can see that."

"Anyway, I think I've reined him in on that possibility… at least for the moment. In the meantime, we'll have to wait and see how the museum responds. It could still get very awkward… and potentially very dirty!"

Ian's supposition proved to be correct. The anticipated reply from Claude arrived in his email inbox at just after 1.30pm. Not a great deal was said but, reading between the lines, he could tell there were definitely lots of people in France panicking! Claude also asked if it was convenient for Ian to attend a meeting at 2pm on the 13th July at the Musée du Autry as well as send him a copy of Courtauld's full report on the museum's painting as a matter of urgency please.

Ian smiled. Yes, he would agree to the 13th July and he immediately emailed Claude a copy of Simon's summary report, including copies of the graphs and x-rays.

About two hours later, and to Ian's huge surprise, he received the following email from Claude:

Hello Ian,

Thank you for your email enclosing the Courtauld Institute of Art's summary report. The Musée des Beaux-Arts d'Orléans have already received their own report directly from Courtauld's.

The meeting you suggested with the museum's senior personnel is confirmed.

I was wondering if you could arrive a little earlier on the 13th July and meet with Albert and I for lunch at twelve noon? Albert will arrange a table at the same restaurant where you and he previously met with your wives.

The Result

Kind regards,
Claude.

Well, well, well, thought Ian. We do live in interesting times!

Chapter 42

Penny and Viktor arrived home early Sunday morning after their overnight flight from St. Lucia. It was less than 24 hours later, at 6am, when Penny switched off the bedside alarm clock. She was anxious to find out what had been going on at Sotheby's whilst she'd been away. She got out of bed, showered and was dressed before 6.45. Two slices of toast for breakfast and she was striding out on her way to the local Docklands Light Railway station. She'd really enjoyed her relaxing 14 days break in the Caribbean sunshine. Lots of peace and quiet, well away from the hectic pressures of Sotheby's and the challenges of the art world. Now it was back to the realities of her usual working day.

Viktor hadn't stirred when Penny left for work. However, he was now awake but still lying in bed. He also felt refreshed but in a different sort of way. Yes, he'd enjoyed the relaxing lifestyle of their holiday, but he'd definitely decided that he wanted more out of his life. More adventure, different challenges and no more routine. The big sticking point for him, though, was where to begin! How does one actually start? He thought of Ian and admired his decision to abandon his career at Sotheby's for something different and a new challenge, something more rewarding and not just from a financial perspective. Maybe he'd give him a ring and catch up, invite him for lunch, or a

197

beer. He suddenly remembered and wondered about the painting he and Ian had viewed in France, 'Fête Gloanec'. Yes, that was something to get the conversation started.

Viktor looked at his watch. It was 8.30. A bit early to make a casual call, so he decided to give it a couple of hours. He got out of bed, put on his dressing gown, walked into the kitchen and switched on the kettle. He then moved into the lounge and across to the windows. There he looked down at the activity on the River Thames. A barge was slowly drifting down the river. Viktor wondered what it was transporting, but he would never know as the cargo was covered by large sheets of black tarpaulin. Travelling in the opposite direction was a big yacht. He'd seen a few yachts this size in the harbour at St. Lucia. He looked closer and could just make out its name, *'No limits'*. Its three white sails were straining with the river breeze as it otherwise glided serenely up the river towards Tower Bridge in the far distance. No limits, thought Viktor. Is that an omen?

At 10.30am, Viktor made his telephone call.

Ian immediately recognised Viktor's number. "Hi, Vic. How's things?"

"Hello, Ian. Good, thanks. I thought I'd give you a call about the painting you took me to see in France. I'm curious to know what the outcome was?"

"Long story, Vic, but I was right. The museum's painting is a copy and Charles's is the original. You remember it from 'Dexter's End'?"

"Yes, of course. You knew straight away that it was the original. So, what's happening to it now?"

"I'm going to Paris next week for a big meeting, to see how we can sort it all out."

"I see," said Viktor, feeling slightly down. Once again, he was missing out on another adventure. "Penny and I have just come back from a holiday. We went to St. Lucia."

"That's good. I hope you both had a great time. How's Penny getting on with Northgate?"

"I think she's getting along fine. She was certainly up and out early this morning, keen to find out what's been going on in her absence."

Ian gave a small laugh. "She's too good for Northgate. He'll use her brains and take the credit. So then, Vic, what are your plans now that you're back from sunning yourself in St. Lucia?"

"I've got two clients to see and a couple of evaluations for Alexander, but otherwise it's all a bit quiet."

"I could do with a hand if you're interested."

Viktor's face immediately lit up. "What do you want me to do?"

"Remember those six paintings I asked you to investigate for me?"

"Of course. I wondered why you were involved with pictures like those. But then you mentioned that Andrei had left them to you."

"That's right. But what he hadn't done was leave the provenances. At least I couldn't find any in the Monaco apartment. So, my question to you is, do you want to see if you can track down the provenances and then maybe find some buyers? I know you've done some exploratory work on them already."

"Buyers are going to be tricky given four are, er... 'tainted', should we say. But I can give it a go."

"You can have 60% of the sale price."

"But they're your pictures, Ian."

"I know, but I don't want them and haven't got the time to allocate for the research. None of them are worth millions, but two do have a value – even the ones on the Commission's listing could have a buyer."

"Are the paintings still in Monaco?"

"Yes. I think that's the safest place for them at the moment. I've taken photographs of all six and they're on my computer. There's some information on the back of three of them too. I'll email you the details, that should help you get started."

"I'll see what I can find out."

Ian noticed that Vic's voice seemed to have a lot more energy now. "No rush, Vic. Just see what you can do."

"Thanks, Ian… and good luck in Paris next week."

"Thank you. Good luck yourself… and, Vic, be careful." Ian switched off the call.

"Was that Vic?" asked Emma. She was looking at Ian from her desk in their home office.

"Yes. Penny telephoned yesterday afternoon. She asked me not to tell Vic, but said she was worried about him as he'd lost some of his focus and enthusiasm. He keeps talking about how successful Andrei and I have been and that he isn't. She wondered if I had any suggestions and warned me he might ring."

"Have you been able to help?"

"I've given him a challenge, something to get his teeth into. It'll certainly be interesting to see what he comes up with."

Chapter 43

The taxi dropped Ian off outside the restaurant. He looked at his watch. It was 11.52am Parisian time. He was in good time for his meeting with Albert and Claude.

He was just about to enter the building when he heard a familiar voice calling his name. He looked along the street and, ten metres away, saw Albert walking towards him.

"Bonjour, Ian," called Albert as he came closer.

"Bonjour, Albert," replied Ian. They shook hands.

"So, why the earlier meeting with just you and Claude? I had to get up in the middle of the night to catch my train!"

Albert laughed, gently touched Ian's shoulder and steered him towards the restaurant's entrance door. "Let's get inside, my friend. I think Claude is already here. We'll explain everything."

The two men entered the restaurant and the maître d' immediately walked over and welcomed them. He instantly recognised Albert and greeted him like a long-lost friend. He explained that the third guest was already here. Albert and Ian followed him towards their table, situated in a nice quiet corner. Claude was reading his menu but, once he'd spotted his two colleagues approaching, he stood up and held out his hand to greet both Ian and Albert. All three then sat down.

"It's good of you to join us, Ian. There are a few things I want you to be aware of before the bigger meeting this afternoon. Firstly, can I get you a drink?"

"A glass of sparkling water would be fine please, Claude. I want to keep a clear head for later."

Albert decided he would have just one glass of Chablis, and the maître d' said he would send a waiter over with the drinks and menus.

Claude started to speak. "I think Albert mentioned to you that I once worked at the Musée des Beaux-Arts d'Orléans."

Ian nodded.

Claude continued, "I won't go into the details now, but let's just say I left the museum against my will. I was accused, unjustly, of things that were happening at the museum, but they were absolutely nothing to do with me. I think you English call it a 'scapegoat'! I was young and naive, but my friend here, Albert, persuaded me to leave without any argument and arranged for me to join my current employers, the Musée du Autry."

Albert intervened. "It was a difficult situation. In the end, the Musée des Beaux-Arts d'Orléans promised not to prosecute if Claude resigned and left quietly. So that's what he did."

Ian again nodded, but wondered why this information was relevant and where the conversation was heading.

"The two people responsible for my problem," interjected Claude, "have long since left the museum, but I've always said that I would like to get my revenge. My revenge is that I want to help you. That's why I've volunteered my time and energy to help you. To be a sort of 'catalyst' between you and the museum.

"I'm sorry to hear this story, Claude," replied Ian, "but I'm working on behalf of my client and all we are looking for from the museum and the catalogue raisonné people is acceptance that my client's painting is the real 'Fête Gloanec'. We're not looking for revenge or punishment."

The waiter arrived with the drinks and handed out two further menus to Ian and Albert.

Once the waiter had departed, Albert was the next to speak. "Ian, we understand your position. What we're going to do is give you some extra information that will help you achieve your, and your client's, aims. At the moment, the muscum's opinion of your client's painting is that it is a fake! They know the facts of Courtauld's investigation, but their stance is still that their picture is the correct 'Fête Gloanec'. The authors of the catalogue raisonné have a very close relationship with the museum and they have decided they definitely will not replace the museum's copy in favour of your client's painting in their next edition."

"I see," responded Ian. "That makes things a lot trickier."

"Let's order our food, Ian, and we'll explain what we think the best approach will be," said Albert, picking up his menu.

Ian slowly unfolded his own menu, but his mind was a million miles away from considering something to eat. He had hoped this situation could be settled with an amicable agreement. It now looked like a possible serious fight, which of course would give Charles reasons to publicise the issue across social media channels – and, knowing Charles's short fuse – in a big way! He was beginning to think that nobody was going to win this war now. Had it all been a waste of his time?

The three men made their meal selections. Ian went for a simple salad. He certainly didn't have an appetite now.

Claude began to speak. "Ian, the museum is aware of all the facts from your investigations but, as we've told you, they have rejected these details completely."

Ian thought for a moment and then said, "So, this meeting

later is going to be a waste of time. My client thought this might be the case and he'll want to expose the whole affair on social media. He may take legal action too. Is that what these people want? Think of the damage to reputations, the bad publicity and people questioning the value and accuracy of the Gauguin catalogue raisonné. Nobody gains anything and everyone's going to be a loser."

"Okay, Ian, calm down." It was Albert speaking. "We said at the beginning, we have a plan."

For the next ten minutes Ian listened to Claude's proposal. He slowly calmed down, gradually realising Claude's ideas could actually make a big difference.

When Claude had fully explained his ideas, Ian sat back in his seat. "You're not expecting me to present these points as well, are you? Because I'm only taking your word that they're true."

"Don't worry about that, Ian," said Claude. "They're most definitely true and I can prove it! What I'm suggesting will neither compromise you or your argument. Present your case as you intend and, depending upon their response, Albert and I will hit them with our retaliation!"

Ian sipped his water and pondered on what he'd just heard. Claude really wanted to get his revenge. He was certainly not the sort of man to get on the wrong side of.

Chapter 44

It was just after 3.30pm when the three members of the Musée des Beaux-Arts d'Orléans team departed the board-room at the Musée du Autry. They refused the offer of coffee and were not very happy at all. They just wanted to get away from Paris as quickly as possible.

Ian, Claude and Albert were still sitting around the boardroom table. They were reflecting, in silence, on what had been said… and what had been achieved.

It was Claude who eventually broke the silence and stood up. "Well, I'm going to have a cup of coffee. Anyone going to join me?"

Both Ian and Albert said they would like a cup too. Claude walked over to a small table where a cafetiere of coffee and several cups had been placed on a silver tray. He poured three cups and carried two over to his colleagues.

Ian said thank you and shook his head. "I hope nobody recorded that meeting because it was blackmail!"

Both Claude and Albert smiled, then Claude said, "Ian, you did not hear any of that conversation. Promise me you will never, ever, repeat it to anyone."

"After what you two guys have just achieved, you have my word."

"Well, they couldn't argue with your facts, Ian," said Albert, putting his cup back on the saucer.

"I know but..."

"Ian," said Claude firmly, bringing his own coffee cup to the table. "It's all done and agreed. That's the end, okay?"

"Yes, okay, sorry," said Ian, apologetically. Then, trying to change the subject, "Is there any more coffee?"

"Of course," replied Claude. "Help yourself."

Ian stood up and walked over to the cafetiere and topped up his cup. He offered the others more coffee but both declined. He returned to his seat. "How should we deal with Charles's painting?"

"Hang on to it for the time being," replied Claude. "Probably safest to wait for the banker's draft to be paid into your client's bank account."

"You seem convinced Charles will be happy with the settlement, Ian," said Albert.

"He will be after I've explained the situation to him. He was hoping for 25 million pounds, but I'm sure he'll be more than happy with 25 million euros."

"Well, gentlemen, I think I had better get back to my office," said Albert standing up.

"Yes, I must go too." Ian finished his coffee and stood up. He looked at his watch. "I think there's a Eurostar train in 55 minutes. Albert... Claude, what can I say? Thank you. This couldn't have been achieved without you two."

Ian walked over, shook Claude's hand, gave him a big smile and said, "You have my word."

"Exciting day, Ian. I'm pleased we got there in the end," replied Claude, smiling and thinking how satisfying it was to finally achieve his revenge!

"Come on, Ian," said Albert, waving his hand. "We can share a taxi and get you back to the Gare du Nord."

The three men left the boardroom. Claude led them back

to the museum's entrance. There Ian and Albert both said their goodbyes to Claude.

Albert hailed a taxi and he and Ian jumped in. The traffic was strangely quiet and they arrived outside the railway station in under ten minutes. Albert stayed in the taxi when Ian got out. Before shutting the door, Ian, once again, thanked Albert for all his help and told him to keep in touch. They both asked for their regards to be passed on to their wives. Ian closed the door and, as the taxi pulled away, he smiled and waved to Albert.

An hour later, Ian was sitting on the Eurostar watching the French countryside flash by his window. He was drinking a glass of Chablis and thinking back to the events of the afternoon. He was personally happy with the outcome, pleased for Charles and satisfied that justice had finally been achieved.

He then thought of Emma and removed his mobile phone from his inside jacket pocket. He telephoned Emma and gave her a brief resume of the day. She congratulated him and said she would collect him at Esher railway station later that evening. Ian agreed to ring her again when he knew which train he would be travelling on from Waterloo.

After the telephone call, Ian sent Charles a brief text. He simply typed: *Great news! Will telephone you in the morning. Ian.*

When Ian switched off his phone, he noticed he was feeling hungry. Since eating breakfast, he'd only eaten the light salad at the restaurant, so he headed off in search of the dining car.

It was just after 10am, the next morning, when Ian telephoned Charles.

When he noticed it was Ian telephoning, Charles became very excited. "Ian, hi. What's the great news?"

Ian explained that the Musée des Beaux-Arts d'Orléans had agreed to buy his painting to replace their own, which they now agreed was probably the copy.

"That's brilliant, Ian. You're the champ!" exclaimed Charles. "What have they agreed to pay me?"

"Charles, there's a lot to tell you, but not over the phone. Have you any plans for today?"

"Nothing I can't change. Why?"

"Okay, why don't you hop on the train and come down to Esher. It's a lovely warm summer's day and there's a wonderful pub nearby next to the river."

"Sounds great."

"Good. There's a train from Waterloo at 11.55. Will you be able to catch it?"

"Absolutely. By the way, I also want you to look at a villa in Portugal that I'm thinking of buying. All the details and photographs are on the internet."

"Fine. I'll be waiting for you at Esher station. Have a good journey."

The 11.55 train from Waterloo pulled into Esher station on time. Ian easily spotted Charles almost skipping down the platform towards him. He had the biggest smile across his face and greeted Ian with a manly hug.

"This is the first time I've ever been to Esher. I hope the natives are friendly," joked Charles.

"Yes, they are… largely," said Ian with a small laugh. "Come on, I've booked a table at a great pub."

The two men walked towards Ian's car, which was parked in the short-term parking area. Ian unlocked the doors and they both got in.

"Come on, Ian, put me out of my suspense. What happened?"

Ian started up the engine and accelerated away. He

explained that the Musée des Beaux-Arts d'Orléans had agreed to pay 25 million euros for his painting.

"Not 25 million… pounds?" queried Charles.

Ian had already prepared himself for what he was about to say… and, more importantly, what he wasn't going to tell Charles. "No. Obviously I had to do some negotiating and they pointed out that if we sold your painting via auction, there would be marketing and commission costs."

Charles thought about this. "Yes, okay. I can see their point but, at the end of the day, they've accepted Courtauld's reports and all our paperwork. That's great… and one up for my great-grandfather!"

"They did query a few points but we eventually got there."

"Ian, you've been fantastic! I won't forget all the time and costs you've incurred. I'll make sure you're well rewarded. We've got a great result!"

Ian smiled. "Thanks… it's been fun."

"Fun!?" announced Charles exasperatedly. "It's been a nightmare! I don't want to go through that ever again."

Ian laughed. "Here's the pub. I think you're in need of a stiff drink."

"Stiff drink!" exclaimed Charles. "I'll buy us a bottle of champagne."

Ten minutes later they were both sitting at a table on the patio overlooking the river. The sun was warm overhead and, after the waiter had taken their order for champagne, he gave each of them a food menu and pushed up their large sunshade. They gazed up and down the river and watched as several pleasure boats sailed slowly by. It was all very tranquil and typically British, thought Charles. A far cry from London… and probably Portugal too.

The waiter returned with an ice bucket which contained their bottle of champagne. Two flute glasses were placed on the table. The waiter picked up the bottle, wiped the bottom of moisture and then the cork was removed with a resulting 'pop'. Both Ian and Charles watched in silence as the waiter slowly filled their glasses to the brim.

After the waiter had walked away Charles picked up his glass and made a toast. "This is definitely a time for celebration. Cheers to you, Ian, you've done a wonderful job."

"Cheers," replied Ian, smiling and clinking Charles's glass with his own. "Thanks for the champagne... but, unfortunately, the job is still not complete. The museum has set some conditions for the sale."

Charles replaced his glass on the table with a thump. His smile had disappeared.

"Nothing to worry about," continued Ian, "but we must follow the conditions properly."

"Okay. So, what do we still have to do?" Charles said with more than a hint of trepidation.

"Well, firstly everything has to be done very quietly and discreetly. The museum and the catalogue raisonné authors are incredibly embarrassed. They certainly don't want their picture, and this sale, to come to the public's attention. It could do serious harm to their reputations if it did."

"I don't have any problem with that. I want to keep it quiet too... now."

Ian continued, "The provenances are going to be another issue for them. I'm not sure how they can change the records without someone asking questions, but that's not our concern. What's more important is that they want to pay you by banker's draft."

Charles shrugged his shoulders. "That's fine with me. I guess they don't want to be seen issuing a cheque in their name or having it go through their account as a bank transfer. I think I prefer their choice anyway. Keeps it away from the prying eyes of the taxman."

"Yes, and talking of the taxman, you need to keep this

money away from your UK bank account. I'll introduce you to my Swiss bank in London. We'll talk about that later."

"Thanks. I was wondering about that. The last thing I want is for money laundering or taxation investigations."

"Anyway, back to their conditions, they want to pay 50% now and the balance when they receive your painting."

"I see. What do you think about that?" Charles assumed it was probably okay, but he wanted to hear what Ian had to say first.

"I think it's alright. We still hold all the trump cards. They also want no further communication with you or me, no reporting to social media, or our legal representatives communicating with them once you have received all the money."

"Hopefully, that won't be necessary anyway."

"Finally, when you're happy that the deposit has arrived in your bank account, you will instruct and pay for the transportation of your picture to the museum in France. They said they'd be quite happy if you instructed Brooklands again."

"Cheeky of them, but okay. What's next?"

"What's next, Charles, is… we need to order our food. There are no more conditions for the sale."

Charles's face lit up. Back came the big smile and a deep sigh. "After we've finished this meal, Ian, I'll show you the photographs of the villa I'm going to buy… in Portugal."

Chapter 45

In between carrying out valuations for Alexander, Viktor continued his investigations into Ian's six paintings and searched a lot deeper into the illegal and murky art world that existed during the 1930s and 1940s. He'd discovered that during this period, many official records containing the names of the correct owners of paintings had 'disappeared' from the art archives and thousands of paintings had been given falsified provenances. A network of corrupt dealers and so-called experts proliferated during this time and they provided new authentications. He was convinced he would find the history of Ian's four 'tainted' paintings buried somewhere in these illegal records. Who were the rightful owners and what were the correct provenances?

The two watercolours, however, he was untroubled with. They were not on the 'Commission for Looted Art in Europe' listing and appeared to still have all the correct and original provenances. They even confirmed that Andrei Petrov was the current owner. Viktor valued them at about £70,000 each and thought he might already know two possible buyers.

It was during the next day of his investigations that Viktor stumbled across the name of Julius Böhler, the notorious Munich gallery owner and dealer. He'd been reading an article in an art magazine about the Zentralinstitut für

Kunstgeschichte (ZIKG) in Munich. ZIKG had, in 2015, acquired copies of Julius Böhler's extensive archives. These archives provided details of huge numbers of transactions that were carried out from 1903. In particular, they highlighted the many suspicious transactions which were completed during the Nazi era. It was well known that Böhler was a central figure in aiding the successful trading of Nazi-looted art. Amongst the names of buyers listed in the archive were Adolf Hitler and many senior members of the Nazi regime. Listed as sellers were a number of high-ranking members of the German Gestapo, the primary 'acquirers' of the looted art from the true owners.

Viktor wondered if the Böhler archive listing was available for public viewing.

He continued to access the internet and flicked through other publications. Suddenly he came across an interesting article which reported on a successful restitution achieved by the 'Commission for Looted Art in Europe'. He jotted down the following summary notes:

Gottlieb Kraus, businessman and honorary consul for Czechoslovakia in Austria.

- *He, and his wife Mathilde, assembled a collection of over 160 paintings.*
- *In 1923, they opened their apartment as a museum, to display the collection to the public. The collection included the painting 'View of a Dutch Square' attributed to the Dutch Old Master, Jan van der Heyden.*
- *In March 1938, about the same time as the start of the persecution of the Jews by the Nazis, Gottlieb and Mathilde Kraus fled via Prague to the USA, leaving their entire art collection behind in Vienna.*

- *On 13 June 1941, all of their property, including the art collection, was confiscated by the Gestapo.*
- *On 8 July 1942, the Van der Heyden painting was sold by the Gestapo to Heinrich Hoffmann, Hitler's friend and photographer. He was also the father-in-law of Baldur von Schirach, the Nazi Governor of Vienna.*
- *In May 1945, the Hoffmann art collection was discovered by Allied officers at Schloss Dietramszell in Bavaria, and sent to Munich where it was inventoried and photographed.*
- *After the war, the Kraus family made efforts over many decades to find and recover their 160 seized paintings, but without success.*
- *In March 1959, the Van der Heyden painting, and several other pictures, were transferred by the Allies to the State of Bavaria with specific instructions to make proper restitution.*
- *The Van der Heyden painting subsequently entered the Bavarian State Paintings Collections in Munich as inventory no. 12891.*
- *In 1962, the Van der Heyden painting was discovered and handed over by the State of Bavaria to Mrs. Henriette Hoffmann von Schirach, the daughter of Heinrich Hoffmann, as a 'return sale' (Rückkauf) in exchange for the sum of just 300DM!*
- *On 14 November 1963, Mrs. Hoffmann von Schirach sold the painting through the Lempertz auction house in Cologne for 16,100DM. The Dombauverein Xanten in North Rhine-Westphalia bought the painting at Lempertz without the knowledge that the painting had previously been stolen from the Kraus family.*
- *In 2011, a restitution claim for the painting was submitted to Xanten by the 'Commission for Looted Art in Europe' on behalf of the Kraus family.*

- *Until 2019, only six of the original 160 paintings had been recovered.*
- *On the 21st March 2019, 'The Commission for Looted Art in Europe', representing the heirs of Gottlieb and Mathilde Kraus, announced the return of the painting 'View of a Dutch Square' to the family.*

Viktor put his pen down and reflected on what he'd written. Just one example of the horrible times that existed on mainland Europe during the Nazis' time in power. How many stolen paintings, he wondered, will eventually find their way back to the rightful owners? Probably not many, unless family heirs are able to come forward and state their claim. Even then, the paintings still have to be found and later properly repatriated. Recent history has shown, however, that as with the Kraus collection, very few paintings are ever found again… and, where they are, there is often a long and tortuous process to be followed before they are finally returned to their rightful owner.

Viktor suddenly felt a pang of conscience and deep sympathy for these poor souls. The more he read and investigated, the more concerned he became with his involvement in Ian's pictures. He knew for certain what Penny would say.

The four 'tainted' paintings didn't belong to Ian, they hadn't even belonged to Andrei. They were legally someone else's property. Property that had been unceremoniously stolen or looted. Whilst Ian and Andrei were not the actual looters, by keeping the paintings for themselves, were they not just as guilty and responsible for perpetuating the crimes and prolonging the misery for the real owners?

Not for the first time Viktor thought how 'dirty' a business the art world could be. So much deceit and corruption and a total lack of integrity.

Whilst holidaying in St. Lucia, he'd made up his mind that he was going to help with the restitution of these stolen paintings, and was going to start by telling Ian that he wasn't prepared to spend time trying to sell his four 'tainted' pictures. Indeed, Ian had to realise that such behaviour was not only illegal, but certainly immoral as well. He didn't want to be party to such a grubby scheme – even if the result was a falling-out with a colleague he so admired!

Chapter 46

Ian and Emma were in their home office. They were discussing possible dates when they could both return to Monaco for a holiday. Emma pointed out that the end of Robert's school term was on the 13th.

"Do you think Robert would want to join us this time?" asked Ian. "I thought Arthur's family had invited him to their holiday home in Cornwall this summer."

"I don't think any dates have been finalised. We'd better ask Robert which option he'd prefer," replied Emma, hoping his preference would be to join them in Monaco.

"I know which one I would have preferred when I was his age," replied Ian, trying to think back to what he was doing when he was eight years old.

"I'll have a word with him when he telephones on Friday," replied Emma, "It's strange him being away full time."

"I know, but he wanted to do it and I think he's really enjoying it. It'll be good for him."

"Most of his friends are full-time boarders, so he's got lots of company and plenty of activities at the weekends as well."

"Okay, I'll check out the flights and availability. However, I'll wait until you've spoken to Robert before I book anything. By the way—"

The conversation was interrupted when the telephone rang.

Ian answered the call. "Hello?"

"Ian, it's Vic."

"Hello, Vic. How's things?"

"Fine, thanks. Can we have a discussion about your paintings?"

"Of course. How are your investigations progressing?"

Emma indicated that she was leaving. Ian waved back and mouthed 'okay'.

"Ian," replied Viktor, "that's what I want to discuss."

Ian noted the seriousness in the tone of Viktor's voice. "Fine. Is there a problem?"

Viktor explained all the details of his investigations to date and the report about the Kraus family's case. He also said he was extremely concerned about the legality and morality of what Ian was doing.

Ian was a little shocked, but not totally surprised. He too had been having second thoughts about these paintings. "Look, okay, Vic. I understand the points you're making. You're right, I'm not the lawful owner and rightly they should be repatriated back to the people who are."

"I didn't really think you'd want to be involved in this sort of illegal business, Ian, but you did ask me to find a buyer."

"To tell you the truth, Vic, I wanted to try and help you. You seemed down when we last spoke and appeared to be hinting you were looking for something more stimulating in addition to your work with Alexander. Those paintings were the only thing I could think of at the time. Maybe I picked the wrong challenge. Sorry."

"You know, Ian, I've been thinking about my career and where I am and what I'm doing. When I left Sotheby's, I had so many ideas and ambitions, but it's not really worked out as I'd hoped. My father told me stories about Andrei and his wealth, his business successes and the lifestyle he lived, and I guess I probably just revered him too much. Maybe him leaving me that fabulous inheritance also put pressure on me to follow his example, to succeed as well. I know now that I'm never going to be another Andrei, we're just not the same type of people."

Ian listened to Viktor's words and thought it could have been him making exactly the same point. "I guess we've both been in danger of trying to live up to the ambitions Andrei set for us, but, as you say, we're not the same people."

"I've been reading a lot lately about the 'Commission for Looted Art in Europe' and I'm considering offering my help in some way. Apparently, they're always looking for qualified volunteers. There are thousands of people and families who lost valuable art collections during the Second World War."

"Well, if you're serious, Vic, you can start with the four paintings we've been talking about. They're currently in Monaco, but I can arrange for them to be shipped to you in the UK."

"That would be great, Ian." Viktor's voice suddenly sounded much more enthusiastic.

"Mind, there would be one condition," said Ian seriously. "The paintings would have to be recorded as being given by an anonymous donor."

As Ian was making this last statement, Emma walked back into the room with two mugs of coffee.

"I'm sure that wouldn't be a problem," said Viktor. He was confident that some of the previous donors would probably have 'gifted' their art work anonymously too.

They finished their conversation after Viktor promised he'd let Ian know more after he'd approached the Commission.

"What's all this about anonymous donations?" asked Emma. She placed Ian's mug of coffee on his desk.

"Do you remember I told you that, as well as the apartment in Monaco, Andrei had left me a few paintings?"

Emma nodded, although she couldn't remember exactly what Ian had told her.

"Well, some time ago," continued Ian, "I asked Vic if he would do some research for me. He did and told me that four of the paintings were listed as lost or missing on the 'Commission for Looted Art in Europe' database."

"Isn't that the organisation that attempts to find stolen paintings and get them repatriated to the rightful owner?"

Ian nodded. "Anyway, Vic's now saying he's going to volunteer to help them. I told him I would be prepared to donate these four paintings, but only if my donation could be done anonymously."

"Are these paintings valuable?"

"Well, that's an interesting question, because the answer is both 'yes and no'. Yes, if the paintings are repatriated back to the rightful owners, but no, except to an unscrupulous buyer, because they're stolen property. No legitimate individual would be interested."

"And Andrei left these stolen paintings to you. That was nice of him."

"It's not like he left them to me in his will. He just said I could do with them as I wanted. There was no written formality to them."

"Even so, I can see why you want to donate them anonymously. I just hope Andrei hasn't left you any more ticking bombs!"

Chapter 47

After speaking with Ian, Viktor decided he wanted to tell Penny about his new plans. He was sure she would have some useful comments to make.

Over dinner that evening, Viktor explained his aim to offer part-time support to the Commission. He spelt out his reasons for wanting to help people to achieve proper restitution of stolen works of art. However, he deliberately avoided mentioning his conversation about Ian's four paintings.

Penny thought his idea was interesting and commendable. She did make two comments and Viktor took them on board. She also reminded him of when they both worked with Ian at Sotheby's, in the early days, and the problems over the McLaren paintings.

"That's right," remembered Viktor. "It was the first case Ian gave you to handle on your own."

"How could I ever forget that obnoxious wife!" replied Penny. "If you remember it was your inspired moment that got the Commission involved with their paintings."

"Indeed. I'll mention that case in my application. Thanks."

The following morning, Viktor contacted the Commission via the email link on their website. He advised them of his personal details, why he thought he could help and made specific reference to the McLaren case. Again, he deliberately didn't mention Ian's paintings. That, he thought, was something for another day.

It was two days later when Viktor received a reply to his email. The Commission said they were interested in his offer and asked if he would attend an interview at their offices, Catherine House, 76 Gloucester Place, Marylebone, London. Three options were given for dates and times.

Viktor was pleased and excited. He immediately emailed back confirming the first of the dates and time.

Ian had two jobs he wanted to do in London, but the main purpose of his visit was to deposit Charles's cheque at the Swiss bank in Leadenhall Street and speak to them about setting up a new account for Charles.

From the very early days of Ian's relationship with Andrei, both he and Sergei had recommended that Ian did not put large amounts of money directly into his or Emma's personal UK bank accounts. Instead, Andrei had opened a special Swiss bank account in Ian's name so that all future large payments, made by Andrei to Ian, went directly into this Swiss account. Ian was warned that UK banks have money-laundering teams constantly monitoring large transaction activity and they might just begin to wonder, or worse, ask, where these extra amounts of income were coming from. From that day onwards, Ian had made sure that only his normal income and payments went through his UK personal bank account.

Sergei had also advised Ian about the Swiss bank branch in Leadenhall Street, London. He recommended that he should only use this particular branch in the UK for deposits or withdrawals of any large sums of money. This bank, and his own bank in Switzerland, were both part of a much larger group, so he could access his Swiss account from this branch… with no questions asked!

Ian walked along Leadenhall Street and approached the Swiss bank from the opposite side of the road. He looked across at the ornate five-storey stone facade. It looked as though it belonged to the 19th century. However, once he'd crossed the road and pushed through the large glass entrance door, there was no doubt this was a serious business, very much part of the 21st century.

When Ian entered the small reception area, he noticed the room was subtly lit and the layout simple but plush. There were no cash or deposit machines, no glass-fronted teller counter and certainly no marketing materials on display. There was absolutely nothing to suggest what was going on in the building. In every respect, this was a very personal and private bank and one that you had to be 'invited' to join. Prospective clients were considered only after being recommended. In Ian's case, it was both Andrei and Sergei that had recommended him. It was simply nothing like any other bank Ian had visited before.

Immediately, an attractive young lady, dressed in a navy blue jacket and matching skirt, approached him. Ian guessed she was probably in her early 20s. He knew she would be a highly qualified graduate because he'd been told that the bank prided itself on being very selective and only employed the very top graduates.

"Good morning, sir. My name is Emilie. May I help you?" said the lady, with a welcoming smile.

"Hello, Emilie," replied Ian. "My name's Ian Caxton. I have an appointment with Jeremy Cameron."

"Would you please take a seat over there, Mr. Caxton." Emilie pointed to a dark blue couch. "I will inform Mr. Cameron of your arrival."

Ian walked over to the couch and sat down. He watched Emilie as she walked to the end of a short corridor and disappeared through the rear door. It was all very quiet and he was on his own. All he could hear was the ticking clock on the wall.

Two minutes later, a tall well-dressed man, wearing a grey double-breasted suit, came through the same door and walked over to join him. He held out his right hand.

Ian stood up, smiled and held out his own hand.

"Ian, so good to see you again," greeted the man. They shook hands.

"Hello, Jeremy, how are you keeping... and Julie?" replied Ian. Over recent years Ian had built up more than just a business relationship with Jeremy. He knew Jeremy was about his own age, married to Julie, had two children and was a keen Chelsea football supporter.

"We are all fine, Ian. Your family too, I hope?"

"Yes, life is very good at the moment, thank you."

"Excellent! Let's go through to my office."

The two men walked towards the rear door, where Jeremy pressed six digits on the security keypad and pushed it open. They walked into a short well-lit corridor. Displayed along the walls were four landscape oil paintings of famous views in Switzerland. Ian knew they were originals. The artist had produced such amazing pictures, which, at first glance, most people would think were excellent colour photographs.

Jeremy stopped outside a green door, turned the handle and pushed it open. He invited Ian to enter first. Ian stepped through and looked around the room. It was lavishly furnished. The desk, chairs, bookcase and a large drinks cabinet were built of American white oak. The room was modern and polished to a very high standard; Ian was not used to seeing such opulence in an office outside of those occupied by chief executives.

Jeremy invited Ian to sit down and then walked over to the drinks cabinet. "Can I offer you a drink?"

Ian sat down and smiled. It was just after 2pm and, as Ian

seldomly drank alcohol so early in the day, said, "No, I'm fine, thank you."

Jeremy sat down behind his desk. "So, Ian, what can I do for you today?"

Ian put his hand into the inside pocket of his jacket and withdrew a white envelope containing Charles's cheque. "I would like to deposit this cheque into my account, please." He passed the envelope over to Jeremy.

Jeremy switched on his computer and pressed some keys.

Ian sat back in silence and watched. He was impressed that Jeremy never had to ask him about account numbers or any other personal details.

"There we go, Ian, all done."

Ian nodded. "Thank you."

"Would you like a print of your latest statement?" asked Jeremy. "The interest has recently been added."

"Yes, thank you." Ian knew approximately what the balance was as he could access his account online. However, he didn't know how much interest had accrued.

Jeremy pressed some more keys and Ian heard the nearby printer suddenly spring into life.

Jeremy got up from his seat, collected the print and offered it to Ian. "Obviously all the figures are in Swiss francs, but I have put today's sterling exchange rate on the bottom."

Ian glanced at the statement and Jeremy returned to his chair.

"Everything as you expected it?" asked Jeremy. He still had his computer open and Ian's account on view. "Obviously, that's just the cash situation. It doesn't include the funds and shares you're invested in."

Ian nodded. "Yes, as usual, Jeremy, everything seems to be fine," replied Ian. He was surprised with the amount of interest that had accrued. Swiss interest rates were obviously much better than those currently applying in the UK.

"Excellent. So, Ian, is there anything else I can help you with?"

Ian said there was. He pointed to the 2.6 million Swiss franc entry on his statement. He briefly summarised the circumstances in which the money had come into his possession. He explained that it was really Emma's money and he wanted Jeremy's advice as to what the best way was of gradually transferring the money to Emma's UK bank account.

Jeremy leaned back in his chair and explained the safest and best way, thus avoiding prying eyes on her UK account.

Ian smiled and confirmed he would go with Jeremy's suggestion.

"One more thing," said Ian, pointing over to Jeremy's desk. "That cheque I've just given to you is from a colleague who'll shortly be receiving about 25 million euros and I've suggested he opens a Swiss bank account with you. Can you do that?"

"If you're recommending him, Ian, we certainly can." Jeremy looked at the cheque again. "Tell... Mr. Owen to telephone me and we'll make an appointment."

Directly after the meeting, Ian telephoned Charles and told him to contact Jeremy Cameron at the Swiss bank in Leadenhall Street. He also gave him the phone number. Minutes later, Charles had made the telephone call and an appointment was agreed for the following day.

Chapter 48

Viktor duly attended the interview at the Commission for Looted Art in Europe's offices in Marylebone and met two of its members. It turned out to be very different to any that Viktor had attended before. He spoke briefly about his background but, most of the time, he just listened and asked a few questions. He was fascinated and enthused, but surprised when he was told many German museums were still reluctant to repatriate thousands of proven looted paintings to the rightful owners. The CLAE's restitution successes were still only just over 3,500, just a small percentage of the estimated hundreds of thousands of items still missing or lost.

It was two hours later when Viktor left the CLAE's offices. He'd signed up and agreed to specifically help uncover lost and stolen paintings and drawings. However, he was also warned that when any suspicious paintings were detected he should not, under any circumstances, try to retrieve them himself. That part could often be very tricky, possibly require legal enforcement and could, occasionally, be extremely dangerous!

After he left the interview Viktor decided to go for a walk through nearby Regent's Park. He wanted to think more about what the CLAE people had said and what he'd signed up to do.

The sun was still warm and when he arrived at the edge of the boating lake he stopped and watched a number of people enjoying the hired pedalo and rowing boats. After a few seconds he continued to stroll along the lakeside path. When he spotted an unoccupied bench, in the shade of a large oak tree, he sat down. After taking a few deep breaths he telephoned Ian.

When Ian answered, Viktor explained how the meeting had gone and told him that he was now one of the CLAE's part-time volunteers."

"Well done. So, what does that entail?" asked Ian. He wondered if Viktor had made the right decision.

"In a nutshell, I've got to look out for paintings and drawings that are listed on their database. It's slightly more complex than that, but essentially that's my role."

"I see. Are you happy with that?"

"Yes. I'm really eager to get started."

"Well, I'm really pleased for you, Vic. Have you told Penny?"

"No, she's in a meeting with Jonathan Northgate this afternoon, so I'll tell her later."

"Send her my regards… and also my sympathy for still having to put up with Northgate."

Viktor smiled. Obviously, time hadn't healed the rift between Ian and Jonathan. "I'll do that. So, what are you going to do about your four paintings?"

"Emma and I are going to Monaco in a couple of weeks. Do you want me to ship them directly to you?"

"That would be great. It will show the Commission that I'm really serious. If you address the shipment to my apartment, the concierge will put the parcel in the storeroom until I collect it. I'll make sure the paintings can't be traced back to you."

"Okay. I'll let you know when I've sent them. Goodbye, Vic… and well done."

Ian switched off the call and stood up from the garden bench. He was in the garden and was about to return to cutting the lawn when he heard Emma call. She walked across the patio with two mugs of tea.

"I thought you might like some tea," said Emma, handing Ian one of the mugs.

"Thanks. Vic's just telephoned. He's been accepted for a part-time role with the Commission for Looted Art in Europe. He sounded really excited."

They both sat down on the bench and sipped their teas.

"So, what's his role?"

"Mainly searching for the paintings on the Commission's database. He's still working part time with Alexander as well, so he might unearth something from those visits."

"Isn't it all a bit dangerous?" asked Emma, thinking of the sort of characters he might come across, "If people own stolen paintings, it's most unlikely they'll want to forfeit them, especially if they've paid a lot of money for them."

"He certainly needs to be careful, but I'm sure the Commission has given him proper instructions. At least I hope so."

Chapter 49

Charles's meeting with Jeremy Cameron had gone well and arrangements were made for a new deposit account to be set up in Switzerland.

Once his Swiss online account was live, Charles kept checking it every day, until finally he spotted a new entry, a deposit of 12.5 million euros. Later that afternoon he telephoned Ian.

"Hello, Ian Caxton speaking."

"Ian, hi. Charles Owen."

"Charles, great to hear from you. Everything okay?"

"Yes, really good, thanks. I thought I'd let you know the banker's draft deposit is in my new Swiss bank account and the painting's en route to France as we speak."

"That's great news. You just need to wait for the balance, now."

Charles smiled. "Patience was never one of my strengths. How long do you think it'll take?"

Ian mentally tried to calculate the journey, unpacking and inspection times. "About a week, probably."

"Right," said Charles hesitantly. He'd hoped it would be quicker than that.

"Any developments with the villa in Portugal?"

"I've got a flight booked to Faro in two days' time. The agent is meeting me at the airport."

"They obviously think you're going to buy this property."

"The agent's name is Estela. Chatted to her several times on the phone. She has a lovely accent, so I hope everything else is just as attractive when we meet!"

"Charles, you're incorrigible. What about your London apartment? Have you got a buyer?"

"No, but I think I'm going to let it out. The local estate agent thinks I'll get a good rental income."

"Okay. Let me know when you receive the balance from France… and good luck in Portugal."

Charles laughed at Ian's comment. "Do you mean the villa or…"

"The villa!" interrupted Ian, "But, I'm sure you'll let me know how everything goes."

"Cheers, Ian, and thanks. Thanks for everything. Keep an eye on your post box."

After this final comment, Ian heard the 'click' at Charles's end of the line.

It was ten days later when Emma heard the postman delivering their mail. She was in the kitchen preparing lunch. She picked up the letterbox key, walked through the hall and opened the front door. After unlocking the box, she removed three envelopes.

"Anything of interest?" shouted Ian, from the office, after he heard Emma shut the front door.

"Only this letter addressed to you," replied Emma as she entered the office. "The other two are junk mail."

Ian was sitting at his desk, looking at his computer screen. However, he stopped when Emma handed him the letter. He ripped open the end of the envelope and pulled out the contents. There was a short note with a banker's draft attached. He read the note:

Ian, hi,

   Received the balance from France! Yippee number 1!
   Bought the villa in Portugal! Yippee number 2!
   Will speak to you soon.
   Thanks for everything. Hope the enclosed banker's draft covers your extra expenses!
   Best,
   Charles.

Ian flicked over the stapled note to look at the banker's draft. "Emma, have a look at this."

Emma, who was just about to return to the kitchen, walked over to the front of Ian's desk and took the letter. Like Ian, she read the note first and then looked at the attached banker's draft. "Wow!" she exclaimed. "Five million pounds. Charles certainly knows how to reward you."

"That comes on top of the one million pounds he gave me earlier."

"He obviously recognises the amount of hard work you've put in to help him. Well done you!" Emma handed the note and banker's draft back to Ian. "What are you going to treat me to?"

Chapter 50

When Robert made his weekly telephone call home, he informed his mother that the holiday with Arthur's family was now definitely on, so he reiterated his preferred option. He still wanted to go to Cornwall. Emma was disappointed, but when she told Ian, he said that boys of Robert's age usually want to go on holiday with their friends rather than their parents adding, "Besides, if this Cornwall holiday goes well, maybe we should encourage him to come on holiday with us and invite a friend as well."

On the 19th, Emma delivered Robert to Arthur's parents' house well in time for the planned journey to Cornwall on the 21st. Ian, meanwhile, had arranged their flights to Nice for the 23rd. He'd just managed to secure the last two business class seats on the late afternoon flight. As a result, it was just after 10pm when they arrived at their Monaco apartment. Just enough time for a late evening drink and a shower, before climbing into bed.

At 7.50 the next morning, Ian was up, dressed and sitting in the kitchen with a mug of tea. His laptop computer was open and he'd been reading incoming emails and sending replies since 7am. His final email was to Bob Taylor. He wrote:

Hi Bob,

I hope you and your family are well.

Emma and I have just arrived in Monaco for two weeks. We were wondering if you and Zoe wanted to join us for a meal one evening. I was thinking of the 'Blue Marlin' again, unless you prefer somewhere different. My treat.

I'm also hoping you could help me package up four small paintings and arrange for your carrier to ship them to the UK.

Cheers for now,

Ian.

Once he'd sent the email, Ian made himself another cup of tea and moved outside onto the balcony. Although this side of the building wouldn't get the full impact of the sun until later in the morning, the temperature was already warm. He sipped his tea and watched the early morning activity in the harbour below. Several yachts and ships were preparing for their day's activities. Deliveries were being taken on board and sails were hoisted. Two ships were already heading out towards the Mediterranean Sea. He smiled to himself and knew he would never get bored with this wonderful view.

A few minutes later, he returned to the kitchen and checked his computer again. Bob Taylor had responded:

Hello Ian,

Great to hear from you again. Yes, we would love to join you and Emma for a meal at the 'Blue Marlin'. We have a regular child sitter for Fridays, so the 27th would be ideal for us.

Concerning packing your paintings, etc., no problem. Just pop down to the gallery any time. Either Zoe or I will be available during opening hours.

Hope to see you shortly,

Bob.

Great, thought Ian. Now all I need to do is get the paintings from the vault.

Emma suddenly appeared from the bedroom, wearing her dressing gown. "You were up early."

Ian looked up from his computer. "I woke up at just after six, so decided to get up. I've emailed Bob and Zoe inviting them for a meal at the 'Blue Marlin'. I also wanted to know if Bob would help me with packing and shipping the four paintings to Vic. He's just replied and said yes to both."

"Good. You can tell me the details later. I'm just going to have a shower," Emma replied, walking back towards the bedroom.

"Okay." He decided now was a good time to collect the four paintings.

It was about 35 minutes later when Ian returned carrying the four paintings in a large cardboard box. After placing the box on the floor close to the door, he walked over to his laptop. There was still no sign of Emma, so he sent a further email to Bob, saying he would deliver the paintings later that morning.

Ian and Emma had a late breakfast together and Ian explained the details of his email exchanges with Bob.

Emma ate the last of her scrambled eggs on toast and said, "It will be nice to meet up with Zoe again, and to eat at the 'Blue Marlin' restaurant. The seafood there is wonderful."

"I'll see if I can book the same table as last time. Have you any plans for this morning?"

Emma thought for a second. "Not really, but I do need to properly unpack my suitcase. Why?"

"I'm going to take those paintings to Bob's gallery," said Ian, pointing to the cardboard box.

"Okay. Should I meet you back here, say about one o'clock? We need to get some extra supplies in for meals. We ought to do that this afternoon."

Ian stood up and placed his plate and empty cup at the side of the kitchen sink. "I'll go now. The sooner those paintings have left this property the better."

Chapter 51

When Ian arrived outside the gallery he could see through the window that both Bob and Zoe were in the display area. Zoe appeared to be discussing a painting with a customer. However, when Ian pushed on the door causing the bell to ring, Bob immediately looked up. He came over and held the door wide open, as he could see Ian was struggling carrying a large box. Ian placed the box on the nearby desk and breathed a sigh of relief.

"Heavy, was it?" asked Bob, after closing the door and joining his colleague.

"Not especially, just awkward," replied Ian, wiping his brow.

"So, how's things? We've not chatted for ages."

"I know," replied Ian. He felt a little guilty. "I don't know where the time goes."

"What are these pictures in here?" asked Bob, pointing to the box.

"A long story but, essentially, I acquired them some time ago. Vic did some investigations and established they'd been stolen by the Nazis during the Second World War. Now, I just want to get them back to their rightful owners."

"That's very noble and community spirited of you," teased Bob. "Are these the paintings you were suggesting I might like to sell?"

"Yes. That was before Vic came up with the bombshell that these four are all on the Commission for Looted Art in Europe's database. I didn't want to put you in a difficult position, so I'm sending them on to Vic."

Bob looked a little confused. "Why Vic?"

"Oh, of course, you probably don't know. He's working part time for the Commission."

"Really!" exclaimed Bob. "Vic! He's working for the CLAE! Bit like the poacher turned gamekeeper, isn't it?"

Ian laughed. "Yes, I was a little surprised too, but it made me think. Hence getting these paintings sent to the Commission."

"Okay, let's get them into the back room and packed. My courier usually arrives at about four o'clock."

Ian picked up the box and followed Bob through the display area and into the packing room. Between the two of them, they managed to parcel up the paintings in about 20 minutes.

"Come and say hello to Zoe whilst I make some coffee." Bob led Ian back into the display area where they saw Zoe saying goodbye to the customer. After the customer had left the premises, Bob called out, "Look who we've got here!"

Zoe walked over with a big smile on her face. She and Ian greeted each other with a kiss on both cheeks.

"It's so good to see you again, Ian… and how's Emma?" asked Zoe.

Bob whispered that he'd make the coffee and walked away.

"She's fine and looking forward to our meal on Friday."

"We are too. We've not been back to the 'Blue Marlin' since the last time with you."

"We had such a good evening, I thought we ought to do it again."

"You and Emma must come over to us for a meal before you go back to the UK."

"That would be nice. I'll tell Emma."

"Is it just a holiday that brings you to Monaco this time, or is there any business involvement?"

"No business, except Bob is sending a parcel to the UK for me. Otherwise, it's just a holiday."

"Here's your coffee," announced Bob, rejoining them. He placed the tray on the desk.

"So, Mr. Caxton, how's the art world treating you?" asked Bob, handing Ian a mug before passing another to Zoe.

"We are doing okay. Emma's more involved now and doing some buying and selling herself. What about you two?"

Bob and Zoe looked at each other wondering who was going to respond. Eventually Bob spoke, "It's been a bit mixed to tell you the truth. We're okay, turnover is good, but it could be better. It's the expenses that are the main issue. It's costly to live in Monaco and the children's school fees keep increasing."

"My father's health has also deteriorated," interrupted Zoe, "so we've been involved with his medical costs too. My brother helps, but it's still expensive for all of us."

"I'm sorry to hear that," replied Ian, with genuine sympathy. "Your father's been unwell for some time."

Zoe nodded and a tear began to appear in her right eye.

"Yes," said Bob, "the old boy has been struggling for a while with Alzheimer's."

"Must be tough on your mum as well."

Again, Zoe nodded, but now she was more composed and able to speak. "My father had to go into a home about four months ago. For my mother, it was a blessing, but with deep sadness."

Ian nodded, "Yes, I can see that."

Zoe was eager to change the subject. "How's Robert now? It's been a while since we last saw him."

"He's getting on well at school, made lots of friends and appears to be enjoying his school work. At the moment, he's holidaying with one of his friends and their family. Said he preferred his pal's company over his parents."

Both Bob and Zoe smiled.

"I recognise that one," said Bob, with feeling.

"Emma's got some photographs on her phone, so I'm sure you can both exchange stories and experiences on Friday."

"I'll look forward to that," said Zoe. "It's quite some time since we've eaten out with friends."

Ian felt sorry for Bob and Zoe's predicament. He just hoped things would pick up again… and quite soon. "It will be a lovely evening, I'm sure."

They all turned around when they heard the gallery's doorbell ring. Zoe made her apologies and went over to speak to the customer.

"I'd better get back to Emma. She'll be wondering where I am. What do I owe you for the packing and postage?" asked Ian.

"That's alright, Ian, don't worry about it."

"Are you sure?"

"Ian, things aren't quite that bad, not yet, anyway," replied Bob, but Ian could sense some worry in Bob's voice.

Both walked towards the door. Ian waved to Zoe and shook Bob's hand. "See you on Friday at 7.30." Ian looked at his friend, but the bubbly character he was used to was definitely not there.

Ian walked slowly back towards 'Harbour Heights'. He was concerned about Bob and Zoe and hoped their money problems were just short term. He began to wonder whether he should try and help them out. The issue with Zoe's father was obviously a financial and emotional drain on both Bob and on Zoe's family.

Chapter 52

Viktor entered his apartment building through the large glass entrance doors and strolled across the expansive reception area towards the security entrance. He was still thinking about the strange viewing he and Alexander had just completed. It was a few seconds before he began to register that his name was being called.

"Mr. Kuznetsov!"

Viktor stopped walking and looked around. He then realised it was Frank, one of the concierge team, who was calling him. He changed direction and walked over to the reception desk.

"You have a parcel, Mr. Kuznetsov. I've put it in the storeroom."

The only parcel Viktor was expecting was the one from Ian. "Thank you, Frank. I'll leave it there for the time being and collect it in a day or two."

Frank nodded. "That's fine, Mr. Kuznetsov, I'll put a note on it to say you've been informed."

Viktor smiled. "Thank you, Frank." He then proceeded towards the security entrance where he presented his security pass and was waved through.

As Viktor entered the elevator he was still thinking about his earlier viewing with Alexander. They had been

241

to 'Chestnut Villa', a large detached Victorian building, located in Twickenham. He'd assumed he was only going to be required to carry out his usual valuation and certainly wasn't anticipating anything out of the ordinary. All he knew was that, up until one week ago, two Russian Embassy employees had been renting the property. However, when Viktor arrived at the front door of 'Chestnut Villa', he found it open and Alexander and the rental agent talking in the hallway. He had heard the agent informing Alexander that the house didn't come fully furnished, so most of the contents were owned by the tenants.

Alexander had spotted Viktor and introduced him to the rental agent, Anil Patel. Viktor shook hands and then listened when Anil continued speaking. "The tenants were present last Monday morning because the postman spoke to one of them. However, by 4pm, they'd packed their suitcases and boarded the 19.42 flight to Moscow. They left this short note on the kitchen table, giving me these details. This note was not discovered until three days later when the cleaner arrived to carry out her weekly clean. Earlier that same morning, the postman informed us, there were several bottles of milk still standing on the step next to the front door. Properties in this part of Twickenham are mostly occupied as short-term rentals. We, like a number of the other local rental agents, unofficially pay the postman a small retainer to inform us if he spots anything out of the ordinary at any of these rental properties."

Viktor was not sure what was going on, but Alexander nodded to Anil, so it was obviously making sense to him.

Anil continued, still flicking the note in his hand from side to side, "I'm not interested in a valuation, I just want a quotation to clear all the contents and temporarily store them. I've got people on my books who are looking for similar short-term rental properties in this area."

Alexander could see the problem. He was prepared to quote for temporary storage until such time as the agent could obtain further instructions from the Russian tenants. However, he also stated that he'd experienced this sort of situation before and insisted the agent sign a storage contract before anything was moved. That way, the storage payment was guaranteed.

Anil had been amenable to this condition as he was holding three months' rent, paid in advance.

The three men had then walked through the property while Alexander and Viktor made their usual notes.

The elevator arrived at the top floor. Viktor stepped out and walked along the passageway to his and Penny's apartment. He let himself in, tossed the door key into a nearby metal bowl and wandered into the dining room, which doubled up as his office. He placed his notebook on the table and, from a small pile of files on the floor, picked up the one titled 'CLAE Database' and placed it next to his notebook.

Sitting down, he opened up his notebook and reread the notes he'd written whilst at 'Chestnut Villa'. He had a really strange feeling about the pictures he'd seen.

However, after reading through all the pages of the database, his investigations came to nothing. None of the pictures were listed. Nevertheless, he was still curious and decided to establish each picture's provenance. Did the two Russians actually own them? They were poor quality. Could they be copies or deliberate fakes? Why would these Russians own such mediocre pictures?

It was about two hours later when Viktor received a telephone call. It was from Alexander and he wasn't pleased.

"Vic, hi," said Alexander. His voice was more serious than normal.

Viktor wondered if he had upset him. "Hello, Alexander," he said, cautiously.

"I've just had a visit from the police," stated Alexander. He now had a slightly angry tone to his voice. "It's about that bloody house we visited this morning. The police wouldn't tell me much, but they did ask a lot of questions. Asked me why we were there? Were we friends of the occupants? Had we taken anything away? Things like that. They really pissed me off and I told them to talk to the agent. Anyway, I thought I'd let you know because they also wanted your name, address and telephone number."

Viktor was shocked and immediately concerned. "Okay... thanks for letting me know."

"If they do call on you, Vic, be careful. I think one of them could be MI5."

"MI5!" exclaimed Viktor. "But we didn't do anything."

"They were going to speak to the agent next, so hopefully he'll explain the background. You might not get the visit, but I thought I'd better warn you."

"Yes, well, thanks, Alexander, I'll let you know if they call."

"Cheers, Vic... and good luck."

Viktor ended the call. What the hell's going on! Suddenly, panic set in. He quickly thought about anything in his apartment that shouldn't be there. After a few minutes, however, he couldn't think of anything that could potentially be construed as incriminating. He slowly began to calm down and made himself a cup of coffee. After all, he thought, I know I've got nothing to hide, for goodness' sake. I'm even part of CLAE. Then he remembered Ian's pictures in the storeroom. What if the police want to know why I have stolen paintings in my possession?

Starting to panic again, Viktor picked up his mobile phone and dialled Anne, his direct contact at the CLAE. After two rings Anne answered his call.

Vic tried his best to calm his nerves and speak in his normal voice. "Anne, good afternoon, it's Vic."

"Hello, Vic," replied Anne, "you sound a bit out of breath. Are you okay?"

"Yes, fine, thanks. I've just been doing some exercises, trying to keep fit and all that," replied Viktor. Even to him, it sounded like a lame excuse. "The reason I'm ringing is I've received four paintings that are on the Commission's database."

"Oh, well done."

"Thanks, but the tricky thing is they've been donated anonymously."

"Okay, I understand. We don't mind how we get the paintings. Nobody here will ask any questions. Are you going to bring them into the office or do you need them collected?"

Viktor hadn't thought about this. "Ah," he replied, trying to make a quick decision. "Maybe it would be safer if somebody collected them. Not the sort of thing to carry around on the Underground."

"That's fine. I'll get David Thomas out to your address later this afternoon. Would four o'clock be okay?"

"Four o'clock would be great. Thanks. Tell David I'll meet him in our reception area."

"I'll do that. Well done, Vic. You're going to make somebody very happy."

"I hope so."

When Viktor switched off his phone he decided his best option, between now and four o'clock, was to get out of the apartment, go for a walk, do anything but stay here. If the police did turn up, he wouldn't be here. That would buy him some time.

Chapter 53

It was 3.55pm when Viktor returned to his apartment building. He walked through the entrance doors and into the reception foyer. He was both pleased and relieved to see that there was only one man standing at the reception desk talking to Frank, the concierge. After what Alexander had told him, he assumed the police, if they did come to see him, would send more than just one person.

He walked guardedly towards the reception desk to enquire if anyone had called and specifically asked for him. However, when Frank spotted Viktor approaching, he immediately pointed towards him and said to the man, "Here he is."

The man talking to Frank turned around and walked over to join Viktor. Viktor thought he was probably about 50. He was tall and well dressed in a dark blue suit, and appeared very fit. Viktor's heart began to race. Was this the police after all? he wondered.

"Hello, Viktor," said the man, holding out his hand. "David Thomas from the CLAE. I gather you've got some paintings for us."

Viktor could have kissed the man on the spot. He held out his own hand and David shook it. "Thanks for coming," said Viktor, breathing a sigh of relief. "Yes, they're in the storeroom. I'll ask Frank to get them."

"You'd better look at this first," said David, who proceeded to remove a plastic CLAE identity card from his wallet. Viktor inspected the card and then nodded as he had a similar card of his own.

Viktor turned around and asked Frank if he would collect the parcel. Frank nodded and walked towards the door marked 'Storeroom'.

"This is a nice place, Vic. Been here long?" asked David, looking all around him.

"Just over two years. Since the regeneration, this part of Docklands has become really trendy."

David smiled. "I can just remember when it was the old port. My grandad used to work here and Dad used to bring me sometimes, usually on a Saturday. I think I was about seven. It's certainly a lot different now."

Viktor nodded and showed David the guide he'd picked up earlier whilst out on his walk. David looked at some of the old photographs and pointed to some of the buildings he remembered.

Frank returned carrying the parcel. Viktor looked at the labels and noticed Bob Taylor's gallery name stamped on the side.

"Yes, that's it. Thanks."

Frank smiled and walked away.

"Let's go over there," said Viktor, pointing. He then lifted and carried the parcel over to a large wooden table. After lightly placing it down, he used his penknife to slit the top open.

The two of them carefully removed the four paintings from their protective packaging, laid them on the table and examined and commented on each one. At the end of their discussions, Viktor used his mobile phone to take several photographs. David, meanwhile, wrote some notes in his book and then handed Viktor a receipt.

As they repacked the box, Viktor said, "That's the first time I've seen these paintings. They're in good condition."

David nodded his agreement. "I understand they've been anonymously donated."

"Yes, I think the owner inherited them. Somebody I know informed him they were on the Commission's wanted list, so he got in touch with me."

"Very honest of him. They must be worth quite a bit of money."

"They will be to the rightful owners. Otherwise they're just stolen property."

"I guess so. Somebody's going to be happy."

Viktor smiled. Not as happy as I am right now, he thought.

David secured the parcel as best he could and picked it up. It was not heavy, just a bit cumbersome. "Well, Viktor, it's been nice meeting you. I'd better be off otherwise the office will be closed before I get back."

Viktor walked with David towards the large glass doors and opened one wide enough for David to step through.

"Have you got far to walk?" asked Viktor. He wondered whether he should go with him.

"No, my car's in your underground car park."

"Okay. I'll walk with you, just in case anyone decides to mug you!"

Both men laughed and then walked down the slope at the side of the building before turning into the underground car park.

Ten minutes later, Viktor arrived back in the reception area and thanked Frank again for his help. To his relief, Frank didn't mention whether anyone else had been asking for him.

Chapter 54

Ian and Emma arrived at the 'Blue Marlin' at 7.25pm. The restaurant's ambience hadn't changed. The walls were still adorned with timber boards painted in different tones of blue and old fishing equipment was hanging, maybe a little precariously, from parts of the ceiling and the walls.

The maître d' walked over and welcomed them. Ian informed him of his booking and the maître d' led them to the same table they'd used before, the one with the lovely harbour view. He ordered two gin and tonics and explained their guests were running late, but would be arriving shortly. The maître d' nodded and said their drinks would be sent over immediately.

Their drinks duly arrived and Ian reminded Emma about their earlier discussions concerning Bob and Zoe's financial situation.

"Yes, I've been thinking about that," responded Emma. Initially she'd been alarmed but now she was worried. "Do you think we should offer Bob and Zoe some sort of short-term financial help?"

"I'd certainly like to help Bob," responded Ian, with genuine sympathy. "He was a good friend to me at university and I think both of them could do with some short-term help."

"It must be very difficult for Zoe. She's got the children

to look after, her mother is living on her own, her father is ill and she's trying to share in the running of a business."

"I want to do something," repeated Ian. "I've been thinking about their situation ever since I left the gallery, but the big question is, what can we do?"

"Do you want me to talk to Zoe? If you suggest it to Bob, he might be too proud to accept our help."

Ian thought about Emma's suggestion and replied, "It might be better coming from you… woman to woman, as it were. Ah! here they come. Are you sure you'll be okay with doing that?"

"I'll have a go," she replied and they both stood up to greet their approaching guests.

Between the main course and desserts, Zoe decided she needed a break and stood up. Emma seized the opportunity and said she would join her. The two men were left laughing and reminiscing about their time at university.

It was about 15 minutes later when the ladies returned, just as their desserts were being placed on the table. As Emma sat down, she glanced at Ian and gave him a smile. Ian assumed the smile was a hint that she'd been able to have a positive conversation with Zoe.

Over coffee, Zoe insisted that Ian and Emma must come to dinner at their apartment before they went back to the UK. She promised she'd prepare a traditional French meal, one her mother had introduced to her. Emma said it sounded wonderful and, after some discussion, it was agreed for the following Tuesday.

A few minutes later, Zoe reminded Bob that their child sitter was due to leave fairly soon. Ian paid the bill, adding a nice tip, and they left the restaurant together. It was still warm outside so they slowly walked alongside the harbour. At the corner of the next street, they all said their goodbyes and Ian and Emma headed in the direction of 'Harbour Heights'.

Ian then asked Emma if she'd spoken to Zoe.

"Yes. She was very surprised that we'd been discussing their financial situation, but I pointed out that, as we were good friends, we were concerned and didn't like to hear there were problems. She then began to relax, but also became a little emotional and explained she was very worried. More worried than she'd let on to Bob. It's all due to the additional cost of her parents. The other costs are okay, they'd always been properly budgeted for but, with her parents, it was more personal and she felt it was unfair on Bob."

When they arrived at the side of the 'Harbour Heights' building, Ian and Emma stopped walking and sat on a wooden bench which looked out over the harbour.

Emma continued, "I told Zoe we wanted to help. I also explained that I was talking to her because we both felt Bob might be too proud to accept our help. Again, she became a little emotional and said it was her family's problem. Bob had been unfairly dragged in. I reminded her of the marriage vows – 'for better, for worse' – and suggested Bob would be just as anxious because of her and the children. Zoe gave me a hug. It's obvious they're pretty desperate."

Ian nodded and bit his bottom lip.

"We finished our discussion when Zoe promised she would think about our offer and tell me their decision next Tuesday."

Ian was still looking at Emma, but wasn't sure what to say. The sea breeze strengthened and they suddenly felt a chill.

"Thank you," said Ian. "It was obviously a difficult conversation. Come on, let's get back to our apartment. I guess we'll just have to wait until next week."

They stood up from the bench. Suddenly Emma gave Ian a big hug and whispered in his ear, "I hope we don't have similar problems with our parents in the coming years."

Chapter 55

For the next few days, Ian and Emma continued to enjoy their time on holiday. They'd been on several local walks, stopping off for lunch or afternoon tea. One day they'd travelled to Nice by train. This journey was a particular favourite of theirs, especially as the route follows much of the Mediterranean coast and affords wonderful views out to sea.

It was now Monday afternoon and, after their latest walk, Ian and Emma found themselves passing Bob and Zoe's gallery. Emma stopped when she spotted a colourful seascape oil painting on show in the window.

"Look at this, Ian," she said, pointing at the picture. "It would look wonderful in the apartment."

Ian stepped closer and stared at the picture. "Mmm, I like it too. Very fresh and Mediterranean. The artist has a nice touch."

"We've been talking about hanging new paintings on the walls for ages, especially to cover where Andrei used to display his collection. The walls look so bare."

Ian nodded. He could see Emma's point. "I wonder if Bob has got any more by the same artist?" Ian looked closer at the painting to try and identify the artist's signature.

"Let's go in and give them a surprise," said Emma. She was eager to have a closer look at the picture.

Before Ian could reply, Emma had pushed open the door and stepped inside. Ian followed and closed the door behind him.

"Well, well, well," announced Bob, when he spotted them. "You're a bit early for dinner. It's not until tomorrow evening… I think!" He walked over to join them.

Emma and Ian laughed and then Emma spoke, "We've just been out for a walk and found ourselves passing your gallery, so we had a look in your window."

"And did you find anything you liked?" asked Bob, hopefully.

"Yes, we did," responded Emma.

"Right, let me guess." Bob walked over to the main window and glanced at the five paintings on display. "Okay," he said, pondering and stroking his cheek, "I think you like the Amelie Moreau… her seascape. Yes, that would be to your taste."

"That's right. How did you know?" asked Emma. She was staggered with Bob's deduction.

"He saw you standing outside and pointing to the picture," replied a female voice. It was Zoe, walking towards them from the display area.

"Now you've spoiled my fun," said Bob, and they all laughed.

Zoe joined them and greetings were exchanged.

"Let me get the painting so you can see it better." Bob reached into the window display area, removed the seascape painting and placed it onto a nearby vacant easel. "There you are. Nice, isn't it?" he said, switching on two soft spotlights.

Emma and Ian stepped forward to have a closer look.

"I really like it," announced Emma, "It's so French… and Mediterranean."

Ian nodded and asked, "Is the artist related to Gustave Moreau?"

Emma looked at Ian and wondered who Gustave Moreau was.

"Not that we're aware," answered Zoe. "I'll have to ask her."

"Styles are completely different," stated Bob, "but, you never know, if they are related, the painting skills must be in the genes."

Ian could see Emma was wondering who they were talking about. "He was a 19th century French artist," he explained. "A lot of his work involved religious and mythological subjects."

"I think I prefer this sort of painting," said Emma, looking again at the picture. "How much is it?"

Bob and Zoe glanced at each other and Zoe said, "We're advertising it for 10,000 euros, but we can give our friends a 10% discount."

"We'll take it!" insisted Emma.

"See," said Bob, removing the painting from the easel, "I said it was to your taste."

They all smiled.

"Have you got any more examples of this lady's paintings?" asked Ian. He was genuinely impressed with the quality of her work.

"Not at the moment," announced Zoe. "She's only 24 years of age, but I think she has real talent and a big future. She's given me a small catalogue of her work and told me she would paint commission work too. I've got her catalogue in my desk drawer... somewhere. Let me see if I can find it."

They all walked over to the desk area and whilst Zoe searched the drawers, Bob placed the painting on the desktop.

"Yes, here we are," announced Zoe, holding a booklet which consisted of just a few pages of colour photographs. She passed it over to Emma.

Emma looked at each page whilst Ian peered over her shoulder.

"As you can see," interrupted Zoe, "her style is definitely suited to coastal views."

"Her work's very impressive. I like these two." Emma pointed to two pictures with similar Mediterranean scenes. "Do you know how much they'd cost?"

Zoe walked across and looked at the photographs Emma was pointing at. "I've got her price list in the drawer as well." She opened the drawer again, found an A4 sheet and ran her finger down the listing. "They're the same size as the painting you've just bought and both are listed at the same price. For you they would be 9,000 euros each. I can telephone her and get the paintings delivered here for tomorrow. You'll be able to see them before we have dinner."

"Do you want me to pack this one up now, or would you prefer to take it with you tomorrow?" asked Bob. He was about to take the picture down to the packing room.

Emma looked at Ian, who said, "Let's leave it with you until tomorrow. That way we can see all three paintings side by side."

Bob and Zoe smiled and then Zoe announced, "I'll telephone Amelie, immediately."

Chapter 56

Although the dinner appointment had been set for 7.30, Ian and Emma arrived at the gallery at 7pm so they could look at the three Amelie Moreau paintings all together.

Bob had just finished rearranging three easels and was now adding the pictures. When he heard the doorbell ring, he walked over to greet his guests. "Nicely on time. Come and see the paintings. I've set them up so you can see what the collection would look like if they were all hanging together."

"Can we put these down first?" asked Ian, waving two bottles of champagne. Emma also had a colourful bouquet of flowers.

Bob took the flowers from Emma and laid them on the desk. Ian placed the two bottles next to the flowers. All three then walked over to the easels where the pictures were being specially lit by soft spotlights.

"I've been looking forward to this moment all day!" announced Emma, excitedly.

"Well, let's hope you won't be disappointed," replied Bob. He had two fingers crossed.

Ian and Emma initially viewed the collection from about three metres away. There they could gauge the impact of the collection side by side. They then stepped forward to look at each painting individually.

"You know, Bob," said Ian, still staring at each painting, "this lady has a real talent. Have you signed up to be her agent?"

Bob stepped forward and smiled. "You're the first people to show such a serious interest, so no, I guess that's something Zoe and I need to try and do… and quickly. She's really Zoe's client."

"I really like them," interrupted Emma. "They look fabulous together. I love the hint of abstract and the colours. So Mediterranean, but also quite subtle."

Bob smiled, hoping for the final commitment.

Ian put his hand into his jacket pocket and pulled out an already completed cheque. He handed it over to Bob saying, "We'll take all three!"

"That's excellent! I'm really pleased. Zoe's going to be ecstatic." He looked at the cheque and his face changed. "But you've made it out for 30,000 euros. We agreed on 27,000."

Ian smiled, and then said, "Worth every euro of 30,000 to us, Bob. This artist has real potential. These three paintings will be worth twice that amount in five, maybe seven, years' time."

"I think this deserves a celebration." Bob was excited for Zoe.

"That's what the champagne's for," responded Ian.

Bob was feeling a little emotional. "Let's collect everything from the desk and we'll go upstairs. Zoe is probably just finishing preparing our meal… she's going to be over the moon when she hears the good news."

Indeed, when Bob explained the details of the sale to Zoe, she was a little emotional. Emma walked over to give her a big hug.

The champagne flowed and the traditional French

chicken casserole, with added Chablis, rosemary and a number of other herbs and spices from Zoe's mother's recipe, was excellent.

After they'd cleared the table and the ladies were in the kitchen, Emma took the opportunity to ask Zoe if she'd been able to speak to Bob about their offer of helping out with their financial situation.

Zoe paused from loading the dishwasher and leaned back against the sink. She looked across to Bob who was in deep conversation with Ian on the far side of the room. "Bob's always the optimist, I'm more realistic, but we did have a long talk the other evening. He thought that if we could increase the turnover, everything else would be alright."

"But surely," interrupted Emma, "that puts more pressure on you. You've still got all your parents' problems, your children to care for and your share in running the business. It's just too much."

"Bob doesn't quite see it that way. His focus is on the business. I'm the one that's juggling all the balls. To be fair though, he does get involved with the children and their school runs. He also covers for me in the gallery when I have to go over to see my mother, or my father. Things were okay until my father became ill. In some ways, Bob blames my parents for the extra pressure being put on us and our outgoings."

"It's not really their fault," said Emma, "most of us get old... eventually."

"I know, and deep down, so does Bob, but it's just the extra financial pressure. We're having to eat into our savings, and they're not going to last forever. You and Ian buying those three paintings has really helped us... at least for a few months."

Emma smiled. At least we have been able to help, a little, she thought. "Ian and I have been talking and agreed that we would like to offer you a loan. You could pay us back when times are much better."

"Bob's been talking to the bank about a loan, but it's difficult because this building, and the two either side of us, are owned by my father. We tried to get him to transfer this building into my name, but his generation doesn't see the benefit of doing that. Now, with his illness, it's all become complicated and he can't make that decision."

"If you don't mind me asking, Zoe, what amount of money was Bob hoping to borrow?"

"We initially applied for 400,000 euros, but that was refused. We then applied for 350,000, and that was refused too. We tried to persuade the bank manager that the business could cover that amount, but he wanted the security of putting that amount of money against the property. Being in Monaco, the bank knows this building is probably worth four to five million euros."

Emma could see their difficulty. "Have you spoken to your brother about financing your parents' situation?"

"We've discussed it many times since father was diagnosed. He's in a similar situation to us. The big problem is our father is property rich but the family is cash poor. I know it's all relative and we're much better off than a lot of people, but…"

Emma shook her head in frustration. "Look, Zoe, please talk to Bob again. We hate to see you in this situation. After all, it's not your fault. We'll gladly lend you the 400,000 euros. Just pay us back when you can."

Tears began to well up in Zoe's eyes. She looked across at Bob, who was still talking to Ian and pointing out through the window. She looked back at Emma and gave her a hug. Zoe whispered, "I'll speak to him tomorrow. I don't know how he'll take it, but, thank you. I really don't know how to thank you enough."

Even Emma's eyes were beginning to moisten.

It was just after 10.30am the next day when Ian and Emma arrived back at the gallery. Bob was waiting for them. He'd already parcelled up the three paintings and they were ready to go.

When Ian and Emma walked through the door, Bob immediately joined them, kissed Emma on both cheeks and shook Ian's hand. He was feeling quite emotional.

"Are you okay, Bob?" asked Ian, with concern.

Bob took a deep breath before speaking. "Zoe told me this morning about your generous offer of a loan. It's so kind of you both but, seriously, I can't take it, not from friends. It's too much of a risk for you."

Ian and Emma looked at each other in surprise. Emma was the first to react. "That's exactly what friends are for. We want to help you both. Think of Zoe, think of the stress she's going through at the moment. There's Antoine's medical costs, Zoe's mother, the children's school fees, the time Zoe's having to allocate to her parents and trying to do her share in the gallery… and looking after you. A lot of women would have had a breakdown by now."

Bob was feeling a bit shell-shocked with Emma's outburst.

Even Ian raised his eyebrows slightly in surprise. "Emma's right, Bob. If this loan gets you back on track, well that's great for everyone. There's no pressure on paying us back either. Just pay us when you can."

Bob looked from Ian to Emma and then back to Ian. "Zoe wants us to take your kind offer, but this is difficult…"

Ian placed his right hand on Bob's shoulder and looked directly into his eyes. "We know it's not easy. You're a proud man, but sometimes you have to think about others too – Zoe and your kids, Zoe's parents and what their family has given you. Look around you, Bob. Did you ever think you would be living here in Monaco, be a partner in this gallery, have such a wonderful wife and kids? Come on Bob, swallow that pride. You owe it to these lovely people."

Bob's bottom lip started to quiver and he could feel a tear welling up. After quickly brushing it away with his hand, he looked at Emma, who was nodding her agreement. "Okay, I know what you say all makes sense and, maybe I'm being too selfish, but it's such a lot of money, I need to do something… "

"No, you don't, Bob," interrupted Ian, continuing his relaxed tone. "We can afford the loan and, more than anything else, we want you and Zoe, our very good friends, to be happy, relaxed and able to carry on without the stress you've both been living with recently. When we next visit Monaco, we want to see the usual happy Taylor faces and the big smiles. Zoe's parents aren't going to live forever so, in the meantime, mate, take our offer to get you through this temporary glitch."

Bob began to nod his head. He then gave Ian a hug.

Tears, but this time tears of joy, were beginning to well up within Emma too. She walked over and patted Bob on the shoulder.

Chapter 57

It was just over two hours later when Ian and Emma were back in their apartment. They'd just finished unwrapping the three new paintings and were deciding where each should be placed.

Since Andrei's departure from the apartment, the only painting left hanging was an oil painting titled 'Rose in a Glass Vase', painted by William Nicholson. This was the picture that Ian had 'acquired' all those years ago in Moscow, but had subsequently sold on to Andrei. Obviously, it was one of Andrei's little jokes to leave it behind to surprise Ian. Emma knew the story about Ian's trip to Russia for Andrei, but she still didn't know the full circumstances or, indeed, the reasons why this particular painting was still in the apartment.

Ian held one of the new pictures against the wall, whilst Emma weighed up whether that was the correct painting for that particular location. This exercise went on for some time until Ian started to complain about his aching arms. Once Emma was happy, she swapped places with Ian and he had a look. Eventually they agreed and, with the use of a hammer and tape measure they'd borrowed from Bob, plus hooks and pencils they'd already found in the apartment, the three Amelie Moreau oil paintings were finally on display.

Emma stood in the middle of the lounge and slowly looked around the room. Yes, she was satisfied with the new paintings and their locations. Also, the bare walls were finally decorated with excellent and interesting pictures.

Ian walked over to stand next to Emma. "They really suit this room. A lovely Mediterranean feel in the apartment."

Emma nodded. "But, we've still got that bare wall over there," she said, pointing to the one remaining wall where there were no pictures. "Maybe we could commission Amelie to paint the view looking back across the harbour with this apartment building in the background."

"It's a thought," said Ian, but he was not totally convinced. "Let's leave it until we come back next time. Then we can see everything with fresh eyes."

"Okay."

Ian nodded and smiled.

"Do you know what I fancy for dinner tonight?" asked Emma.

"What? The fridge is almost empty."

"Seafood at the 'Blue Marlin'. It's our last evening and these paintings have given me an appetite for a Mediterranean fish meal."

Ian smiled. "I'd better see if I can book a table."

In Antigua, the extension building work to Oscar's villa had been completed. All that remained outstanding was the final coats of paint to the internal walls and ceilings. May had spent many hours on the internet and visiting shops in St. John's. She'd been looking at various furniture items, fittings, curtains and other decorative accessories.

Oscar had earlier been involved with the selection process and made his own suggestions. However, after serious debates with May, he eventually decided that, in the interest of a continuing harmonious relationship, he'd let May decide for herself. He would only make a stand where he really didn't like something. Fortunately, Oscar soon realised that May had really good taste when it came to interior design.

The existing front bedroom, previously being used as a temporary office and dumping area for most of May's possessions, had now been converted into a dressing room complete with a bank of fitted wardrobes for all May's clothes and shoes. The new extension contained a purpose-built office for both Oscar's and May's use, an extra ensuite bedroom for guests and a substantial garage and workshop.

Interspersed between the time spent on choosing all the new furnishings, Oscar and May's art businesses continued to grow and flourish. May's marketing of the Caribbean paintings in China and Hong Kong was slowly paying dividends. Wesley, the owner of the 'Shell Gallery', was impressed to see his turnover figures increase by 30%.

After another busy day, Oscar and May had decided to have a relaxing early pre-dinner rum cocktail on the patio. They were now sitting on loungers and watching the sun slowly set over the sea. Other than when it was raining, this event had become a nightly ritual ever since May had made her first visit. She adored the constantly warm evenings and was fascinated by the sounds of nature in the background, the sea breeze rustling through the palm trees and the dusk calls made by the various species of tree frogs. It was all so different to her experiences living and growing up in Hong Kong. There, the road traffic sounds and people's voices were the dominant and constant noise. Now she felt more at peace, relaxed and happy with her life.

Oscar sipped his rum cocktail and reflected on a successful day. He'd just finished decorating May's new dressing room. He took a deep and satisfied intake of breath.

May looked across to him and smiled. "Happy with

yourself, now that you've finished my dressing room?" she asked.

"I will be after tomorrow, once we've relocated your dressing table and the rest of the furniture in there," said Oscar.

"We can then start on the extension properly," responded May. "There'll be a lot more room in the office now and we can get on and decorate it. Then we can put the office furniture and equipment into their proper places."

Oscar's idea of a brief respite from all his manual activity had suddenly vanished. He could make an excuse by saying he had to visit a client but, deep down, he wanted to get the extension completed as quickly as May did. "Slave driver!" was his immediate response but when he saw May sit up with a stern face, he replied, "Okay. It'll be great to get the office up and running properly. Definitely better than trying to work from the kitchen table."

May resumed her position on the lounger and closed her eyes. Her mind focused once more on the soothing chatter of the tree frogs. Suddenly, she heard a large thud. "What was that?" she asked, immediately sitting up again.

"Just a coconut falling from that tree," announced Oscar, pointing to a coconut palm about ten metres away. "We've now got some fresh coconut milk for breakfast."

Oscar got up from his lounger and walked across the patio to where the coconut had landed. He picked it up and walked back to May. "I'll take this into the kitchen, then get started on the salad for dinner. It'll take me a few minutes to dress the crab."

"Okay. I cooked it this morning. It's in the fridge, so it should be cool enough by now," said May, picking up her drink. "I'll join you in a few minutes."

Oscar strolled towards the villa carrying the coconut and his cocktail.

May sipped her drink and then placed the glass back

on the small wooden table at her side. She lay back on the lounger and closed her eyes again. Her mind began to wander. She thought of her mother, so frail now, old, partially deaf and living in a care home. She had not seen or spoken to her for nearly a year, although she'd sent her letters and received a few in return. Whilst it was nice to read her mother's news, it was always a challenge trying to control her emotions. Even now, just thinking about her mother, a small tear appeared in her left eye. Unrealistic, she knew, but it would have been wonderful for her mother to see her new life.

May brushed away the tear, sat up and took another sip of her drink. She looked back at the villa, the new extension and then spotted Oscar through the kitchen window, preparing her meal. She knew he would call her when everything was ready, so she placed her drink back on the table, stood up and slowly walked towards the coconut palm. She stared up at the remaining bunch of coconuts slowly swaying back and forth. The evening breeze was now a little stronger so she decided to move away and stroll over to the clipped hibiscus hedge. Here there was an uninterrupted view of the beach and the Caribbean Sea. It was almost a full moon and the reflections lit up a white streaky glow on the inky black water. May watched as the small waves rose up before quietly collapsing on the sandy beach. A small line of surf temporarily remained on the seashore, before slowly disappearing into the sand. She and Oscar swam in this lovely warm water almost every day. She took a deep breath of the lovely fresh sea air. This was her new life. She felt so lucky… and, finally, so happy.

Suddenly she heard Oscar calling.

Chapter 58

It was ten days after Ian and Emma had returned from Monaco when Robert arrived home from his holiday. When Emma asked him what he'd been doing in Cornwall, Robert listed swimming, surfing, horse riding, beach-buggy racing, walking and tree climbing… in the woods at the back of Arthur's parents' holiday home. In summary, the holiday was brilliant!

Emma was astonished and realised Robert wouldn't have been doing those sorts of activities in Monaco. "Would you like Arthur to come on holiday with the three of us?" asked Emma, but she already had an idea what his reply was going to be.

"I don't know," Robert replied seriously. "The apartment is nice, but there's not much to do. Maybe if we went somewhere more interesting, where there's more for Arthur and me to do."

That's probably a fair comment, she thought. Whilst there is the possibility of swimming in the Mediterranean, maybe Ian and I need to focus more on holidays where there would be more activities for Robert and his friends.

"Where's Dad?" asked Robert, as he started to walk away.

"He's in London, on business. He'll be back later this afternoon. Did you want to speak to him?"

"No… just wondered where he was."

Later that evening, after Robert had gone to bed, Ian and Emma were sitting at the breakfast bar with two glasses of Chablis. Emma summarised the discussion she'd had with Robert and also mentioned her concern about the rest of his summer holiday.

"He's got a point," responded Ian. "We can always take our trips to Monaco during school term time. When it's school holidays, we ought to give him greater consideration. Any suggestions?"

"We did say we'd take him to Oxford for a day out, but would an eight-year-old boy really be interested in going there? I know we would, but I'm not sure about Robert."

Ian nodded. "Difficult, isn't it? I think we ought to make a list of possibilities and ask him for his own thoughts. He'll probably have a few ideas of his own."

Over breakfast the next morning, Ian asked Robert, "Is there anything special you'd like to do before you go back to school?"

Robert stopped eating his muesli and looked across at his father. "I would like to invite Richard over to stay with us for a few days. He lives too far away for us to meet just for a day. Over the weekends, at school, we play a brilliant computer game, so it'd be great to do that here."

Ian looked at Emma and she responded, "We can arrange that, if that's what you want. Is there anything else?"

Robert was a little shy in making his next comment. "I'd like to visit the art galleries in London, with Dad."

Both Ian and Emma were staggered. Until that moment, Robert hadn't shown the slightest interest in his parents' business, or in art generally.

"I'll gladly take you," replied Ian, wondering where his son's comment had come from. "What's suddenly given you this interest?"

"Last term we started to study the history of art and my favourite artist is Canaletto. His paintings are fabulous, just like photographs of history. Also, I know you and Mum make a lot of money from selling paintings."

'Little children with big ears' was the phrase that immediately sprang to Emma's mind.

Ian laughed and looked at his son in a new light. "Yes," he said, smiling, "but our money doesn't just come from good luck or a fluke. We've had to work very hard for it, over a number of years."

"I know, Dad, but Arthur's father owns three art galleries and he's rich too."

Ian smiled at his son. He couldn't remember being like this when he was eight years of age. He was still into Lego, football and cricket then. "Okay, I'll take you for a day out in London. We'll go on Tuesday. The National Gallery has a good collection of Canaletto's pictures."

"That would be great, Dad," said Robert excitedly, "because I've got a project to start before next term. It's all about Canaletto's paintings." Robert then finished his breakfast and went off to his room.

Both Ian and Emma stared at each other, somewhat bemused.

"I don't believe what I've just heard," said Emma. "School's changed a lot since I was there."

Ian shook his head. "Well at least it looks like we've got a large part of the rest of Robert's holiday sorted."

"All this time he must have been listening to our conversations and discussions… and never said a word," said Emma, a little horrified at the thought.

"I know," replied Ian. "I wonder what else his ears have picked up over the years."

On the following Tuesday morning, Ian and Robert travelled to London, leaving Esher station on the 10.05am train. At Waterloo, they caught the Underground and alighted at Charing Cross station. From there they walked the short distance to Trafalgar Square and then into the National Gallery. Ian explained that, although the building's name is a gallery, it's actually a museum and has a collection of over 2,300 paintings. However, it would be impossible to display all of them at the same time, so most are kept in store and some are rotated. The very special ones are on permanent display.

They spent most of the morning in rooms 38 and 39. Robert made numerous notes in his pocketbook about the Canaletto pictures he'd viewed. He also read the information notices provided against each painting and added these details to his pocketbook.

As they looked at each picture, Robert asked questions and Ian also pointed out some particular special feature or characteristic of the painting. Ian certainly felt he was being seriously challenged.

It was just after 1.30 when they sat down for a break. Ian took the opportunity to tell his son more about Canaletto. "Canaletto was born in Venice and was famous for capturing precise and atmospheric views of his city. He'd quickly realised that many of the tourists who came to visit Venice were fascinated with his work and wanted to take a painting home as a memento of their visit. Even all those years ago, people liked to hang paintings on the walls in their home. After all, there were no cameras or mobile phones to capture the views as there are today."

Robert smiled and continued to make notes.

Ian continued his tutorial. "As Canaletto became more popular, he employed apprentices, and other skilled local artists, to help him keep up with the growing demand for his work. Like most artists, he wasn't afraid to add an element of 'artistic licence' to his work either. It wasn't his intention just to record the actual view, like a camera would, he wanted his compositions to have more impact. Customers much preferred this approach because then the whole of the painting was full of interest."

After their break, they moved on to visit other parts of the National Gallery. Robert was particularly intrigued to know why some artists painted pictures that were so different to others.

By 3.30pm, they were both hungry; Ian was certainly feeling the strain and in need of a rest. Although Robert wanted to carry on, Ian said it was time to get something to eat. However, before they finally left the building, Ian took Robert to the museum's shop as he'd promised him a souvenir. Robert decided on a print of Canaletto's painting 'A Regatta on the Grand Canal'. He said it would look cool on his bedroom wall.

When they eventually sat down at the Espresso Bar by Muriel's, for a cold drink and sandwiches, Robert told his father he'd had a fabulous day. Ian was still amazed with Robert's enthusiasm and was especially pleased with his observations and inquisitive questions. So much so that he suggested another trip to London in a week's time, to visit some more interesting museums.

Chapter 59

During the rest of Robert's school holidays, his friend Richard came to stay for three days and Robert and his father visited London several more times. They visited the Courtauld Institute Galleries, the National Portrait Gallery, the Queen's Gallery, the Tate Gallery and Tate Modern. On their trips to the National Portrait Gallery and the Queen's Gallery, Emma joined them. She had never been to either of these galleries before.

From these visits, Robert was slowly formulating a list of his preferred artists. Canaletto was still his favourite, but he also liked many of Turner's atmospheric works, L. S. Lowry's 'matchstick men' and some of Wiiliam Hogarth's funny and satirical caricatures. He now began to understand that, although all artists painted different subjects and with different styles, there were some common elements that applied to most of the paintings he'd seen. These were talent, hard work and enthusiasm. However, after his visit to the Tate Modern, he really couldn't understand how so many weird pictures and canvases, some just containing lots of splashes of paint, could be considered proper works of art. On the train journey home from the last London visit of his holiday, Robert made this very point to his father.

Ian explained that what was 'deemed to be art' was very

much a personal opinion. He quoted Jackson Pollock's work as an example. "His paintings are abstract art and produced by laying a canvas on the floor. Then the paints are either poured or dripped onto the canvas. But is this really art?" he asked his son.

Robert looked at his father and remembered seeing some of Pollock's work at one of the galleries they'd visited. "They're colourful, but I could do that. It isn't talent or skill, they're just boring – nothing like the quality of Canaletto's paintings!"

Ian smiled. He had some sympathy with Robert's comments but wanted to give him some exposure to all areas of the art world. "Abstract art doesn't attempt to try to reproduce an accurate view of say, a landscape or portrait; instead, abstract artists focus on shapes, colours, lines and splashes, to create their work."

Robert shrugged his shoulders. He was still not impressed... or even convinced. If he could produce a similar effect then it was not really proper art as far as he was concerned! "Do you think they're good paintings?"

"Some are," replied Ian. "Some are clever. Take Turner's later work, for example. They often included elements of abstract painting."

Robert nodded. "I like his paintings. They're exciting!"

Interesting observation, thought Ian. "At the end of the day, paintings are for two groups of people. The first group are the connoisseurs. These are the people who want to own a picture because they really like the composition and appreciate the artist's talent. The second group are the investors. These people buy and sell paintings solely to make a lot of money."

"But how do you know you can make a lot of money?"

"That's the tricky one and can often be a big gamble. There are lots of factors that have to be considered, but they usually fall into two categories. The first considers who the artist is. Is their work popular, what sort of prices have their earlier paintings been sold for and is there still a demand for this artist's work?"

Robert nodded. He decided that all this made sense.

"The second category," continued Ian, "is more to do with timing. When people are wealthy, they have a lot more money to spend. When the world economy is good, there are more wealthy people in the world. More wealthy people results in more people having the ability to pay higher prices. This increased competition drives up prices. However, when economic times are not so good then the opposite happens and prices go down."

"So, are Canaletto's paintings worth a lot of money?"

"They are worth many millions of pounds, but they rarely come up for sale. Lots of people would love to own one of his paintings so, if one came up for sale, there would be a lot of people wanting to buy it. The price would then go sky high due to the increased competition."

"What about abstract pictures? Nobody's really interested in them, are they?"

Again, Ian smiled. "Remember I mentioned Jackson Pollock?"

Robert nodded.

"Well, in 2016, one of his paintings was reportedly sold for 200 million US dollars in a private sale."

"Oh, wow! Is it any good?"

"Again, that comes back to personal opinions. Some people would say everything that Jackson Pollock painted was good… or even brilliant. Why? – Because they're worth lots of money!"

Over the last few days of his holiday, Robert put together the written report for his school project. When he'd finished, he asked his father if he would read it. Ian did – and he was impressed. So much so that he suggested to Emma that she should read it. She was amazed with the detail of her son's report and told Ian that she was learning a lot more about art – from her eight-year-old!

Robert was really pleased with his father's positive feedback and was looking forward to handing in his report to his teacher.

To Viktor's relief, he didn't receive a visit from the police. During a later telephone conversation, Alexander told him that the police didn't need to speak to him again. "I was relieved," continued Alexander, "But I did ask the policeman what was going on? He told me it was none of my business. However, I reminded him I was still storing the tenants' property, so it certainly was very much my business!"

"What did the police say to that?" asked Viktor.

"They just told me to continue to store the contents and they would make contact again. You know, Vic, there's something very fishy going on here. Why would these Russkies just up and leave like that?"

Viktor smiled at Alexander's derogatory term about Russians. He obviously hadn't thought about where Viktor's surname had originated. "I think we're best out of it, especially if MI5 are involved."

"Maybe, but I've still got their possessions for at least another two weeks."

"I'm surprised the police didn't want to see them. Have you looked at them yourself?"

"Only when we packed them. Nothing unusual other than some strange bits of clothing."

"I tried looking into the history of the paintings but, to be honest, they're worthless. The question is, why did two reasonably wealthy Russians own such a poor collection of pictures? The furniture and the rest of the contents all seemed quite valuable."

"Yes, they are. As I say, something dodgy is going on. Maybe some of the property has been stolen."

"The paintings don't appear on the CLAE database. Besides, they look too modern. Any chance I can have another look at them?"

"Why do you want to do that?" asked Alexander. He was keen just to get rid of all the property, not to encourage Viktor to poke his nose in.

"You mentioned that things may have been stolen. That's given me an idea."

"Okay," responded Alexander, reluctantly. "When do you want to come to the warehouse?"

"What about tomorrow morning, about eleven o'clock?"

"I won't be here then, but ask for Bill. I'll tell him you're coming."

"Thanks, Alexander." Viktor closed the call and sat back in his seat. Slowly a smile appeared on his face and he said to himself, this could just be a wild goose chase, but you never know!

Chapter 60

When Viktor arrived at Alexander's warehouse the next morning, Bill was waiting for him.

"Morning, Vic," greeted Bill, a short and muscular man with long dark brown hair pulled back into a male ponytail. "Alexander said you were coming. You want to look at those Russkie paintings?"

Viktor smiled to himself, but decided not to comment on the 'Russkie' description. "That's right. I hope they're easy to find."

"No problem. Come on." The two men walked into the deep and cavernous building. "I got 'em all out earlier."

"Thanks. It's quiet here today."

"Yeah. The rest of the guys are out on a delivery. I 'urt my wrist last week so I'm 'ere 'olding the fort."

Viktor nodded and looked at the strapping on Bill's left wrist. "Does it hurt now?"

"Nah, only when I twist it a bit. Right, 'ere we are."

They'd arrived at the side of a large stack of wooden crates. A notice pinned to one of the crates said 'Buckworth', which was the rental agency's name. Bill pulled out two smaller wooden boxes from the side of the crates. "The pictures are in 'ere," he said.

Viktor looked around him and spotted another crate

standing on its own. "Let's put them over there. So I can get a better look."

Viktor picked up one box and Bill the other. They then carried them over to the larger crate. Bill put his box on top and Viktor placed his on the floor.

"You looking for anythin' special?" asked Bill, as he opened the first box.

"I'm not sure, Bill. Something's just been niggling me."

Viktor removed the three paintings from the first box and laid them down alongside each other. All three were oil paintings. Using a small torch, Viktor bent down and more closely inspected each painting.

After about a minute, Bill asked, "Anythin' yet?"

Viktor stood back up and pointed at the far picture. "What do you think of that?" He shone the torch beam at a section of the picture.

Bill looked closer to where Viktor was pointing. After a few seconds he turned and said, "It's damaged."

"Anything else?" asked Viktor, still pointing the beam to the same spot.

Bill bent back down again and blew on a small piece of dried paint. "There's somethin' underneath!"

"Mmm, that's why I wanted to inspect them closer. I think there's another painting underneath."

Bill looked closer again. "You might be right. 'Ow's that?"

"Sometimes, when you want to hide or smuggle a valuable painting, one way to disguise it is to paint another picture over it. You can get special paints that will cover the original. That way there's no permanent damage to the painting underneath."

"That's crafty. So, anyone just glancing at the picture would never know what was really underneath. Yeah, sneaky!"

Viktor smiled. "I've heard of valuable stolen statues being

covered with plaster. To completely disguise and hide the original."

"So, 'ow's the original uncovered without damagin' it?"

"The top coat can be washed off with special cleaning solvents. The original would have probably had a temporary protective varnish added as well."

"You learn somethin' everyday."

Viktor removed his mobile phone from his pocket and took several photographs of each painting. He then said, "Let's put these back and have a look at the others."

Bill repacked the paintings carefully and put the wooden box on the floor. Viktor picked up the second box and placed it on the crate. Bill stepped forward and opened and unpacked it. Viktor looked at two further oil paintings and one watercolour sketch. He then laid the three pictures side by side.

"This one's a watercolour," announced Bill, pointing. "'Ow do you cover that one?"

"I think this is an original, not very good and unlikely to be worth anything. Probably just included to emphasise an uninteresting collection."

"Sneaky!" said Bill again. "Looks like somebody's gone to a lot of trouble."

Viktor removed his pocket torch again and leaned over the first oil painting. This time Bill took a closer inspection as well.

"Look in the corner there," announced Viktor, pointing the torch beam to the top left-hand corner.

Bill looked even closer and again blew a dried speck of paint. "Looks the same. There's another picture underneath." He leaned back and looked at Viktor, who had just picked up a spent matchstick he'd spotted on the floor.

Viktor swapped his torch to his left hand and, with the matchstick in his right, he gently prised away another loose piece of dried paint. Immediately another small section of the underneath painting was revealed.

"What you goin' to do now?"

"I'm not sure. Let's have a look at this other picture." Viktor put the matchstick in his pocket and returned the torch to his right hand. He then closely examined the next painting. However, there were no obvious bits of flaky paint this time. Again, he took several photographs of the three pictures.

Bill leaned down and had a quick look. He couldn't see anything either.

After a few seconds of thinking, Viktor said, "These paintings need to be X-rayed. It will then be possible to identify exactly what's underneath."

"Can you do that?"

Viktor smiled. "Not me. This is a job for an expert. Let's get these packed up again."

Bill packed the second box in his usual professional style and the two wooden boxes were returned to the 'Buckworth' storage section.

"Before we go any further," said Viktor, scratching his chin, "I need to speak to Alexander."

The two men began walking back towards the office.

Bill looked at his watch. "It's ten to twelve. 'E said 'e'd be back about mid-day."

"Better keep all this information to yourself for the time being, Bill," said Viktor, as they approached the office. "The police will have to be involved."

"Okay, I'll keep shtum."

The two men walked into the office, but nobody else was there.

"Fancy a coffee?" asked Bill, walking over to the coffee machine.

"Thanks. Black with no sugar, please."

Just then, Alexander entered the office. "So, you're still here. Find what you wanted?"

"Hello, Alexander. Yes, I think so. Do you have the name and contact number for the policeman who interviewed you?"

"The police! What have you two been up to?" asked Alexander, somewhat surprised.

Bill gave Viktor his mug of coffee and asked his boss if he wanted one too. Alexander declined.

After a brief sip of his coffee, Viktor explained what he and Bill had just discovered.

"So, you think there may be something more valuable being hidden?"

"Could be, but we'll not find out for definite until after the pictures have been X-rayed."

"Things are finally making some sense," replied Alexander.

Both Viktor and Bill looked at each other, somewhat surprised.

Alexander continued, "I've just met the rental agent again and, guess what? He's received an email from Moscow. The two Russian tenants want their paintings to be shipped on to them… asap!"

Alexander telephoned Detective Sergeant Andrew Baker, one of the policemen who'd interviewed him previously. He explained Viktor's findings and the detective said he would call in later that day. He also insisted that under no circumstances should the paintings be moved or shipped on to Moscow… and he wanted to speak to Viktor.

When Alexander finished the call, he relayed the detective's instructions to Viktor. Viktor said he didn't want to hang about at the warehouse for the rest of the day and, if the police wanted to speak to him, they could telephone him on his mobile. Besides, he didn't have any information to add to that which Alexander had already given them.

Nevertheless, it wasn't a surprise when Viktor received a telephone call from Detective Baker. He answered all the detective's questions and managed to establish that the police had removed the six pictures from Alexander's warehouse and they would now be subjected to forensic investigations.

Ten minutes after Viktor had switched off this call, his mobile rang again. This time it was Alexander. "Vic, hi. Have the police been in touch?"

"Yes, just a few minutes ago. Detective Baker asked a lot of questions and I gather they've now taken the paintings away for examination."

"Yes, that's what I was going to tell you. The same three coppers came to the warehouse as before. One, I definitely think, is MI5 or MI6. All a bit James Bond!"

Viktor smiled. "It's not really surprising, diplomatic immunity and all that. Have you told the rental agency guy?"

"Yes, he's quite alarmed. The police had just arrived at his office whilst I was speaking to him, so he had to cut short our conversation."

"Hopefully we'll hear more in due course. I really want to know further details about the hidden pictures. My guess is there's theft and smuggling involved. Probably been going on for some time."

"You might be right. The problem I now have is that I'm still storing all the Russians' furniture and contents. I've got a feeling this is all going to get very messy… and for certain, I don't want to be involved with either the police or the Russians."

"Maybe the police will want to take the furniture away," replied Viktor, hoping to cheer up Alexander.

"Let's hope so. I just want to get shot of it all."

Chapter 61

It was a week after Robert had handed his project report to Mr. Connolly, his History of Art teacher, when he was asked to stay behind after class. Robert didn't know if this was good or bad news.

"Well, young Robert," said Mr. Connolly, after the rest of the class had left the classroom. He was holding Robert's report in his hand. "This is quite a comprehensive piece of work. Where did you get all this information?"

Robert explained how Mr. Connolly's presentation of Canaletto's paintings had really sparked his interest. Then he mentioned his father's involvement with the art industry and their trips to many of the major London museums and galleries during the summer holiday.

"You have been busy. You obviously like your art."

"Most of it, yes, sir, but I'm less keen on modern art. Most of it's pointless."

Mr. Connolly smiled and thought about 'old heads on young shoulders'. "You know, Robert, I'm going to show this report to the headmistress. It's a well-researched and skilfully composed piece of work. You obviously have a keen interest and strong opinions about the art world. Well done."

"Thank you, sir, but it was your initial talks that gave me my interest and enthusiasm."

"I'm pleased to hear that someone appreciates my classes."

"We do, sir. Most of my friends are interested too. We think your presentations are really fascinating. We have arguments about Turner, Monet and other artists. Now that I've actually seen a lot of these paintings for real, I can really appreciate what you've been telling us."

Mr. Connolly raised his eyebrows. He was slightly taken aback but gratified with Robert's comments. "Well, keep up the good work, Robert. I'm expecting more good reports from you in the future."

Robert stood up from his chair and looked at his teacher. He gave him a smile and said, "Thank you, sir, I'm looking forward to writing them."

After Robert had left the room, Mr. Connolly reflected back on their discussion and Robert's obvious confidence and enthusiasm. He predicted a bright and fascinating future for this precocious young man.

Emma was in the office when she heard Ian's car arrive in the driveway. Seconds later he appeared in the office and placed his briefcase on his desk. "I've got a painting in the car for you to look at. I'll just pop back out and bring it in."

She stood up when Ian returned carrying a parcel wrapped in brown paper. He laid it down on his desk and removed all the wrapping.

Emma stepped forward to get a much better look. "It's certainly dirty. An oil painting, landscape, doesn't appear to be signed… or it might be hidden under the grime." She pointed to the painting's right-hand side. "These areas are damaged – well, the paint's peeled. The frame is scratched. Not overly inspirational is it?"

"At face value, I largely agree."

"But," interrupted Emma, "you think there is more to this picture than meets the eye."

Ian smiled and slowly nodded his head.

Emma looked back at the picture. She scrutinised it more carefully this time and turned it over to see if there was any more information on the back. There was just an old piece of paper attached to the frame. Yellowed and torn with age, it just said 'veda' and '78'.

"Other than suggesting it could do with a good clean… and some restoration work, I've no idea," replied Emma, a little disappointed.

"Remember old Arthur Jenkins in the High Street? He died a few months ago."

"Of course. He had the old antiques shop. I called in a couple of times. Not very good, mostly junk," responded Emma, without enthusiasm.

"There's a closing down sale sign in the window, so I decided to go in. His son, Tony, is trying to sell all the stock. He's inherited the business but has no interest in antiques. We chatted for a while. He just wants to get rid of as much stock as he can because there's a new tenant lined up. The tenant wants to convert it into a cafe. Anyway, I had a browse but nothing caught my eye, so I asked Tony if there were any more pictures that weren't on display. He said there were a few in the basement and I was welcome to take a look, so I did."

"And you came across this," responded Emma, pointing at Ian's picture.

"There were about eight pictures stored together, all covered in old hessian sacking. This one was the only painting worth anything, so I offered Tony a hundred pounds for it."

Emma raised her eyebrows, smiled and then laughed. "Okay, tell me it's an undiscovered Gainsborough or a Constable!"

It was Ian's turn to smile. "No, I'm afraid not, but, in my opinion, it might have been painted by a similar quality artist."

Chapter 62

Ian spent the next two hours in the office exploring the internet and checking his reference books. When Emma brought him an afternoon tea, he was more certain than ever of his judgement.

"Thanks, Emma," he said, as she placed the mug on his desk. "Do you want to know what I've found out?"

Emma pulled her chair away from her desk and sat opposite him. "I'm all ears."

"When I first saw this painting, I thought it looked like a picture that could have been painted by a man called Joseph Wright or 'Joseph Wright of Derby' as he's better known. I've seen lots of his paintings and visited the Derby Museum once, but that was some time ago. The museum owns a large collection of his works. Joseph Wright mostly lived and painted in the Derbyshire area during the mid-18th century, although he did live, and paint landscapes, in Italy for a short while. He was one of the first painters to record life during the early days of the industrial revolution and painted some wonderful group portraits of people working in an industrial setting. Two of my all-time favourite paintings are 'A Philosopher Lecturing on the Orrery' and 'The Iron Forge'. 'The Iron Forge', incidentally, is displayed in Tate Britain. When I pointed it out to Robert, he described it as 'cool'!"

Emma smiled and said, "Wright must be really good then!"

Ian sipped some of his tea and continued. "What Wright was most famous for was his use of light and shadow. Many of his pictures focus on new inventions and industrial technology. Sometimes his paintings appeared to be lit by candlelight. The light in 'The Iron Forge', for example, was produced by the white-hot glow from a lump of iron whilst it was being beaten by a large industrial hammer."

Emma nodded, but decided industrial paintings didn't sound very interesting to her.

"However," continued Ian, "Wright was also a skilled landscape artist and often painted night scenes. He could then emphasise the contrast of the light and darkness produced by moonlight or at sunset."

"Ah," interrupted Emma, pointing at Ian's painting, "I can see the contrast with this moonlit picture. It's very clever." This was far more interesting, she thought.

"That's right. I'm fairly sure this is one of a number of night paintings he did in Dovedale. That's a picturesque valley about ten miles from Derby." Ian now pressed some keys on his computer. "Look here."

Emma walked around to Ian's side of the desk and looked over his shoulder. She saw a moonlit view of a dark rock-sided valley with a flowing river in the foreground. Located high in the sky, a full moon was lighting up the surrounding billowing clouds and reflecting light directly on to the river below.

"This painting's called 'Dovedale by Moonlight'," said Ian. "It was painted in 1784 and is owned by an art museum in the United States. Do you recognise the similarities?"

Emma nodded. "Yes, they do look alike."

Ian pressed some more keys and another painting appeared. "Now this painting here is titled 'View in

Dovedale'. It was sold by Christies in 2007 as part of a pair, for about 300,000 pounds. Again, recognise the likeness?"

Again, Emma nodded. "Do you think these have all been painted as a group?"

"Wright would often paint these sort of pictures in twos, one showing the same view by day and the other, lit by moonlight. Now then... let's look here." Ian picked up his painting, turned it over and pointed to the scrap of paper attached to the back. "I'm having to guess a bit here, but I think the 'veda' is part of the name Dovedale and the '78' could be part of the year it was painted, 1784, or there-abouts. As you say, it's similar to 'Dovedale by Moonlight'."

"You should have been a detective," announced Emma. "That's brilliant!"

Ian smiled and then took another sip of his tea. "I thought I already was... an art detective! It certainly pays better money."

"What are you going to do next?"

"It obviously needs a good clean. We'll then be able to get a better look at the signature and I can then decide whether it's worth restoring. There are areas where the paint's peeled anyway, but I'm hoping it's not too bad and can be restored. If that's all okay, then we'll need to get it authenticated. However, that's more tricky because, other than Arthur Jenkins' antiques shop, I don't know any of the painting's provenance. Tony's promised to look into his father's records, but I'm not optimistic. Mind, I did promise him another hundred pounds if he came up with some of the painting's history."

"If it is all okay, and restorable, what do you think it might be worth?"

Ian hesitated. "Wright's work sells for a variety of prices. The Americans like his work, so, if I auctioned it in, say, New York, I might get, maybe, 200,000 dollars after commission."

"Not a bad return on 100 pounds."

"But firstly, I need to establish the painting's name, its provenance, check for a signature and decide whether it's worth restoring. A lot more work still to do."

"Is there anything I can help with?" asked Emma. She didn't know what, but wanted to be involved.

"You could see if you can find this painting on the internet or in my reference books. I've not got that far. Look for 'Dovedale' in the title, dated in the 1780s. I'll have a word with Peter Jarrett and get it cleaned."

It was five days after Ian had delivered the painting to Peter Jarrett's studio for cleaning that he and Emma walked into the same studio's reception area. Ian announced he had an appointment with Mr. Jarrett. The receptionist smiled and said she'd go and get him. A few moments later she returned and was accompanied by Peter Jarrett. Emma guessed he was probably in his mid-fifties. His long greying wavy hair and thick black spectacle frames made Emma smile. She thought he looked more like a scientist!

Greetings and introductions were made and they all walked through the rear door, down a short corridor and into, what Emma thought looked like, a small laboratory. Ian immediately spotted his painting. It was clamped to an easel and illuminated by two spotlights. They all walked over to have a closer look.

"It doesn't look like the same picture," announced Emma. The grime and dust that the picture had collected over many years had been removed and, bar a few areas where the paint had flaked away, the painting looked in reasonable condition.

Ian smiled. "Peter's a perfectionist," he responded to Emma, and then turning to Peter he said, "You've done an excellent job." He leaned much closer and pointed at the damaged areas. "What do you think? Can this be repaired?"

Peter stepped forward and looked at where Ian was point-ing. "Yes, I would think so. That part needs some special attention, the rest is just superficial. The picture has enough existing colours for me to match it properly and enough features that are similar to Wright's authenticated Dovedale work."

Ian looked away from the picture and said to Peter, "Emma has found what looks like our painting on the inter-net. The entry suggests a title 'Moonlight over Dovedale'. Unfortunately, the report also states 'whereabouts unknown'."

Peter nodded his head. "What do you want me to do?"

Ian walked back closer to the painting again. He could now see the signature, but concentrated his inspection on the seriously damaged section. "You say you can restore this part to look like the original?"

Peter also looked closer at the damaged area. He adjusted his spectacles, pointed and said, "This small area here will need a base covering to hide the bare canvas. I'll also look at 'Moonlight over Dovedale' on the internet to get an idea of the cloud shapes. Fortunately, the damaged area is only small and part sky and cloud, so it should be easy to follow the other existing areas of sky and clouds to match the colours."

Ian and Emma both peered at the area Peter was pointing at.

"As I say, the rest is mostly a straightforward restoration," continued Peter. "Tiny dots of matching paint will sort that out – just superficial. It will take about a week, ten days at the most, because I'll need to wait for the base covering to dry properly before I apply the paints. About two days of actual work."

Ian looked at Emma, but she said nothing.

Ian looked back at Peter and said, "Okay, let's get the job finished."

Chapter 63

Alexander received another visit from the police. They wanted to take all the Russians' furniture and contents away. They showed Alexander a warrant and explained that the rental agency was aware of the situation. Alexander didn't mind. He was pleased to be shot of the whole business and even offered his men's help to load up their lorry.

When the police had finally left the premises, Alexander telephoned Viktor. "Vic! Good news. The police have collected all the Russians' property. Thought you'd like to know."

"Okay, thanks," Viktor replied. "Did they say anything about what they've found out about the paintings?"

"No, they did ask me some more questions but I told them to speak to you."

"Thanks for the tip-off."

"Just looking at a possible job in two weeks' time. Are you about?"

Viktor knew he would be. "Yes. Let me know when."

"Will do, bye."

"Goodbye," replied Viktor, and made a note in his diary.

It was about an hour later when Viktor received a telephone call from Detective Sergeant Baker. The detective asked Viktor some questions, but Viktor thought he'd previously given this information. Nevertheless, he took the opportunity to quiz the detective about what had happened to the paintings.

Detective Baker was a little guarded, but said, "I know you've been extremely helpful, Viktor, and without your involvement we wouldn't have uncovered this crime, but, I can't tell you too much because there's still a full investigation going on and, of course, the two suspects used to work at the Russian Embassy."

"I'm not really interested in the politics and your criminal investigations, but I would like to know the details of the five hidden paintings." He then went on to tell the detective about his involvement with CLAE and how important it was to identify stolen paintings.

"Look, all I can tell you is the experts are still inspecting each painting. I'll let you know when I'm able to tell you more."

"Okay, thanks," responded Viktor, a little disappointed.

It was three weeks later, whilst Viktor and Alexander were viewing a property in the Weybridge area of London, when Viktor received his next telephone call from Detective Sergeant Baker. He immediately walked out the building and into the rear garden to take the call.

"Viktor, hi. I promised you an update when one was available," said the policeman. "There's still not much I can say, but we've traced the owners of the real paintings. They were stolen from a house in Edgware about eight months ago. The profile of the crime matches similar thefts committed over the last four years."

"I see," replied Viktor. "So you think the theft of our paintings was not a 'one-off'?"

"We're checking that out. I'm afraid I can't tell you the details of the paintings because the real owner is now known and obviously wants it to be kept private."

Viktor was disappointed, but could understand the owner's situation. "I can see that. He wouldn't want just anyone to know about his valuable possessions."

"Anyway, thanks to your keen eye and initiative, we've hopefully stopped this gang from future thefts and smuggling valuable paintings out to Russia."

"I don't suppose you'll be able to arrest them now they're back in Moscow."

"No, but we'll keep their details on file. Anyway, Viktor, I must go. Thanks again for all your help."

"Thank you for letting me know."

Viktor switched off the call. He was still standing on the patio and staring down the long garden. He was disappointed not to have been told more.

"All okay, Vic?" It was Alexander calling through the open patio doors.

Viktor walked back towards the house and said to Alexander, "No news about the original pictures but, one positive is, I think I've just established a useful contact at 'The Met'!"

Earlier that same day, Ian had collected his 'Joseph Wright of Derby' painting from Peter Jarrett. As usual, Peter's restoration was excellent. He even had to remind Ian which parts of the painting had been repaired. When Ian arrived home, he took the painting into the home office and called Emma. He then stood the painting on his desk.

When Emma walked into the office she immediately spotted the painting. "Are you pleased with it?" she asked, leaning over to have a closer look.

"I'm very pleased. What do you think?"

"I can't see where it's been restored."

"You're not supposed to. That's why it's been restored by an expert."

"He's very good," replied Emma. She was now standing back up to her full height. "What are you going to do with it now?"

"How do you fancy a few days in Derbyshire?"

"Derbyshire!" exclaimed Emma. "Why Derbyshire?"

"I thought you might like to see Dovedale, where this picture was painted. There are some lovely towns in the Peak District and I want to take you to the Derby Museum. I think you'll be impressed. Besides, it would be useful to get the museum's opinion on this painting. If they think it's a genuine piece of work by Mr. Wright, that would certainly make a big difference."

"When are you thinking we should go?"

"I'll need to speak to the head curator first and see if I can make an appointment."

"We'd better check our diaries too."

Ian made a note of the groups of days they were both available and telephoned the museum. He was put through to Mrs. Lucy Johnson who, he was told, was the senior curator of art. She was the key person to speak to when it came to discussing Joseph Wright's paintings. Ian explained to her the details of his painting and asked if it was possible for her to inspect it and give him her opinion. Mrs. Johnson said she was intrigued and would be pleased to take a look. They then agreed on a date and time for the appointment.

Emma checked the internet and decided that after they'd visited the museum, they'd stay in Derbyshire for a short break in the picturesque town of Bakewell. She'd found a nice local pub which provided both accommodation and meals.

Four days before their planned trip, Ian suggested it would be better if they travelled to Derby one day earlier. That way they'd be able to allocate more of their day to the museum. Emma agreed and sought some additional accommodation much closer to the centre of Derby. She eventually found a double room in a hotel. It also had car parking facilities and was just a short stroll to the museum.

Ian volunteered to drive and, as they travelled northwards on the M1, Emma read out to Ian sections of her Derbyshire visitor's guidebook. She also told him she would like to visit Matlock and Ashbourne. Ashbourne, in particular, as it was very close to Dovedale.

It was just after 6pm when they arrived in Derby city centre. Following the satnav, they arrived at the hotel a few minutes later. It was a Monday evening and the hotel was relatively quiet. They were on their own sitting in the lounge, close to a lovely warming log fire. The weather outside had deteriorated and was damp and gloomy. Fog had been forecast so they decided to try the hotel's restaurant for dinner. Besides, thought Ian, tomorrow was a big day and he wanted to get an early night's sleep.

Chapter 64

The following morning, at 10.25am, Ian and Emma arrived at the reception desk of the Derby Museum & Art Gallery. Ian told the receptionist they had an appointment with Mrs. Lucy Johnson at 10.30am.

The receptionist smiled and, after announcing her name, Alice, she called to a colleague to cover at the desk whilst she led Emma and Ian into the museum. After passing various display rooms they eventually arrived at a door marked as 'The Joseph Wright Study Room'.

"This is a special study room," explained Alice, pushing open the door. "It is dedicated to the life of Joseph Wright. As well as all his paintings, this room holds a large collection of the artist's drawings, prints, letters and other personal materials."

Ian was impressed. Emma nodded and glanced around the room, staring at all the items on display.

Sitting at one of the desks was another lady who immediately stood up when she spotted the entrants. She was smartly dressed in a grey suit and white blouse and strode across towards them with an air of confidence. Ian guessed she was probably about 40 years of age.

"Good morning," she said, holding out her right hand. "You must be Mr. and Mrs. Caxton. Welcome to the Joseph

Wright Study Room, I'm Lucy Johnson, the curator. Please call me Lucy."

Ian and Emma both shook her hand and Ian announced their first names. "It's really good of you to see us," said Ian. He lifted up his trusty canvas bag. "I've got the painting in here."

"Excellent. Let's go through to my office. I can then have a proper look."

After saying their goodbyes, Alice left them, and Emma and Ian followed Lucy into the office.

"Please put the painting on that easel for me," said Lucy, pointing to a large wooden easel. She reached across to the wall and pressed two light switches. Immediately the easel was illuminated by two soft spotlights.

Ian laid his bag on a small empty table, unbuckled the three straps and removed the bubble-wrap encasing the painting. Once the picture was uncovered, he placed it on the easel and secured it into place.

Lucy put on a pair of blue-framed spectacles and picked up a book which was already open. She carried it over and closely looked at Ian's painting, then compared it to the photograph on the open page.

Ian tilted his head and read the front cover of Lucy's book: 'Joseph Wright of Derby: Painter of Light by Benedict Nicolson'.

"Well, Mr. Caxton… Ian," said Lucy, breaking the silence with a slightly louder voice which made Emma jump. "I can only see a small section of restoration work, so you obviously used a competent restorer. You wouldn't believe some of the botched jobs we see. It looks good and has a lot of the features typical of Wright's style. It precisely matches the photograph of 'Moonlight over Dovedale' in this book."

Emma smiled and Ian gave a quiet sigh.

"We were gifted 'Moonlight by Dovedale', another of Joseph Wright's paintings, in 1945. I think this painting could relate to that same series. Probably painted at a similar time." Lucy looked back closely at the painting again. "Unlikely to have been painted by a follower of Wright. We call them 'not quite Wrights'!"

Ian and Emma both laughed.

Ian stepped forward and pointed to the area where the major part of the restoration work had been completed. "Would you be happy with this level of restoration work?"

"Oh, yes. As I say, it's been done very well. In our storeroom we have some of Joseph's collection which have not been restored as well."

"Would you say this picture has definitely been painted by Joseph Wright?" asked Ian. He had his fingers crossed.

"I couldn't say that exactly. I would need to be satisfied with the provenance and see the results of any forensic reports first. However, I'd say you're probably 80% there. But, of course, it's not me who has the final say. It's these people you'll have to convince." Lucy tapped her fingers on her book's front cover.

"I'm pleased you're quite positive," said Ian. "At least I can go forward with more confidence."

"Were you planning to stay at the museum for most of today?"

Emma nodded and Ian said, "Yes. I want to show Emma the paintings in the Joseph Wright Gallery and, with your permission, look at your archives in the Study Room."

"Good. By all means you have my permission to visit the Study Room. We're rather pleased with it. The thing is, I have another appointment at 12.30 with a colleague who is very knowledgeable about Wright's paintings. I'd like to hear his opinion on your picture… if that's alright with you?"

"Certainly," responded Ian. "We're due in Bakewell this evening, so we plan to leave here at about four o'clock."

"Excellent. I recommend our 'Coffee House' for lunch. We

have a new chef and he's just revamped the menu, so I'm sure you'll find something that will be of interest to you both. What about coming back to my office… say at three o'clock?"

Both agreed and Ian asked, "Is it alright if I leave my bag here too?"

"Yes, just leave it where it is."

After the meeting, Ian and Emma walked back into the Joseph Wright Gallery where they spent the next two hours. Emma was fascinated by the quality of the paintings. She couldn't believe they were all painted 250 years ago. She especially loved the 'A Philosopher Lecturing on the Orrery', in particular, the way Joseph Wright had captured the light and warmth emanating from a lamp that supposedly represented the sun. She also smiled at the expression on the children's faces, so captivated, staring at the philosopher whilst he was presenting his explanation of the orrery.

Ian told Emma how Wright had a serious interest in science and had been involved with the 'Lunar Society of Birmingham'. This group consisted of leading industrialists and pioneering scientists of the day. As well as Joseph Wright, two other famous members were Josiah Wedgewood and Richard Arkwright. The group would gather on a regular basis to discuss science and philosophy and Wright recorded many of the group's early experiments in his paintings.

Later, they found the painting 'Moonlight by Dovedale'. Ian pointed out all the similarities he could see with his own painting. Emma nodded and agreed.

By 1.15pm, they decided to take Lucy's recommendation and visit the 'Coffee House' for lunch. They found a modern and well-lit room and both agreed the quality of the food certainly warranted the curator's praise.

Just after 2pm they returned to the Study Room and read about Joseph Wright's life. They also looked at some of the museum's collection of Wright's drawings, prints, letters and other pieces of his personal memorabilia. A knowledge-able gallery assistant helped Emma to access some of the visual displays and answered her many questions. At three o'clock Lucy left her office and joined them, saying, "I hope both of you are impressed with our archives."

"They're excellent," said Ian. "Very well put together... and so informative."

Emma said, "I hadn't realised Joseph Wright was involved with so many important scientists and industrialists of his time. His life was so fascinating."

Lucy smiled. "Yes. I know I'm biased when it comes to Joseph, but he's quite a hero of ours. Come into my office. I know you want to get away shortly."

Emma said thank you to the gallery assistant and fol-lowed Lucy and Ian into the office. They all walked over to Ian's painting, which was still fixed on the easel.

Lucy started to speak. "The appointment I had, just before lunch, was with a colleague called Ernest Bristow. He's a bit of a celebrity around this area but, more importantly for you, he's also a serious collector of Joseph Wright of Derby's paintings. He owns about 27 paintings and drawings."

Ian raised his eyebrows in surprise. "Quite a collection."

Lucy continued, "He likes your painting very much and thinks it's definitely painted by Joseph Wright. He also thinks it's the missing painting that the catalogue raisonné states as 'whereabouts unknown'."

"Well, that's great news," said Emma, smiling. Ian turned towards her and smiled too.

"It is indeed," responded Lucy, "because Mr. Bristow would like to purchase the painting from you."

"I see," said Ian, trying to keep calm. "Did he say how much he was prepared to pay?"

"Yes, 125,000 pounds!"

Chapter 65

Ian and Emma stared at each other in surprise.

Ian then asked, "Do you mean Mr. Bristow is prepared to pay that amount of money now, without provenance and without forensic examinations?"

"Yes, indeed. He's quite happy that this painting is the one in this catalogue. The catalogue states the full provenance from 2001 back to the 1780s. Your information that the antique dealer purchased it in 2004 seems to tie up nicely, although there's the niggle of the three-year gap."

Ian nodded. "I need to discuss the offer with Emma."

"Of course you do. I've got to speak to somebody now so, you two stay here, and I'll be back in a few minutes," said Lucy. She departed the room.

"What do you think?" asked Emma. "It's a good offer… isn't it?"

Ian smiled. "Tempting. I need a minute to think this through."

Emma initially stayed quiet. She was thinking about the added costs if they decided to sell the painting at an auction. "Auctioning costs in New York, insurance and transport would be expensive. You always said not to be greedy."

Ian nodded. "Yes. Even if I keep it there'll still be added

costs and, of course, there's no guarantee I'd get significantly more at auction."

"I agree."

"You think I should take Mr. Bristow's offer?"

Emma nodded and then said, "Yes, it seems fair."

"Okay. When Mrs. Johnson returns, I'll tell her yes."

Emma smiled and gave Ian a kiss on his cheek. They walked over to the painting together and had another look. A minute later Mrs. Johnson returned.

"Have you made up your mind?" she asked.

Ian smiled. "You can tell Mr. Bristow he has a deal!"

"Oh, excellent. He'll be so pleased. Now, you said you are travelling on to Bakewell later. Are you on holiday for a few days?"

"Yes," replied Emma. "We wanted to see some of the lovely Peak District towns. We can be back here on Thursday afternoon."

"Good. Well, what I suggest, and I know Ernest will go along with my idea, is for you to leave your painting with me. I'll give you a receipt and put it in our secure storeroom. I'll also ring Ernest, tell him his offer has been accepted and ask him to arrange a banker's draft. He can bring it here on Thursday. Should we say three o'clock?"

Ian and Emma looked at each other and nodded. "Yes," said Ian, "three o'clock will be fine."

"Excellent. You had better leave a mobile number with me, just in case," said Lucy. She walked over to her desk and picked up a pen and notepad. Emma called out her own mobile number and then Ian's.

"Do you want me to repack the painting in my bag?"

"No, you can take your bag with you. The picture will be properly protected."

Ian picked up his bag and said, "I hope you don't mind me saying, but you do seem to be going to a lot of personal trouble."

"Mr. Caxton, I promise you, it's no trouble at all. Mr. Bristow has loaned and donated pictures to us in the past and he's promised us the rest of his collection in his will. So, as you can see, we have a very special relationship."

Over the next two days, Ian and Emma enjoyed their time in the Peak District, especially Dovedale. Despite the dismal weather, Emma managed to tick off all the places she wanted to visit. They promised themselves another holiday in the area in the summer when, they hoped, the weather would be much better.

On Thursday at just after 2.40pm, Ian parked his car in the multi-storey car park in Derby city centre. From the car's satnav information, he estimated it was about a ten-minute walk to the museum. He and Emma arrived in the reception area at 2.56pm.

As they were expected, they were immediately escorted through the museum and into the Joseph Wright Study Room. There, Lucy and an elderly gentleman were looking at one of the display screens. Lucy noticed Ian and Emma walking towards her and spoke to the gentleman. Both stopped what they were doing and walked over to greet Emma and Ian. Introductions to Mr. Bristow were made and they all made their way into Lucy's office.

Emma guessed Mr. Bristow was in his late 70s. Slim and well dressed in a smart tweed overcoat, he had an air of confidence that reminded Emma of Ian's father.

"Welcome back to Derby and our museum," said Lucy, with a smile. "I hope you had a lovely time in the Peak District."

Emma gave a summary of their visits and finished by saying they were going home with a bag full of Bakewell puddings for the freezer. Everybody laughed.

Ian's painting was displayed on the same easel where he'd placed it three days ago. They all walked over to inspect it.

"It's an excellent painting," said Mr. Bristow who then pointed to the restored area. "I can see there's been a small amount of restoration work, but it's obviously been done by a professional. Someone who cares and knows what they're doing. Doesn't distract from the painting's quality, or its value, in my opinion."

Ian couldn't identify Mr. Bristow's accent, but there was just a hint of one. "The restorer is Peter Jarrett. He used to work for Sotheby's when I worked there. He now works on his own and has a long waiting list of clients."

"Well, young man, here's your banker's draft for 125,000 pounds." Mr. Bristow produced the draft from his overcoat pocket. "Don't spend it all at once!" Everyone laughed.

"Thank you, sir," said Ian, glancing at the draft. "I hope the painting gives you many years of pleasure."

Mr. Bristow laughed. "Lucy here, and this museum, they're the ones that will get the pleasure... when I've popped my clogs. They'll inherit all of my Joseph Wright collection."

"Not for many years yet, we hope, Ernest," said Lucy, with feeling.

"Are you people going back to London tonight?" asked Mr. Bristow.

"Yes, we've got plans for the weekend. Mind, we want to come back here again in the summer. It's a lovely part of the world."

"Travelling by car?" Mr. Bristow's question had a slightly more unsettling tone.

"Yes," said Ian, hesitantly. "We've parked in the multi-sto-rey. We'll be going back via the M1."

"Just be careful. The weatherman has predicted more fog between here and Leicestershire tonight. Could be a pea-souper."

"Thanks for the warning. I think we'd better make a move."

They all shook hands and said their goodbyes. Ian and Emma left the museum and headed back towards the car park.

The predicted thick fog was already rolling in.

Chapter 66

Later that same afternoon, Richard Caxton, Ian's father, had just entered the lounge and was checking the time on his wristwatch. It was just after six o'clock. Damn, he said to himself, I'm missing the evening news. Watching the Six O'clock News on television was a habit with Richard. He liked to keep up with what was happening in the world.

He pressed the remote control and sat down on the sofa. A few seconds later the first picture he saw was of a multi-vehicle pileup on a motorway. He turned up the volume.

The commentator was describing the huge crash that had occurred at about 4.30 that afternoon. "It occurred in dense fog," he was reporting, "between junctions 23 and 22 on the southbound carriageway of the M1. It is an extremely serious accident and first estimates say there are numerous casualties. Many people have either died or been injured. This section of the motorway cuts through the dense Charnwood Forest, so it happened at a particularly difficult section for the rescue services to attend. The police have closed the northbound carriageway at junction 22 so they, the fire brigade and ambulances, from both Derby and Leicester, can attend. Two rescue helicopters have just landed…"

"Oh, my goodness. Elizabeth!" shouted Richard. Ian's mother immediately came into the lounge.

"What's that?" she asked, looking at the television and rubbing her hands on a tea towel. She'd been preparing dinner.

"A big pile up on the M1. Somewhere in Derbyshire. Lots of fog in the area."

"Oh dear. Anybody hurt?"

"Man reckons lots of people have died or are injured. People drive far too close and too fast nowadays, especially in fog!"

Elizabeth sat down next to her husband. She had a worried look on her face. "I do hope nobody we know is involved!"

The story continues in

'The Reprisal'

Volume 6 in the Ian Caxton Thriller series

DISCOVER THE FIRST FOUR VOLUMES OF THE IAN CAXTON THRILLER SERIES.

'THE OPPORTUNITY'

Ian Caxton is a senior manager at Sotheby's. After successful career moves to Sotheby's branches in New York and Hong Kong, Ian is now based in London and earmarked for the top position. However, following a chance meeting with Andrei, a very rich Russian art dealer based in Monaco, Ian suddenly reassesses all his plans and ambitions. Even his marriage is under threat. The Opportunity charts the tumultuous life and career of Ian Caxton as he navigates the underbelly of the art world, one of serious wealth, heart-stopping adventure and a dark side. The big question is, will Ian take The Opportunity? And if he does, what will the consequences be, not only for him, but also for his wife and colleagues?

'THE CHALLENGE'

The art world is full of pitfalls, mysteries and risk. It is a place where paintings can be bought and sold for millions of pounds. Fortunes can be made… and lost! For those whose ambition is to accumulate wealth beyond their wildest dreams, expert knowledge, confidence, bravery and deep pockets are certainly needed! Ian Caxton is being tested by fake paintings, a financial gamble on the artwork of a black slave, his wife's life-changing news and a series of mysterious emails that suggest he's being watched. More dramatic events, mental conflicts and soul-searching decisions. How will Ian cope with all these extra demands?

This is the big question, that is The Challenge.

'THE DECISION'

A worrying letter from a dead colleague, a Gainsborough painting downgraded by the experts, a new partnership opportunity, an unexpected statement from his boss and his wife's announcement of her new ambitions. These are just some of the new challenges we see Ian Caxton having to grapple with this time. The answers and consequences of which lead ultimately to his bold life-changing decision!

In Antigua, Oscar joins up with a new business colleague, but soon discovers a world of fraud, deception and murder. Penny experiences unforeseen changes to her life and Viktor is informed of an amazing surprise.

Another page-turning tale of adventure, intrigue, greed and risk, where millions of pounds routinely change hands. Welcome to the exciting, mysterious and sinister happenings that continue to occur in the art world!

'THE GAMBLE'

Ian Caxton has committed to a major change in his career, but will the gamble prove to be a success? More challenges face Ian and his colleagues as they attempt to unravel new mysteries within the art world. Who painted the valuable pictures of 'Sir Edgar Brookfield' and 'Mademoiselle Chad' and which famous artist is hiding behind the name of 'Madeleine B'? Why does Ian think a prized picture on display at the Musée des Beaux-Arts d'Orléans is a fake!?

Who murdered Millie Hobbie and why is Ian's nemesis, Jonathan Northgate, back in his life?

Another gripping page-turning story of adventures, risks and rewards, where paintings once considered lost are now worth millions of pounds.